The Maids of Chateau Vernet

A Soldier Lost in Time

Steven Landry

&

Katie Rae Sank

ISBN: 9781731098122

DEDICATION

This novel is dedicated to the estimated 72,500 French Jews who died in the Holocaust, the 257,500 who survived, and the 3,995 French non-Jews who were awarded the *Righteous Among Nations* honorific for risking their lives to save the survivors.

FOREWORD

"Fiction cannot recite the numbing numbers, but it can be that witness, that memory. A storyteller can attempt to tell the human tale, can make a galaxy out of the chaos, can point to the fact that some people survived even as most people died. And can remind us that the swallows still sing around the smokestacks." — Jane Yolen, author of *The Devil's Arithmetic*

It is estimated that about seventy-five percent of the Jews living in Metropolitan France survived the Holocaust. Perhaps that is why the role of the Vichy Government and French Police in feeding the Nazi death machine has been little noted by history. This novel is set during that time.

The authors would like to thank the members of the Harford Writers' Group @ The Library for their reviews and encouragement during this project, and especially our first reader, Larry Garnett.

Part I

1

0400 hours, Sunday, May 15, 2050, Wah Cantonment, Islamic Republic of Pakistan

"Go, Go, Go!" Staff Sergeant Hiram Halphen rushed forward at the jumpmaster's command and leapt into the night sky twenty-five thousand feet above the garrison city of Wah. A sniper in the *Sayeret* Special Forces Company of the 35th Paratroop Brigade, Israeli Defense Forces, Hiram had been tasked to support a Mossad operation in Pakistan.

Eight Mossad paramilitary agents followed Hiram off the CV-6 Speed Agile stealth transport. Hiram was a skilled night flyer, capable of precise maneuvering in his wing suit. One of the agents, less well trained on the new wing suits, crashed into the perimeter fence moments after Hiram touched down. Alarms blared throughout the nuclear weapons storage facility.

Hiram, followed by his assigned spotter Jacob, sprinted for the shadows along the wall of the nearest building. They found a ladder leading to the roof and scrambled up while gunfire erupted throughout the compound.

At the top of the ladder, Hiram paused and peeked out over the edge of the roof. Two Pakistani soldiers stood on the far side of the roof, both visible in his sixth-generation night vision goggles, scouring the area for the intruders. Hiram swung his M22 assault rifle up into position, settled the laser aiming dot on the back of the nearest man, and fired. With barely a whisper, the electro-magnetic rail gun launched a nine-millimeter bullet at nine-tenths the speed of sound and the Pak soldier pitched forward and off the roof. His companion spun around just in time to catch Hiram's second shot in the chest. He fell back against the low wall, slumped to a sitting position, gasping for breath.

Jacob followed Hiram onto the roof, and they ran to the southeast corner of building. Hiram put his assault rifle down and pulled the ancient, but still effective M2010 precision sniper rifle from its harness on his back. The weapon had been handed down from his grandfather and was the only tangible memento he had left of the man who had taught him to shoot. Meanwhile Jacob set up his night spotting scope and began calling out targets. Hiram went to work.

Ten minutes later, the Mossad team leader called "Masada" over the squad radio net. Hiram glanced down at the combat communication and information digital device, or C2ID2, on his wrist. The counter was winding down from five minutes. When it reached zero, a Mark XII hyperbaric nuclear weapon would reduce the Pak nuclear complex to radioactive dust, taking out a significant portion of the newly established Islamic Republic of Pakistan's nuclear arsenal.

Hiram looked up in time to see the wink of machine gun fire from a distant guard tower. Both he and Jacob dove for cover behind the low wall that rimmed the roof, but Jacob wasn't quite quick enough. Two rounds punched through his body armor, killing him instantly. His C2ID2 display confirmed that Jacob's heart had ceased beating. The device also reported that the other seven Mossad agents were injured or dead.

As bullets continued to fly above his head, Hiram low-crawled across the roof to a spot where he could engage the machine gunner and his assistant. Neither man saw Hiram rise up until it was too late. The gunner's head exploded with Hiram's first shot. To his credit, the gunner's assistant tried to man the weapon himself rather than duck for cover. It was a fatal decision.

With a little more freedom of movement, Hiram ran to a spot where he could get a view of the nuclear weapon emplacement site. The counter on his wrist showed two minutes until detonation. The Mark XII remained in place, three dying Mossad agents around it. Pak soldiers advanced towards the nuclear weapon. Hiram gave them reason to be cautious, picking off several with his sniper rifle as the counter continued toward zero.

At thirty seconds, he judged the Pakistanis wouldn't be able to reach the weapon in time, so he turned and sprinted back to where Jacob's body rested. Hiram pulled off his pack and activated the portal to the combat logistics pod within it.

He wrestled Jacob's body through the portal, dumped all of his and Jacob's gear in after him, and then jumped through himself, a moment before the weapon detonated.

Hiram's disassociated molecules converted to electro-magnetic energy, slipped through time and space, converted back to matter, and reassembled. Simultaneously, the trans-dimensional portal within the hyperbaric nuclear weapon opened, releasing a pressure wave of supercritical water with the energy equivalent of fifty kilotons of TNT with a small side of neutron radiation. The downward oriented pressure wave burrowed through the concrete and steel bunker beneath the device, compressing everything in its direct path into dust, including the Pakistani nuclear stockpile.

2

A temporal artifact of May 6, 2050

Hiram landed on the floor of the combat logistics pod as the sixty-six-centimeter ceiling-mounted portal snapped shut above him. He had been transported through time and space to a fifteen-meter-long, three-meter-tall, by four-meter-wide container located in a temporal artifact of May 6th, 2050, the day the logistical plan for the Wah mission had been finalized.

The inter-dimensional transit portal in the ceiling of the pod was a companion to the one in his backpack. He had travelled from the rooftop in Wah, Pakistan to an artifact of the IDF staging facility deep in the Negev desert, at the speed of light.

The container held everything an IDF infantry scout and sniper platoon could ever need in combat, from food and water to small unmanned aerial and ground vehicles, kayaks and inflatable boats, to twenty-five different types of individual and crew served weapons, along with ammunition, explosives and pyrotechnics. It even contained a fully equipped bathroom and a kitchenette.

Hiram walked to the opposite end of the container, stepping over Jacob's body, where a second, larger portal was mounted vertically on the wall. The two-meter-diameter portal was meant to transport him to its companion at the IDF logistical facility in normal space. However, when he activated the unit's controls, they didn't respond. He ran a diagnostic test, which failed to identify the problem. "Destination not found," blinked on the control screen in bold, red letters.

He tried the aerial projection portal located on the floor in the center of the pod. Its virtual companion opened in the sky exactly 5,000 meters above the portal in Hiram's backpack. The platoon had occasionally used the aerial portal as a means of crossing large obstacles such as rivers or guarded

3

perimeters. Get as close to the obstacle as safely possible, jump into the pod, then back out into the sky, and glide across the obstacle using a parachute or wingsuit. This one also balked at returning Hiram to Israel, or anywhere else in 2050 for that matter.

Hiram spent an hour trying to get either system working without success. With each passing moment, his level of concern grew. Living creatures could only occupy temporal artifacts for a short period of time. Natural cell death accelerated the instant an individual stepped into the pod, like a mountain climber venturing beyond twenty thousand feet, dying bit by bit. The body struggled to make the myriad of tiny repairs necessitated by the breakdown. Someone had called the effect Hagar's Curse, and the name had stuck. Disorientation began to set in after about six hours, degradation of fine motor skills at about seven hours, partial paralysis took hold afterward, and by the ninth hour the effects were both irreversible and so severe that the sufferer would be unable to help himself. An automatic timer built into his C2ID2 helpfully chimed, indicating his remaining dwell time was down to five hours.

Frustrated, Hiram returned to the other end of the pod and set about placing Jacob's body in a cadaver bag and stowing his equipment. He put one of Jacob's two ID tags into his own jacket pocket, leaving the other around Jacob's neck on its chain. He then turned his attention to the portal on the ceiling of the pod. If he exited that way, he expected to find himself back in Wah, at ground zero of a hyperbaric nuclear blast, and likely in the middle of a major mobilization by Pakistani Taliban security and emergency response forces. He had little choice but to at least check it out.

He donned a set of protective coveralls and a face mask. The outfit would do little to stop the neutron and gamma radiation sure to be flooding the area, but it would keep him from breathing in any radioactive particles and keep any beta particles off his skin. The plan had been to orient the weapon's portal downward, maximizing the amount of residual neutron activation products created, thereby contaminating the immediate area without creating a substantial downwind hazard. That plan worked against him now.

When all was ready, Hiram activated the unit and, while standing on the third rung of the ladder leading up to the portal, stuck the probe of a radiation meter through the opaque opening. The probe disappeared from view as if it had been dipped into a bowl of milk, smooth ripples flowing away from the point of contact. The meter showed only normal background radiation, which surprised him. Using one arm, Hiram lifted one of the small recon robots up through the portal and placed it on the ground outside before quickly withdrawing his exposed limb. He activated the robot's camera using the C2ID2 and saw nothing on the unit's auxiliary nine-by-nine-inch monitor but bushes and grass, where there should have been a smoking hole in the ground surrounded by a burning industrial complex.

4

He sent the little robot moving away from the portal in a spiral pattern, but still saw nothing but bushes, grass, and eventually a cultivated area about a mile to the northeast. The robot's on-board radiation meter continued to show only background radiation.

3

0548 hours, Friday, May 15, 1942, The Punjab, British India

Satisfied that he wouldn't be fried or fired upon the moment he passed through the portal, Hiram climbed out into the real world and confirmed the little robot's observations. He also confirmed the absence of any GPS signal. Hiram returned to the pod and removed his protective clothing.

He retrieved a small aerial recon drone from its storage locker and climbed back through the portal. He launched the drone into the air and sent it out from his position in a widening spiral. The drone had a dual mode onboard navigation system – one mode using GPS coordinates and the other an electron spin gyroscope, which provided positional information relative to its launch point. With no GPS signal available, only the latter mode was functional. Two hours later the drone was fifty kilometers out at 5,000 meters. Hiram sat in the shade of a young banyan tree surveying the terrain through the drone's sensors. The local landforms, mountains to the west, a river to the east, told him that he was in the same place geographically as when he last entered the pod. Except that the Wah military garrison was gone, along with any trace of the Islamic Republic of Pakistan.

Hiram launched a second drone, this one designed to listen, rather than look. He picked up an English language radio broadcast. At first, the broadcast made no sense. *The Battle of Coral Sea? The Doolittle Raid on Tokyo?* An hour later, he concluded that he had emerged from the pod in British India in May of 1942 at the height of World War II. Before India became independent. Before the civil war that resulted in the formation of Pakistan. Back when Wah was a part of the state of Punjab in British India.

He had jumped almost three dozen times before without incident. Even with the technology still under development, he hadn't experienced a transport that cost him any more than ten milliseconds. Now, he sat at the exact location of the facility he destroyed with a nuclear weapon less than eight hours ago, but one hundred years before the device ever existed.

How in hell do I get home? He laughed. *Maybe I don't.*

His father Moshi and sister Rachel waited for him back home. He wouldn't make tonight's scheduled video call with them and, if he didn't think of another way out, he doubted ever making the call again. Like his mother, who had been killed in a terrorist attack in 2040, one of the many events that prompted him to join the IDF, Moshi and Rachel would become part of Hiram's irretrievable past.

Hiram climbed back through the portal and into the pod. He checked each storage compartment, opened every door in search of something that might help to throw him back to his own time. His head ached, an unfortunate symptom of Hagar's Curse. Inside one of the cabinets, he found the small wooden box his father had handed him before Hiram had taken off on his first mission almost ten years ago. The finish on the box had been worn away near the latch. He sat down on the floor of the pod and pushed open the discolored and worn brass latch.

A young Rachel smiled up at him from inside. The picture was old, almost twenty years. The edges had softened by wear. He picked up the stack beneath and cycled through the memories. More photos of Rachel, of his father, of the family before Hiram had grown up and joined the military. A family picture, taken the day he graduated basic training at Bakum, highlighted the family traits: light blue, almost hazel eyes, brown hair, rounded cheeks, and long necks, as well as the disparities. Hiram had inherited his build from his mother's side. At almost 90 kilos, he was a much larger man than his father, despite their similar, average height. The IDF had packed still more muscle on him since and his hair had eventually grown back, though he kept it short nowadays. Rachel and Moshi both looked so proud of him that day.

"In case you need us and we can't be with you," his father had said. "I know. I could have dropped them all in some virtual storage facility or posted them to one of those family media sites. But I wanted you to have a hard copy. Just in case."

"Thanks Dad," Hiram said out loud. The pod seemed too empty. He wanted to go home.

He flipped through the stack one more time and stopped at an old black and white, plastic coated photo of his father as a child. A woman who resembled Rachel held him close. Three names had been written on the back of the image:

Jonah, Danette, and Silas Halphen – May 7, 1938

"Well, you're not my father," he said. He turned the photo over and stared at the smiling, faded faces. He had gone through the pictures a hundred times, maybe more, and never read the notation on the back of this single image.

He scolded himself for not paying closer attention. But now that he travelled farther than he ever imagined from home, he wanted their support. He needed his family with him.

The alarm in the pod dinged for the second time. Two hours. The intensity of his headache blossomed at the sound. He closed his eyes and took a few breaths before sealing the pictures back in the box. He gathered a bit of camping gear, tucked the wooden box inside his pack, and climbed out of the pod. Tonight, he planned to sleep beneath the stars.

He settled in at the edge of the woods, started up a small camp stove, and prepared an MRE labeled chicken and rice. As he spooned food out of the desert colored pouch, Hiram looked through the box of pictures again.

He stopped on the old black and white photo again. *1938.* "Family is family" his father had once said during his early genealogical research. Moshi always rooted for their family. They had all survived terrible times because of his support and encouragement. The happy family stared back at Hiram from the plastic-coated image as if waiting for him to catch on to a master plan not yet disclosed to him.

"Family," he said. "I've got family here!"

Hiram pulled up his father's most recent version of their family history. Moshi Halphen held a professor of history position at Tel Aviv University and had been compiling a detailed study of the Halphen family's history. Each time he discovered a new branch of the family or found a saucy bit of information, he sent it on to both Hiram and Rachel, highlighting the installment's most intriguing contents. Hiram appreciated the small gifts more and more as he grew older. As he read the current revision date on the file, he realized this version would be the last.

He scrolled through the early years of the Halphen family until he reached a section titled World War II. The bolded words made his heart stop.

Hiram searched the text for each of the names scribbled on the old photo. Jonah had passed without warning in 1939. As things started to turn sour in Europe, young Silas had been shipped off to live with relatives in America. Danette Halphen, Hiram's great-great-grandmother, crossed France in one of the Holocaust trains headed for a camp in Upper Silesia, Poland in August of 1942. *Auschwitz.* Hiram stopped reading. He picked up the picture again and touched the face that resembled his sister Rachel.

A small section beside the text highlighted Moshi's research effort. "I spent the afternoon searching though the archived prisoner manifests for the Holocaust trains that moved the deportees from Drancy to Auschwitz. I discovered that Danette Halphen, your great-great-grandmother, spent less time at Drancy than I originally thought. After four months at Camp Joffre in Rivesaltes, she was transported via convoy to the internment camp in Drancy. She arrived at Drancy on August 13, 1942. Just fifteen days later, on August 28, 1942, she was transferred to Auschwitz on Transport 25, Train

901-20." If his father's research was correct, at this very moment Danette would be in a Vichy internment camp near Rivesaltes in the department of Pyrénées-Orientales, in the unoccupied French State, more commonly known as Vichy France.

Hiram was a soldier and it would take a physicist to figure out how he had been thrown back in time, though he surmised the nuclear explosion had something to do with it. He'd first been taught the physics of temporal artifacts in high school, knowledge that had pretty much gone in one ear and out the other. Like the C2ID2, he knew how to use the pods, but didn't really understand how they worked. He recalled a discussion about the *Butterfly Effect*, which postulated that even the tiniest change to the past would have tremendous effects on the future. Hiram reasoned that he had changed the future just by exiting the pod in 1942. He was one man. What kind of damage could one man really do? "Step on a butterfly," he said aloud. A small creature wriggled in the tree above him, the threat seeming to make it nervous. "I haven't done anything yet," he yelled at the animal.

He stared at the faces in the image one more time. He had to take the chance to save his great-great-grandmother. And then he would see what could be done about Vichy and the Nazis.

4

1320 hours, Early Afternoon, Monday, July 6, 1942, Pyrénées-Orientales Department, Vichy France

Hiram waited in a covered and concealed foxhole on a slope overlooking a mountain road near the junction of the French, Andorran, and Spanish borders. He followed the progress of an approaching convoy via an overhead drone's video feed to the C2ID2's auxiliary monitor, which rested on his knees. The C2ID2 connected to his other two companions: a small wheeled recon robot watching the road a kilometer to the east of his ambush site; and a larger armed combat robot watching the ambush site from the other side of the road with its weapons sighting sensors. The remote devices returned images from each viewpoint along with a myriad of other unnecessary data. Other than a fat fox, nothing travelled the road.

The road below made a sharp turn from south to east and ran parallel to a stream. Voluminous evergreens lined the far bank of the stream in front of him, backed by jagged, white-capped mountain crests. The forest extended all around him, interrupted only by the mountains and the well-worn dirt road. One of the heavy trees lay across the road, preventing any vehicles from passing.

The dry heat he had become accustomed to had slowly given way to a cooler, wetter climate during his journey west. In the cooling shadow of his foxhole, he considered reaching into the pod for a blanket or a heater. He figured he'd find one. Whoever prepped the damn storage bin had thought of everything.

The genius behind the pod provided Hiram with all the tools he needed to escape with all the prisoners in the convoy. Access to dated maps and historical references provided a time and place to set the plan in motion. The never-ending supply of gear, including food, water, and clothing, would be necessary to support the needs of those he intended to rescue. He had yet to find any limitations on what the pod made available. Up to this point, he found the pod's most valuable asset was the electric-drive, rigid-hull inflatable boat, or RHIB. He had used the boat to cross the sea from India to the Gulf of Aqaba. When the waterway ended, he had trekked across the Sinai Desert, travelling only at night. He avoided the extreme heat of the day by hiding inside a camouflaged cool flow blackout tent that converted the outside heat into a power source for a cooling unit. When he reached the Sinai coast, he climbed back into the RHIB and made his way to southern France.

The approaching convoy consisted of three vehicles – a command car followed by two trucks. As usual, the French police sergeant in charge of this detail had settled his 300-pound frame in the command car's spacious rear compartment. Three other policemen rode in the command car. A civilian drove each of the open-backed trucks, both hauling two policemen and eighteen exhausted female prisoners.

The convoy had set out an hour earlier from a chateau high in the Pyrenees bound for Camp Joffre, the internment camp at Rivesaltes. The women, all Jewish, were forced to serve as maids at a weekend retreat for Vichy government officials in the spa town of Vernet-les-Bains. Weekday business lacked the volume to justify keeping, or feeding, the women. So, they made the seventy-kilometer journey to the chateau each Friday afternoon and returned to the camp on Monday.

The women would return to J block which held all the other Jewish women and children well after the evening meal had been served. At the chateau, the meals provided to the women had been fresh, the bread still soft. And, unlike the near starvation rations at the camp, food had been plentiful. Sleep, on the other hand, had not. The women worked day and night.

Hiram had observed the routine for more than three weeks with his drones. The number of prisoners, the strategic positioning of guards on each truck, and the route the convoy followed remained consistent. Despite his recon effort, he prepared contingency plans to support changes in the number and arrangement of vehicles, presence of additional guards, varying arrival and departure times, and weather conditions. He continued to track the convoy's approach toward his ambush site.

The command car rounded the bend below Hiram's position and came to a skidding halt on the hard-packed dirt road to avoid hitting the large tree that Hiram had dropped across it. The two trucks that followed came to a more controlled stop behind the command car but were unable to preserve the desired distance between the vehicles, as Hiram anticipated.

With one push of a button on his C2ID2, Hiram initiated four blasting caps. The first detonated a satchel charge buried under the stopped command car. The explosion blew the vehicle and its occupants apart, the remains of the vehicle chassis settling upside down in the stream. The next explosion dropped a large tree across the road behind the second truck, cutting off any attempted escape by the remaining vehicles. The final two explosions created large craters at natural choke points in the road, approximately two kilometers in each direction from the ambush site. The narrow road remained the only route to or from the chateau. Any response the Vichy forces might mount would only get by those choke points on foot.

In less than a minute Hiram killed three of the remaining guards and one of the truck drivers with his sniper rifle. The remaining guard from the rear of the front truck and the driver of the second truck had taken refuge behind the lead truck, out of Hiram's sight line. The guard rose up and fired a wild burst in Hiram's general direction, causing him to duck. An anguished scream burst from one of the female prisoners in the lead truck. The prisoners in the second truck huddled with their heads down, some crying, some screaming.

Hiram put down his sniper rifle and turned his attention to the C2ID2 screen controlling the combat robot on the other side of the road. He adjusted the robot's position, then swiveled the gun platform a few inches, sighting on the two remaining men. At his command, the robot's nine-millimeter machine gun barked a six-round burst and both men crumpled to the ground.

"Stay in the trucks and keep your heads down," Hiram shouted twice, first in Hebrew, then in French, as he scrambled down the slope with his assault rifle in one hand and a nine-millimeter pistol in the other. Despite his French heritage, Hiram spoke only Hebrew and English. His great-grandfather Silas had abandoned all things French when he immigrated to Israel after the war because of France's complicity in the Holocaust. During the trip from India, he'd learned and then practiced a few French phrases using the real-time translator everyone called the *Babel Fish* in honor of the great English writer

Douglas Adams. Hiram thought Adams would've had a number of witty things to say about the present incarnation of his idea for a universal translator. Although accurate, the slow translations provided made the tool awkward in conversation and unacceptable in fast-paced situations like in the one Hiram now found himself. Whether or not the women understood his words, the maids complied with his direction.

Hiram approached each downed policeman and shot him in the head. The women in the trucks screamed some more. Unable to find one man, Hiram presumed the body was entangled in the remains of the command car.

Turning his attention to the women, he shouted "Danette Halphen, identify yourself!" in Hebrew, then French. That phrase almost exhausted his French and revealing the Babel Fish to these women promised to raise questions he didn't want to answer.

"You must help us," one of the women in the first truck said. "Elsie's been shot."

Hiram sprinted over to the first truck. He climbed into the cargo bed. One of the prisoners clutched her upper abdomen, blood oozed between her fingers. He didn't expect her to survive long, even with his 21st Century medical supplies.

After a quick examination, he turned to the women and said in Hebrew, "I can ease her suffering with a pain killer. She's going to bleed out quickly. I'm sorry." One of the maids passed along the message to the others. He pulled an auto-injector full of morphine from the medical kit on his belt and jabbed it into her thigh, then applied combat gauze to the wound, which did little to staunch the flowing blood. He said, "I'm sorry" once more. Someone touched his arm, and he turned.

She pointed to herself and said, "Danette Halphen."

Hiram closed his eyes and opened them again. He had traveled here for the woman in the picture. Nothing prepared him for the shock of seeing his great-great-grandmother standing before him. Her young, rounded cheeks were accentuated by a beautiful, comforting smile so much like Rachel's. He forced himself to focus on her, the adrenalin made it difficult.

"Your cousin David in America sent me to rescue you." Hiram had practiced the story a hundred times along the way, often employing the Babel Fish to test his rusty Hebrew. With Danette's son Silas living with David and his wife Eliza in America – a wise decision made after the "Night of Broken Glass" that took place in late 1938 – Hiram thought the rescue scenario viable. Explaining time travel to a woman who had not yet heard of an atomic bomb, or the liftoff of a shuttle headed for the stars, seemed less believable.

A woman repeated his story in French. A few others exchanged quiet words.

"I'll take you and anyone else who cares to come, but we need to leave now."

"You are here to save us?" one of the women said in well-practiced Hebrew.

He hadn't taken his eyes off the woman claiming to be Danette. "Yes, we need to go now."

The corner of Danette's lips lifted and he saw his sister standing before him for an instant. He returned his attention to the group, reassured his great-great-grandmother was among them.

"Please come with me if you want to live. I suggest we all get moving."

The women in the trucks hesitated, looking at each other for reassurance. After a moment, most climbed down and gathered a few meters away. A few of the women remained by the fallen woman's side.

"They won't leave Elsie behind." A woman approached him, her Hebrew distorted and uncomfortable, not native. "You save the families?"

"If we stay here much longer, we won't have a chance to save them," Hiram said.

The woman looked at him for a moment, as if his words made no sense. "You save the families?" A wisp of curly brown hair had escaped her green scarf and swept across her face as a welcome breeze slipped past.

"I'll do everything in my power to save them," he said. *As long as Danette stays safe.*

She nodded and headed toward the women by the truck. She spoke quietly to them and still they refused to come along. Hiram worried they might tell the French police what happened. About a stranger coming to the rescue. About a stranger with a tie to Danette Halphen. After a few minutes of argument, the woman with the green scarf returned to Hiram defeated. "They stay. We go now."

He looked back at the five women huddled in the truck with Elsie, all thin and terrified, then focused on those willing to leave. "You'll translate for me?"

"*Oui*. Yes," she said.

Hiram directed the thirty remaining women down into the stream. They whimpered as the cool mountain water encircled their bare legs. Around the bend and out of eyeshot from the road, six inflatable boats and one kayak waited for Hiram's return. Each boat held up to six women, the kayak only two. Since six of the thirty-six women that travelled on the two trucks wouldn't be coming along, they would use only five of the boats. Getting the women loaded into the boats from the waist deep water took a few minutes, but they all managed to get in. Once they settled in the boats, Hiram considered giving a lesson on the life vests stored in each boat. Time wasn't on his side.

"This will be easy," he explained. "All you need to do is guide the boats downstream." He used a paddle to demonstrate. "A half-kilometer from here the stream will cross under a bridge then diverge from the road, heading off into the wilderness to the north. About three kilometers from there you'll see a spot where a large tree has fallen across the stream. If I haven't caught up to you by then, wait for me in the still water behind the tree. Stay in the boats – do not get out on shore."

"Where are you going?" the woman in the green scarf said.

"I have to clean up this site so we can't be followed," he replied. "I'll be along as soon as I can." He severed the ropes securing the inflatable boats in place with his combat knife and pushed the boats downstream. "Now get moving – you need to make it be past the bridge before anyone comes up the road from the east."

Hiram sent a recall signal to the ground recon robot and the larger combat robot, then took hold of the remaining boat and cut its anchor line before dragging it to shore. He collapsed the boat by removing its internal ribs and deflating the internal bladders. Hiram waded back into the river and retrieved the six boat anchors, carrying them two at a time to a large boulder near the far shore. He laid his backpack out on the rock, activated the portal within, and dropped the anchors into the pod. The collapsible boat and its paddles followed. He lowered in his sniper rifle, attaching the weapon to the mount on the wall nearest the opening. When the combat robot arrived, Hiram activated the robot's portability mode and the device began to fold in on itself. The machine gun arm retracted and the six road wheels rotated and disappeared into the robot's belly. He pushed the device through the portal as the recon robot arrived. Hiram scooped up the smaller device, along with his backpack. He slung the assault rifle over his shoulder and made his way back to the kayak still waiting in the waist deep water. Once the rifle, robot, and pack had been stored and sealed in the cargo hatches, Hiram climbed in himself, pulled up the anchor, stowed it in its storage compartment, and set off downstream.

Three kilometers past the bridge, Hiram caught up to the five inflatable boats, all huddled close to the fallen tree partially blocking the stream. Several of the women held on to adjacent boats, keeping them from drifting farther downstream alone. As he floated toward the cluster, he stowed his paddle and pulled the C2ID2 auxiliary monitor from its storage pouch on the front of his combat vest. The view from the aerial drone showed a swarm of French policemen filtering through the choke point coming from the chateau. The policemen carried small caliber weapons and no watercraft. Any immediate search for the missing women would be conducted on foot.

"I hope you've had a chance to get used to the boats," Hiram told them once he had paddled into their midst. "The water gets a little rougher from here. We'll be moving deeper into the wilderness as we go, so we'll be less visible."

He reached into the storage compartment of his kayak and pulled out a metallic bag, then held it up for the women to see. The bag held enough high-protein meal bars to satisfy at least ten of these women. The bars were labeled with English food names like beef wellington and grilled tuna, none of which matched the actual taste of the thing inside. Every food he pulled out of the portal tasted the same, smelled like animal feed. He assumed the pod caused the unsavory flavor. "This is food. You will find one of these bags in each of your boats. You open it like this." He pinched the tab at the top of his package and pulled the seal away. "Eat. You'll need your strength."

The woman in the green scarf translated for the other women, showing them how to open the bags just as he had.

"Your name?" Hiram asked the woman.

"Deborah Lowenstein," she said.

"You speak French?"

"Most of us do. Much better than Hebrew. Except for Maria, she speaks better Spanish."

Hiram nodded, disappointed. He never learned a bit of Spanish.

"What about English?" Deborah said in English.

Hiram smiled. "Everyone speaks English too?"

"No, but Sarah and I do." She pointed to another of the women who held up her hand.

"It will have to do." He kept his eyes on Deborah. "You tell them what I say when they need to know."

Deborah nodded.

"Go on. Eat," he said. Though Hiram detested the protein bars, the women seemed to savor each tiny bite. He caught a glimpse of a few pleased smiles with brown flecks of food stuck between their teeth.

The remaining journey downstream was quiet. Hiram supposed the joy of a full belly paired with the prospect of freedom contented the former prisoners. If nothing else, they paddled hard and took direction well. The little flotilla covered another twenty kilometers downstream before the sky began to darken. Hiram directed the exhausted women toward a rocky slope at the water's edge. Each boat came to stop amid a hurried mix of splashing and whimpering as the women jumped out into the frigid water and began pulling the boats to shore.

After grounding his kayak, he jumped out and pulled his gear out of the storage compartment. He laid his pack on the rocky shore, away from the women, and spread it open. Reaching into the kayak, he removed the ribs that gave the kayak its shape, so it collapsed into an eight-foot long pile of canvas and plastic stays. After another two folds, the kayak was portable.

"We need to do the same with your boats," he said. Hiram showed them how to remove and fold the ribs and deflate the boats. Each boat compacted down to the size of a briefcase. The five boats sat lined up on the rocky shore. Thirty women walked about the low-lying area working out the stiffness of sitting for so long.

He opened his pack and activated the portal, exposing the white surface inside. One by one, he picked up each of the compacted boats and began to send them through the portal. His pack did not grow fuller. He pushed two of the boats through without question, but the third drew attention. Deborah spoke up first. "How can-What is-?" She stepped back from him. "Magic?"

"No, not magic. I mean it looks like magic." He paused for a moment, uncertain if the truth would hurt the situation. "In basic terms, it's a portal, like a door to someplace else."

"To where?"

Some of the other women ventured closer, watching. He picked up another boat and pushed it through the portal.

"It's a storage area. A place I can keep things." He reached in and felt around for something detachable and pulled out a spare spotter scope

17

mounted near the portal's location in the pod. "Until I need them."

Deborah reached toward the milky white surface. "Can I try?"

"No!" He stepped between Deborah and the open portal.

She jumped back. "I didn't mean to-"

All of the women watched now, curious and uncertain.

"The portal only works for me. I don't know what would happen if you tried." He lied. After the incident with the dog...

Deborah picked up the last compacted boat in line and held it out to Hiram. "I can help then."

Hiram relaxed and knelt back down on the ground beside the pack. "Yes, of course." He accepted Deborah's offering and slid it through the portal.

She then handed him the smaller kayak.

"Let them know," he closed his pack. "No one touches my pack."

Deborah nodded and said a few words in French to the women.

One of the others, a short woman with a dark brown braid that swept across her lower back, asked a question. Hiram looked at Deborah, hoping she'd translate for him.

Instead, Deborah looked to the short woman and as she spoke, the woman shook her head and seemed to slump at the retort. Then Deborah looked at Hiram, waiting for the next direction.

"Let's get moving," he said.

None of the women questioned the order. They nodded, looked away from the water, and began climbing the small, rocky incline.

He led the group into the woods, following a deer trail cut into the overgrown vegetation, urging the women to duck under the low-lying branches. Once the group entered the thick cover of the trees, he returned to erase any sign of their passage. He dragged a heavy branch along the shoreline, spreading loose pebbles and erasing footprints. He covered the marks left by the climb up the embankment by moving around a few leafy vines and a fallen tree branch. *Not perfect, but good enough.* He made his way back to the maids, covering his tracks along the trail.

"We'll spend the night here," he announced once he rejoined the women. Deborah translated. No one argued.

"I'll need to go through the portal for supplies," he said to Deborah.

She signaled for Danette to join them. "We'll watch your pack," Deborah said.

After Deborah translated, Danette nodded and aligned herself on the opposite side of Hiram's pack, which he had placed on the ground.

Hiram looked around at all of the women who stared at him. Each one weary from the long journey.

"Go on," Deborah said. "It's your turn to trust us."

* * *

When Hiram returned from setting the motion detectors up around the camp, he found all thirty women huddled in a circle around the dull glow of the heat unit he had procured from the pod. Some held blankets over their shoulders, others reached out to touch the phantom fire before them. They talked amongst themselves. Deborah and Danette sat side by side, Hiram's pack on the ground between them, just as he'd left it.

He took up a place on the ground beside them, thanked them for protecting his gear. A woman brought Hiram a serving of pot pie in a metallic bag, then returned to her spot in the circle.

The short woman, shortest among them, he had observed, said something to him in French.

Deborah looked at him. "She wants to know who you are. They all do."

He hesitated. "You can call me Hiram."

Deborah translated for the others.

Danette spoke and Deborah translated her words for Hiram. "He knows my family. The ones in America."

"You are an American?" Deborah said.

"Not exactly. I grew up in the Sinai but immigrated with my family to America in 1936 when the *Society of Muslim Brothers* began harassing Jews living on the peninsula. Right after the Arab Revolt started in Palestine."

Deborah shortened his response for the benefit of the group. The women's eyes moved from Hiram to Deborah to Danette, curious and uncertain.

"I spent some time in America when I was young. My father taught biology at Brandeis University," Deborah said.

"I –" Hiram started.

The short woman spoke again, Deborah translated. "Barbara wants to know why you came for us."

Hiram looked at Danette and back to the short woman Barbara, her eyes dark, almost black.

"I was sent by a man named David Wiseman," he said. "A journalist in Washington."

"His family is taking care of my son," Danette confirmed. "He's my cousin."

"Wiseman's got a source in Army Intelligence with the American War Department. The Americans intercepted communication about a Nazi plot to exterminate all the Jews in Europe, not to mention a few other supposed undesirable groups. From what they've gathered, Hitler's calling it the Final Solution." A few understood his words, Deborah translated for the rest. Heated conversation broke out among them. Disbelief. Fear. Anger. A few began sobbing.

"The camp you were headed back to – Camp Joffre, is caught up in this mess. The prisoners in F and J Blocks are to be shipped out in August. The plan is to move the group to an SS run camp near Paris and then to an extermination camp in Poland." He stuck as close as possible to the truth. When Deborah completed her translation, Barbara stood with fists clenched and rattled off a few fiery accusations.

Danette talked back to her this time, almost spitting her retort. For two minutes, the two women barked at each other.

Finally, Hiram stood up, put a hand on his great-great-grandmother's arm. "I am here to help you, and to help your families. I need you to trust me." It sounded wrong. He was already hiding so much.

Deborah took a moment to translate.

"I need your help. Together, we are going to rescue them all."

"We have no weapons," someone said.

Yet another woman addressed her. She said something about a "porter."

"Portal," someone corrected.

"He has to have more guns?"

"We don't know how to fight," said another.

"He'll teach us," Danette said.

For a time, the women continued the discussion. They talked, they argued, and, more than once, they even laughed. Deborah continued translating the statements of importance and Hiram offered words of agreement.

He had formulated a plan, the start of one at least.

Despite the energy the women around him mustered, Hiram felt the day's activity wearing him down. He settled back down to the ground and leaned against the tree behind him. On his wrist, the C2ID2 monitored the motion sensors. As he drifted off, his great-great-grandmother laid a blanket over him.

5

2130 hours, Monday, July 6, 1942, Pyrénées-Orientales Department, Vichy France

Sarah Mandelson, former professor of physics at the University of Paris, watched from the other side of the campfire as Danette laid a blanket over their would-be savior. Everything Sarah understood about the physical universe contradicted Hiram's technology. *His portal seems impossible, yet it exists.*

She had to accept what she had witnessed. She had touched the ground where Hiram laid his pack, thinking – no, hoping – for evidence of a magician's trick. Whatever kind of science explained his magic was well beyond anything published before the damn war. *Necessity is the mother of invention. The Nazis have certainly provided the impetus.*

So here she sat, in the middle of the forest, with twenty-nine women and a strange man, being hunted by the police. And, if they believed Hiram's story, all marked for death. She was relieved that her brother had taken a position in a bank in Switzerland a month before the roundup began. His wife and young son had relocated with him. Sarah had been offered a place in their new apartment, but she refused to abandon the family home. A ridiculous choice now that she thought about it. She believed Hitler and his Gestapo wanted to destroy the Jews, but she doubted Vichy cooperation in the mass murder of millions of men, women, and children. They all found it hard to believe. *Still, they rounded us all up and stuck us in that camp. To what possible end? And if I hadn't returned to my family home in Narbonne after being dismissed from the University, I'd probably already be dead.* She would never forget the day the department head stepped into her lab and told her the Jewish were no longer allowed to hold academic titles. She missed teaching.

"We cannot trust him!" Barbara's hiss pulled Sarah's attention back to the discussion around the heater.

"We have no choice," Deborah said. "He has the weapons and knowledge we need to save our families."

"What if he's lying?" Ellen asked. "We could go back on our own. The Vichy said they would only hold us until the war ended so we didn't hamper the war effort."

"What if he's telling the truth? Then we all die like dogs," Danette said. "Better to go down fighting."

"Easy for you to say," Frieda said. "You don't have family back there."

"Neither do I," said Rosette. "You can do what you want; they're going to have to drag me back to that camp. I'm not even Jewish! I was born and raised Catholic. I was no threat to anybody. They arrested me anyway. The police said I was a Jew because one of my great-grandparents was Jewish. They just wanted to get rid of me."

"What about his portal or pod, or whatever it is?" Ellen asked, nodding towards the pack lying between Deborah and Danette.

"I never would have believed it if I hadn't seen it with my own eyes," Sarah answered. "I have no idea how it works, but it does. It lends credence to his story. That level of technology almost certainly came from the Americans. I heard they entered the war a few months ago. If the Axis Powers had that capability the war would be over by now. Same with the British and Russians."

"She's right," said Ester, who had only arrived at Camp Joffre a few weeks earlier.

Sarah had listened to the officer's conversations back at the Chateau, all the while serving tea or afternoon meals. She lingered during those times, searching for information that might give her fellow detainees hope. The officers spoke openly at the Chateau. Sometimes they talked about their wives, sometimes their children. On occasion, she heard them talk about defiling the maids, though none had made an effort to do so. They shared news from every corner of France, of resistance, and of unsatisfactory leadership. Once in a while she heard about defeat, a thing they all feared. They exchanged somber words about the lost lives of fellow countrymen. Not the Jewish ones though. Except there had been a man who talked about how he missed the Jewish woman who used to bake the sweetest bread. The way he said it, Sarah swore he missed the woman more. But news of American involvement, that had been scant, almost non-existent. "According to what I've heard, the Americans haven't done much of anything. They fought in a big naval battle at Midway and defeated the Japanese. Little good that's done for us."

"If we hide and wait, they'll come and free France," Ellen said.

"If Hiram speaks the truth," Sarah said, "they'll be too late. Everyone in Drancy is scheduled to ship out in August, including our families. And I, for one, will do everything in my power to prevent that from happening. If that means trusting a Yiddish wizard with a magical Tinderbox, then that's what I plan to do."

6

1510 hours, Monday, July 6, 1942, Perpignan, Pyrénées-Orientales Department, Vichy France

Captain Louis Petain, Chief of Police for the Pyrénées-Orientales Department, hiked down a mountain road that supported the passage of a full-sized cargo truck up until an hour ago. The climb over the fallen tree that blocked the road had left a sizeable hole in the side of his uniform pants. Thick, heavy cakes of mud stuck to his polished boots. If the current situation hadn't demolished his pleasant mood, having to cancel this week's date with his delicate young morsel of a mistress finished the job.

"What in hell happened here?" he barked at the first man he saw at the site.

"An ambush, sir," the underling said.

"I can see that, fool. Where are the prisoners?"

"Thirty of them are gone, sir. We caught five, and one died of a gunshot wound."

"And my men?" Petain's anger swelled. "What about my men?"

"Seven of our men are dead, sir. As are both the hired drivers. Corporal Leveque is barely alive. He was blown out of the command car and wound up in a tree. We got him down and four of my men are carrying him to an ambulance at the roadblock west of here."

"What did he tell you?

"Nothing sir, he was unconscious. But the remaining prisoners are willing to talk. Said something about a man dressed as a soldier."

THE MAIDS OF CHATEAU VERNET

"One man did all this?" the captain said.

"That's what the women said, sir. They said he spoke Hebrew, not French. He led the other prisoners east, around the bend in the road. We found tracks leading down to the water, but we haven't found an exit point yet. I've sent for dogs."

"Keep searching."

"Yes, sir." The underling stood in place.

"Get on with it."

"Sir, one of the women said the man was somehow connected to a prisoner named Danette Halphen. He called out to her after the attack."

Petain rolled the name around for a minute. "Name mean anything to you?"

"No sir."

He dismissed the younger man and the policeman sped off to execute his orders. Lieutenant Lebeau, his most trusted subordinate, arrived a few minutes later.

"Lebeau, I want you to take charge of the five remaining prisoners. Question them closely; they may still have useful information." Lebeau nodded his understanding and moved off without a word.

Petain spent the next several hours prowling around the ambush site. He found remnants of satchel charges and discovered the mysterious soldier's foxhole. Inside he found only four shell casings. He expected more. Two odd sets of tracks, one from a small four-wheeled cart and another from some type of small tracked vehicle, added to the confusion. A nuisance ran loose in Petain's jurisdiction. He intended to deal with him before he caused any more trouble.

Before leaving the site, Petain found Lebeau with the five remaining maids, his stance more relaxed than acceptable considering the situation. Several of his comrades lost their lives because of these damned Jews. The maids leaned against the back of the truck with the least damage. They straightened up as Petain approached. Lebeau met Petain halfway.

"Any new information?" Petain said.

"No sir."

"Do you mind if I have a moment with them?"

"Of course not, sir."

Petain approached the women, stepping around the dead one on the ground gathering a compliment of flies. Someone had covered her face with an apron, the ties sprawling away from her head. He stopped for a moment and looked at the body, reflecting for his audience's benefit and not his own. "My condolences for your loss," he said to the women. "We lost a few good men today as well. Such a tragedy."

He approached the woman to the left of the truck. Petain took her hand and guided her up in to the truck. "Have a seat." He ushered the others in, helping them climb up into the back. "We'll get you back to camp soon. I'm sure you wish to see your families."

Once they were all seated, he climbed up into the truck with them and sat near the back. "I know that Officer Lebeau has been kind enough to gather information from you all." Lebeau waited outside the truck, watching. "If you don't mind I'd like to ask you a couple of questions myself before we get you out of here."

A woman beside him spoke up. "What do you want to know?"

"Where did this mysterious soldier come from?" Petain asked.

"I don't know," she said.

"Do you know why he killed my men?"

"No sir."

He put a hand on her shoulder, gripped her tight. Without another word, he pulled out his pistol, cocked the hammer, pointed it at the woman's head, and pulled the trigger. He let go of her shoulder and the body slumped over onto the woman beside her.

The other four women in the truck whimpered. When asked, each one rattled off the same information Lebeau had gathered. When he shot the fourth woman, the remaining maid jumped out of the truck and started running. She tripped over the body with the apron covering its head. Lebeau approached the woman as if he intended to restrain her.

"No need Lebeau." Petain aimed and shot the woman in the back as she made it to her feet. He hit her just below the right shoulder blade. After a quick examination of the pistol, he decided he needed to schedule some target practice. He would have his assistant block out some time when he got back to the office.

"Lebeau, clean up this mess." Petain jumped down out of the truck.

"What should we do with the bodies?"

Petain pulled out his kerchief and wiped the sweat off his face. It came away dotted with pink. "Bury them, burn them. I don't care."

Petain headed back to his car with mud caked shoes, torn pants, and Jew blood speckling his uniform. His irritation grew.

Returning to his office in the provincial capital of Perpignan failed to improve his mood.

"Call my wife and tell her I'll be late," he said to his secretary. "And get that criminalist Locard over here, *tout de suite.*"

"Yes sir," the woman said as Petain disappeared into his spacious office.

Emile Locard arrived ten minutes later, flushed from a brisk two block walk to Petain's office. "You wished to see me sir?"

"Have you heard about the escaped prisoners and murder of seven of our men?" he asked.

"I heard nine," Locard replied.

"Yes, yes, seven policemen and a couple of civilian drivers returning a group of maids from Chateau Vernet." He handed Locard the four bullet casings he found near Hiram's foxhole. "What do you make of these?"

"High quality. Thirty caliber cartridges, but I'll have to measure to make sure. The markings on the base are not familiar – SXP300WM. American Winchester, I suppose."

"The bodies will be here tonight. Dig the slugs out of them, cut them up, or whatever it is you people do with them. I don't care, but I want you out at the ambush site at first light. The damn road should be fixed by then. Don't even think about sleep. I need to know what I'm dealing with before I get a call from the Marshall's office."

Louis Petain's granduncle, Marshall Philippe Petain, popularly known as the *Lion of Verdun,* had been appointed French Prime Minister in 1940, negotiated the French surrender to the Nazis, and became head of state in unoccupied Vichy France. A report regarding the loss of seven policemen and two civilians would cross his desk in the next couple of days, followed by the news of thirty escaped Jews from Camp Joffre. The Marshall's staff, who had seized the opportunity provided by the Germans to rid France of the Jewish lice, would look to hang someone's hide on a wall. Captain Louis Petain planned to make damn sure the hide in question belonged to someone else.

7

0630 hours, Tuesday, July 7, 1942, West of Vingrau, Pyrénées-Orientales Department, Vichy France

Hiram scratched out a crude map in the dirt beneath the towering pine trees. "Camp Joffre is about twenty kilometers by road from the harbor at Port Leucate," Hiram said. "The docks are lightly guarded. A number of the docked cargo vessels are large enough. Should be easy to take one over. With only a few guards on duty at the camp, freeing the prisoners should be pretty simple too. The hard part comes with moving the prisoners from the camp to the dock. We'll need to hold off any response from the camp while we make our way past the harbor defenses. Once we sail out into the Mediterranean, we're looking at about thirty nautical miles – that's three hours – to the nearest Spanish port. We can bribe our way ashore."

Danette stared at Hiram, eyes wide when she spoke. "You want to steal a ship?" Deborah translated.

"With a large enough diversion, we have a chance," Hiram said.

Barbara lit up as Deborah spoke. "Like freeing the other five thousand prisoners at the camp?"

"Exactly," Hiram said.

"How much time do we have?" Sarah said.

"Not much," Hiram said. "According to Wiseman's source, the inmates in F and J Blocks will be moved to Drancy in mid-August." Hiram prayed that the recent events surrounding the escape of the thirty maids wouldn't accelerate the timetable. He planned to keep an eye on the camp.

* * *

Shortly after breakfast, Hiram led his thirty new recruits deeper into the wilderness. Adaptive camouflage uniforms with matching body armor and helmets replaced the delicate cotton blouses and skirts the women wore the previous day. Dress shoes were set aside in favor of hefty black boots that altered their once feminine gait. Although the location they spent their first night offered suitable cover, he wanted more distance between them and their pursuers. The new campsite he had selected rested miles from any settlements, near the abandoned village of Périllos. On the hike to their new temporary home, Hiram, with Deborah's help, talked to his troops about maneuvering through the woods, about keeping an eye on their surroundings and on the others in the team. His unfamiliarity with this version of the world made it hard to assume anything. He couldn't be sure if hunters moved through these woods or if wolves sought out easy prey. His mini-lessons kept them safe from French Policemen, while his eyes searched for more native predators.

* * *

After two hours of hiking they reached a small break in the forest. While the women rested and drank from water bottles, Hiram deployed one of his aerial drones to detect any intruders long before they became a threat. He opened up the portal and reached in. With the exception of his sniper rifle and the nine-millimeter pistols, most of his weaponry consisted of nearly silent rail guns like the M22 assault rifles – an IDF standard. Training the women in the isolation of the woods wouldn't attract too much attention. He retrieved an M22 assault rifle for each of his would-be soldiers.

He issued a rifle to each woman, removing the standard holographic sites since it would take several days to train the former prisoners on their proper use. Despite their light weight, the weapons seemed bulky and awkward against the thin build of most of the women. But a few of the women held the carbon fiber and steel rifles with confidence, as if today were just another day out in the field.

The remainder of the morning was spent familiarizing the women with the weapons. Safety had been Hiram's main concern in turning over such powerful tools to such green hands. "Don't point a weapon at anything you don't intend to kill," he told them over and over again, with Deborah by his side translating. "Don't put your finger on the trigger unless you are ready to fire." They listened well and learned quickly. By lunchtime, Hiram began to trust his new team without much hesitation.

It took most of the afternoon for the women to become comfortable with the weapons. The M22's quiet design and minimal recoil certainly helped. After the initial how-to on proper loading, Hiram allowed for a short period of target practice. He walked behind them, Deborah at his side, watching them at work. Firing. Reloading. Firing again. A few of the women fired tight shot groups after only a handful of rounds. By the time he made the call to end the exercise, he had identified the best shots among them: Ester, Lea, Frieda, Ellen, and even Danette. Hiram intended to test their skill. He wanted all thirty of these women, otherwise inexperienced in combat, to be able to protect themselves. Even if they presented little skill in the initial session, he needed them all to know how to put down an assailant. He needed to make sure Danette made it out of this mess alive.

Hiram was second in line as they resumed their hike through the woods, with Sarah just a step behind him. The short woman, Barbara took point in front of him. While her small stature made her an asset in that position – he thought her more likely to see someone before they saw her – the loaded weapon she carried was the real reason Hiram kept her in sight. He guided her whenever they came to another branch of the deer trails they followed.

Hiram's C2ID2 held topographical maps of Europe, circa 2050. During his long journey from Wah to Rivesaltes he had learned to compare and contrast the images sent by his aerial drones with the maps, picking his way past man-made and natural obstacles. On occasion he missed one.

Barbara signaled a halt and everyone crouched down, weapons at the ready. Hiram made his way forward to see what had spooked her. A steep embankment that led down to a dirt road below blocked their path. A heavy overhead canopy of oak and maple branches prevented the drone from detecting the obstruction.

He looked up and down the road. Avoiding the exposed climb required a long walk around the embankment. He decided to take a chance. It would be a worthwhile training exercise.

Barbara crossed first. She set up an overwatch position in the woods on the far side of the road to match his own on the near side. One by one, the women clambered down to the road, then scampered across into the forest. Twenty of his soldiers made it across when Hiram heard the sound of a motorcycle.

Ester stood exposed at the bottom of the small cliff. She flattened herself into the shrubs along the roadside as the bike came into view. Too late.

Two French soldiers rode the motorcycle, the driver and a passenger in the sidecar. It roared up the road, then skidded to a halt adjacent to Ester's position. Hiram didn't hesitate. He shot both men before they even dismounted.

Concerned that a larger convoy followed the motorcycle, Hiram signaled his soldiers to "Stay down." He cursed as he flicked an icon on his C2ID2 to switch the drone's camera from visible to infrared. Infrared made it more difficult to spot natural obstacles, but he missed the cycle's approach because of that mistake.

The display remained devoid of any other man-made heat sources. He reassured himself that any others nearby would have revealed themselves or fled after he killed the two soldiers.

Hiram turned to the remaining women arrayed along the top of the embankment. "Let's continue the crossing. Frieda, help Ester move that motorcycle into the woods." Deborah interpreted his orders and crossed, followed by Hiram. Now he had two dead soldiers and a motorcycle with sidecar to address. The soldiers would be reported missing, and soon. He removed his pack, laid it open on the ground, and activated the portal.

"Deborah, give me a hand. The rest of you keep watch." They wrestled the soldiers' bodies through the portal, then turned their attention to the motorcycle. The heavy bike was too big to fit through the portal without first breaking it down into much smaller pieces. Hiram decided to push it further into the woods. The uneven terrain made the move slow but with Deborah at his side, they managed to get the motorcycle out of view from the road. As an added precaution, Hiram covered the bike with a camouflage net from his pod. After deactivating the portal, Hiram lingered over the bag. He scolded himself for his mistake.

Deborah put a hand on his shoulder. "We should keep moving,"

* * *

Barbara continued to walk point, followed by Hiram and Sarah. Deborah followed ten meters behind Sarah, close to Hiram in case he needed a translator. Danette walked behind Deborah. Ester took up the rear, almost three hundred meters back. From the moment he had handed her the M22, she seemed the most comfortable.

"Your pod and the weapons inside are beyond my comprehension," Sarah said. "The existence of such things is a physical impossibility."

"And yet they exist," Hiram said.

"Well yes, but how? Where do they come from?"

Hiram expected this question and had formulated an answer reasonably close to the truth, but decades off in timing. "Have you ever heard of the Skunk Works?"

Sarah remained silent for a moment. "I don't think so. Of course, military equipment like yours probably isn't presented in the university's physics texts just yet."

"Were you a student?"

Sarah stopped, reached out a hand to Hiram. "Sarah Mandelson. I used to teach physics at the University in Paris."

The greeting shocked him out of focus. Hiram shook the woman's hand. Once he let go, she returned her attention to the woods around her and continued walking. Hiram did the same.

"So, tell me about this *Skunk Works*," she continued in English.

"It's an American weapons development facility – top secret. I've been told they employ the best scientists of our time."

"Like Albert Einstein?" she asked.

"People like him, although I'm not sure if he's involved himself. Oppenheimer is the guy in charge." In 1942, the Manhattan Project was still in its infancy and he doubted Sarah had any knowledge of it.

"J. Robert Oppenheimer? The professor from Berkeley? I met him once," Sarah said. "An astrophysicist, isn't he?"

Hiram winced. He had no intention of building a myth on unstable ground. "Maybe. You have to forgive me. I'm a simple soldier of fortune. I know how to make the portal work and access the pod, not how it actually functions."

"Its resources seem to be limitless," she replied.

"Essentially, they are. The pod resets itself each time I open the portal, unless I tell it not to. Every time I enter, the weapons magazines and larders are full. It's quite handy, unless you get stuck inside." Hiram remembered his growing panic right after the Wah incident.

"Does that happen often?" Sarah said.

"I don't think so," he said. "Only happened to me once. You've got about six hours before you start getting really sick. Stay beyond nine and you can kiss your ass goodbye."

32

"Too bad we can't all travel through the portal to somewhere else," Sarah said.

"It would certainly make life easier if we could." Hiram shrugged. "No sense worrying about it I guess. We have to make the best of the tools we have, and the pod is a quite useful tool." *But will it be enough?*

"Except you are the only one who can use it." Sarah ducked under a tree branch as they walked. "If anything happens to you, we'll have to kiss all of our," she paused as if trying to find the right words, "all of our asses goodbye."

8

0800 hours, Thursday, July 9, 1942, south of Périllos, Pyrénées-Orientales Department, Vichy France

"Set the device by depressing the switch." He handed the C2ID2 auxiliary display to Ellen. "When the sensor detects a change in the surrounding environment you'll be notified here." He waved his hand over the device and the monitor chirped. On the screen, a small red dot flashed in correlation to their current location on the map. Several green indicators were spread out on the view, all idle.

"What about this one?" Ellen pointed to the blue dot.

"The blue dot is the location of the C2ID2 monitor. The green ones are surveillance bots set up around camp. You want to make sure you and the monitor are well out of range before setting off one of the charges." He sent Ellen off with the monitor and Rosette and Barbara off with additional simulated satchel charges.

Deborah sat down on the ground beside Hiram. She handed him a protein bar – this one labeled blackened tuna. He cringed, recalling the last time he'd tasted the so-called tuna, but accepted the snack. "They are learning well?"

"And quick. I thought the technology would be a problem. Most have taken to it easily." He took a bite of the protein bar. "Emma and Justine's ability to pick up the maintenance procedures on the combat robots surprised me."

"They both worked as forced laborers in a Vichy munitions factory before being sent to Camp Joffre," Deborah said. "Those places are dangerous. The foremen probably made them fix the machines themselves rather than risk Gentile lives to a random spark."

"Well they both know how to turn a wrench, which could come in handy down the road."

"Do you think we'll be ready when the time comes?"

"I am amazed at how far they've come already."

"What did you expect? You've given us a reason to fight. If not for our lives, then for those of our loved ones. Now we have the means as well. We certainly don't feel helpless." She leaned over and kissed Hiram on the cheek. Then she was up again, moving, distributing high protein, high carbohydrate snack packs to her fellow soldiers.

He touched his cheek. Hiram had been at war too long - even before this time travel incident. How long had he been fighting? How many years had he been at it? He remembered a girl back home, the one he'd seen blown to bits by civil unrest. She had been the one to suggest he join the damned service in the first place. She had once kissed him like that.

Soon, these women would be reunited with their families and Hiram could focus on what to do about his situation. Maybe he could take a chance at a normal life here in 1942. He laughed to himself. He was a soldier. He didn't have time for such things – not now.

* * *

1930 hours, Friday, July 10, 1942, Pyrénées-Orientales Department, Vichy France

Hiram's CDID2 chimed. He pulled up the infrared view. One of the drones detected an intruder four hundred meters north of the campsite. An armed man headed straight towards their campsite, moving with purpose.

Hiram switched to the daylight camera. The man carried a primitive shotgun and he appeared to be tracking something. A hunter!

His soldiers provided an audience. They had heard the chime, knew what it meant. Deborah joined him, translating for the group.

"A wolf?" Rosette said.

"No. We've got company. Turn down the lights."

Frieda made it to the small control unit at the center of the camp and turned down all the surrounding glow lights. Hiram watched the display. The hunter paused when the lights went out, then continued at an even quicker pace.

"Kak," Hiram said. *Shit.*

Deborah said, "What do we do?"

"We don't take any chances." On Hiram's signal, the women assumed their preplanned defensive positions around the perimeter of the campsite as they had during the previous day's exercise. Hiram found a spot along the hunter's presumed path and waited with his Taser in one hand, pistol in the other. He hoped to take the man alive and decide what to do with him later.

As the hunter passed Hiram's location, the unmistakable zip-zip of an M22 rail gun cut through the air. The hunter spun around on impact, blood blossoming from his chest. Further along the path, almost hidden from his line of sight, Barbara knelt under a low hanging branch.

"He would betray us," she said, her weapon now lax in her arms. "We must save our families."

* * *

1935 hours, Wednesday, July 15, 1942, Pyrénées-Orientales Department, Vichy France

Barbara sat close to the heater. Three other women, Danette among them, sat nearby as well. They spoke to one another quietly. Hiram made out a few of the words, though the topic of their discussion eluded him.

After the incident with the hunter, Hiram doubted his judgment in training all of the women with weaponry. The look in Barbara's eyes after she had taken the shot concerned him. He told himself fear forced her to pull the trigger.

They had buried the French hunter four days ago in a subtly marked grave about a kilometer from camp. Each of his soldiers gathered around and offered prayers for the man who now lay beneath the dirt. Barbara's prayer seemed sincere. Still, her eyes worried him.

Deborah shot out of the woods behind him, out of breath. She crouched next to him and lifted the sixth-generation night vision goggles away from her eyes. "I wish I had these when I was a kid. I could have been the cache-cache champion of the village."

"Cache-cache?"

"Hide and seek."

"And the others?" he asked without taking his eyes from the four women seated around the heater.

"We surrounded the camp. They'll be popping up-" She paused a moment, then said, "Now." Four women walked into the camp, surrounding those by the heater.

36

"Did you find the mark?" Hiram said.

Deborah pulled out a surveillance sensor Hiram had hidden before the exercise began. About an hour ago, he sent the women out in search of the sensor with only the night vision gear and a pre-programmed map of the area around the camp. He monitored their progress on the C2ID2.

"Good work," he said, not taking his eyes off Barbara.

"Want to know what they talk about?" Deborah said.

Hiram looked at her, the flush of her cheeks obvious even in the pale glow of the lights. He nodded.

"They miss their families," she said. "Sounds like mostly their husbands. Barbara said she would give anything to hear him snoring in her ear once more."

"You're joking."

She shook her head. "Danette lost her husband well before this hell started. Ellen's husband had a heart attack when the police came and rounded them up. Barbara's husband disappeared from the camp. At least that's what she heard."

"And Rosette?"

"Rosette won't talk about it."

Hiram touched Deborah's hand as she passed him the sensor. "What about you?"

She giggled, almost childlike. The adrenaline still pumped through her from the recent game of hide-and-seek. "No husband for me. My father tried to arrange a marriage once. Complete disaster. He didn't try that again."

He tried not to laugh. "Not the marrying type?"

"I don't plan on being an old maid if that's what you're asking. One day I suppose." She dug something out from under her fingernail and flicked it aside.

After a moment, Deborah took the C2ID2 from Hiram. This particular unit spent time in everyone's hands. "Is the drone still grounded?"

"Yup. Fog this morning, wind this afternoon. Feels like we've got a storm moving in now."

"What about him?" She pointed to the small recon robot. The women decided to name him Souri, or mouse, after seeing how he fit into tight places.

"Too far away. He'll never be able to cover the distance before we need to move in."

"Then we pray for clear skies tomorrow." She put her hand on his for a moment, then stood, pocketing the surveillance sensor. "I'll go prep for the next group of seekers."

Deborah flipped down the goggles and took off into the darkness.

Laughter had replaced the serious conversation going on around the heater. Barbara turned to Hiram, smiled, and fell right back into the discussion.

9

0915 hours, Thursday, July 16, 1942, Perpignan, Pyrénées-Orientales Department, Vichy France

Captain Petain sat at the head of the polished mahogany conference table, sipping an espresso as Emile Locard organized his presentation. To his right sat Lieutenant Lebeau and on his left Officer Thibult, one of the officers who had been at the scene. He wondered about the reliability of Locard's report given his oft-expressed distaste for the government's collaboration in the Nazi-ordered roundup of the Jews and Gypsies in the Free Zone. Despite Petain's distaste for the man, he might provide information of use.

Petain knew better than to resist. With his granduncle running the country, his potential for advancement remained unlimited. He followed his orders and pushed the men beneath him to do the same.

So far, his men had found no trace of the escaped maids. A pair of soldiers had been reported missing, but their disappearance seemed disconnected from the missing women. *Probably passed out drunk somewhere, or deserted.* His team had visited every inhabited building in the area since the two failed to report for duty, still nothing. Over the past few months, his men gained unparalleled experience in search and seizure after the Nazi-inspired pogrom that tore through his quiet town. This little woman hunt should have been easy, simple.

"On with it," Petain said before taking another sip, the small cup uncomfortable in his large hand.

"Well sir," Locard said. "The three men in the command car died instantly, a result of the explosive device detonating under the vehicle. Corporal Leveque died two days later from injuries sustained in the same blast. Three of your men and one of the drivers were shot with thirty caliber rounds and I'd presume all shot by the same rifle." He slid a small manila envelope to the side.

"Why do you say that?" Petain asked.

"Two reasons, sir. First, you reported that you found all four casings in the same foxhole, and second, the striations on both the cartridges and the slugs themselves display similar characteristics."

Petain nodded.

"This is where it gets interesting." He picked up one of the small envelopes and dumped the contents into his hand. "Patrolman Leblanc and one of the hired drivers were killed with multiple nine-millimeter shots like this." He held up one of the slugs.

"These little fellows are unlike anything I've ever seen. You see, they have fins. Implies they exited a smoothbore machine gun, not a rifled weapon. Still, they struck with amazing power and tore the two men apart. I found no crimp point for the cartridge casing and we found no used casings on the ground. We're dealing with a new type of weapon here."

Petain glanced into his now empty cup. "What about the tracks I found?"

Locard tapped his finger on a piece of paper before him. "Based on the location of Patrolman Leblanc and the driver in comparison to the tracks, and the location of the foxhole relative to the stopped trucks," he stopped for a moment considering the drawing. "My guess: the mysterious nine-millimeter weapon was mounted on a cart of some kind, the depth of the impression implying it's quite heavy. And, not so easy to hide."

"A second man operated the weapon?" asked Lieutenant Lebeau.

"Perhaps, though the only additional shoe prints found at the scene belonged to women. The second man may have ridden in the cart, meaning it's self-propelled."

"The prisoners we caught didn't speak of another man, or of a vehicle," Officer Thibult said.

"The tracks led away from the scene along the tree line. They may not have witnessed it," Locard said.

"And the other set of tracks?" Petain wanted to steer the conversation away from the five prisoners he'd executed.

Locard reviewed the image of the second set of tracks once more. He said a few quiet words to himself that Petain found indistinguishable. "You don't know what it is."

"I'm afraid not." Locard pushed all of his papers back into a single pile, setting the odd shaped envelopes containing the bullets on top. "I'd like to question the remaining prisoners about the incident."

"That's not going to be possible."

The criminalist's look of disappointment took a sudden turn toward anger as he comprehended Petain's statement.

"You're dismissed. Now move along," Petain said.

10

0100 hours, Friday, July 24, 1942, Rivesaltes, Pyrénées-Orientales Department, Vichy France

Hiram jumped through the aerial portal at one o'clock in the morning. He snapped the aerial portal shut using his C2ID2, then stretched his arms and legs so the wingsuit caught the air. The enormity of the camp filled the view of his night vision goggles as he approached. He drifted toward J block, scanning for guards as his target grew.

After a light touchdown, he noticed an open entry point in the barracks to his left. Deborah, backed by a few of the other women, had told Hiram the barracks doors remained closed and barred after dark. The open door surprised him.

Weapon at the ready, he edged his way along the building wall and stole a glance inside. The barracks appeared to be empty. Hiram slipped inside and soon confirmed that the building was deserted.

He made his way through the next building in J Block. Nothing. Twenty minutes later he determined F Block was empty as well, confirming his worst fear. *His actions* resulted in the prisoners' move to Drancy ahead of the known timeline.

Hiram approached the guard shack at the gate that separated the special camp from the remainder of the compound. He found a lone French policeman flipping through a woman's lingerie catalog, not paying attention to his duties.

The policeman never expected a Taser.

"All teams, this is Hawk, respond, over," he called over his radio, an encrypted digital system, immune to tracking or eavesdropping using 1940's era technology.

"Hawk, this is Team One, over," said Anna. While Danette led the team ready to breech the outer camp's perimeter, her lack of a common language with Hiram required her team have a Hebrew speaker on the radio. Danette's team prepared to distribute hundreds of pistols to the gypsies, Spanish refugees, and the others imprisoned at Camp Joffre, as they made a break for freedom.

"Hawk, this is Team Two, over." Sarah checked in from the cargo vessel *M.V. Calais* at Port Leucate.

"Hawk, this is Team Three, over." Deborah waited by the nearest police barracks with a rocket launcher.

"Team Three – abort, I say again abort. Head to the rally point. Team Two, detonate the satchel charges around the shore batteries and cast off immediately. Head due south for twenty kilometers, then circle. I'll provide further instructions shortly. Team One, I'm headed to exit point alpha with a prisoner. ETA five minutes. Provide cover fire if I'm detected."

"What the hell happened?" Sarah said.

"We're too late. F and J Blocks are deserted. My prisoner may be able to tell us what happened. Team Two, your position is untenable without the planned diversion. I don't want to release the larger prison population until I know what happened to our people." Hiram hefted the policeman over his shoulder. "You have to go now!"

Twenty minutes later Hiram and Team One met Team Three at the rally point northwest of Camp Joffre. They headed back into the wilderness as fast as they could go carrying the half-conscious French policemen.

* * *

The policeman stirred as they arrived back at their campsite. He fell to his knees when Isabelle and Diane let him go. He surveyed his captors, disoriented and afraid.

Hiram knelt in front of him. "Where are the Jewish prisoners?" Deborah translated.

The policeman stuttered.

Hiram backhanded the man. "Where are they?"

The policeman held his hands up to Hiram and started talking.

"He says they were sent away by train. Two days ago. Captain Petain's orders said Drancy," Deborah said. The concentration camp in Drancy put the prisoners one stop closer to Auschwitz – and extermination.

"Captain Petain?' Hiram recognized the surname. "Any relation to the Grand Marshall?"

The policeman nodded. "His granduncle, I think."

Danette stepped forward, leaned over the prisoner, and spat a few words.

"She's asking about the five women from the convoy?" Deborah said.

The policeman's eyes shifted between Hiram and Danette.

Deborah kept her eyes on him while she passed his words on to Hiram. "The maids from the Chateau. He guesses they are dead. Thirty-six women from the labor roster were reported dead. Petain told his men they killed the guards and drivers trying to escape. After they were all captured, he had them disposed."

Danette's voice grew louder.

"She asked if we look dead to him," Deborah said. "He doesn't believe so many of us are here."

Danette kept pressing the sniveling policeman, her anger building. His response did not satisfy her. "Enfoiré!" Danette hit the man with the butt of her weapon. Frieda pulled her away before she landed the second blow.

"Keep an eye on him," Hiram said before stepping away from the group.

He made his way out into the woods. Even with the dull light of the glow lamps visible in the distance he could no longer make out the individual forms of the women. He knelt, placing his pack on the ground in front of him. He opened the upper section, exposing the portal.

"What are you going to do?" Deborah said. Her presence surprised him. She moved with stealth, a skill she learned well before Hiram began her training.

He wanted to be alone, to brood on his failure. He ignored her and activated the portal to the pod.

"So, you are going to hide inside your pod as if you've been defeated?"

"That's the plan."

Deborah came around in front of him. She knelt across from Hiram, the active portal sitting between them. "It's not a very good plan."

He shrugged. "Do you have a better one?"

She reached into her pocket and pulled out a flask. "Our guest had it on him when he arrived. Must have been early in the shift. It's still full." She shook the flask, the sloshing of the liquid audible in the quiet night.

44

He grinned. "I think your plan is better."

Deborah opened the flask and took a sip. She cringed at the taste. "I've had worse." She passed the flask over to him.

Hiram held the flask for a moment and took a drink anyway. Warmth crept through his body, overriding the angry heat brewing since his discovery at Camp Joffre. He passed the flask back.

Hiram deactivated the portal, closed the pack, and sat beside Deborah. They faced the glow of the camp.

"We can try again," she said. "How far away is Drancy?"

"Almost seven hundred kilometers. But that's not the real problem. It's too far from the coast to escape with thousands of prisoners in tow."

"Then what do we do?"

He looked at the flask when she handed it back. "I don't know. Perhaps we finish this off and see if our heads are any clearer."

Deborah let out a small laugh. When he turned to hand the flask back to her, her eyes met his and his heart beat faster. Blood rushed to his cheeks. Her smile faded and even in the dim light from the camp he could not resist that look. Hiram leaned over and kissed her, gently. As he started to pull back, she wrapped her left arm around his neck and pulled him in close to her. Their lips remained locked together as she shifted until she sat on his lap, her legs wrapping around his back. He embraced her. The flask fell over, forgotten. The contents leaked out on to the dirt. Without another word, she pulled him deeper into the woods, away from the sounds of the camp,

When at last they broke apart, their breathing desperate, wanting, Hiram let out a small laugh.

"What's funny?" She unbuckled her belt, the movement rushed.

"An old joke." The two continued awkwardly discarding weapons, body armor, and camouflaged uniforms. "How do porcupines make love?"

She kissed his neck, stopping to whisper in his ear. "How?"

"Very carefully," he said.

She pulled back to face him and shook her head, smiling. Then Deborah pushed him down on the ground.

For a time, they forgot about plans.

* * *

When Hiram and Deborah returned to the encampment hours later the French policeman was no longer tied to the tree where he'd left him.

"Where's the prisoner?" he asked Danette.

She said a few calm words to Hiram and smiled.

Deborah stepped closer, hesitant. "She said don't trouble yourself about that Nazi-loving pig."

11

1845 hours, Saturday, July 25, 1942, Aboard the M.V. Calais in the Mediterranean Sea

Waves rocked the boat as Hiram took hold of the knotted rope that led up to the deck of the *M.V. Calais.* Sarah watched him tie off the smaller boat and begin his weary climb into the commercial fishing vessel. The soldier's journey warranted his exhaustion.

Sarah was not feeling well herself. She had ordered the ship's captain to travel in circles once darkness fell on Friday evening, limiting Hiram's search when he rendezvoused with Team Two. A storm had emerged from the Atlantic before sunup on Saturday morning and roiled the Mediterranean Sea all day. The storm proved to be a blessing. Aircraft had been grounded and the ships at sea were too involved in their own survival to worry about the *M.V. Calais.* The waters, along with Sarah's stomach, finally stopped churning. "I haven't seen that design before," Sarah said as Hiram climbed on to the deck.

"It's a rigid hull inflatable boat, or RHIB. Better suited for open water than the kayaks, especially through a storm like that."

"You're soaked," Sarah said.

"But alive."

Simone peeked her head out of the cabin, followed by Nora. The members of Team Two were anxious to hear news of their families. "Couverture?"

Simone nodded, disappeared for a minute, and came back cradling a woolen blanket. Sarah draped the fabric over Hiram's shoulders.

"Thank you. Let's talk somewhere private," he said. Sarah led him into the Captain's day cabin located behind the bridge.

"The plan's a bust. Since there're only eight of you, we don't need this big ship. We'll keep heading down the coast for a couple of hours, then disable the ship. We'll take boats ashore and find a good hiding place for your team until I figure out our next move. I assume you've already disabled the ship's wireless set?"

"Yes, and the backup we found as well," she replied. "But what are we going to do about our families? Where are they?"

"According to a guard we questioned, they were shipped to Drancy two days ago."

Sarah slumped into a chair as her chest tightened. Her voice waivered as she held in her tears. "But you said we had two weeks to rescue them."

"I know. Your escape may have escalated the timetable."

"What are we going to do? We can't let them die."

"I don't think there's anything we can do for them just yet. I don't know how…" Hiram trailed off and drifted toward the map fastened to the wall of the cabin. "Unless, we can end this terrible war."

"What are you saying?" Sarah joined him at the map. The edges were worn, preferred routes permanently traced on its surface.

"We have to stop the war," he touched Auschwitz on the map. "Before they end up here. It won't be easy."

"A nineteen-year-old Serbian managed to start the Great War all by himself," Sarah said. "You have thirty maids to help stop one. You'll figure something out. I need to go brief my team."

Sarah left Hiram staring at the map and returned to the bridge, where Ester and Maria watched the bridge crew. She brought both women out onto the flying bridge where they could watch the sailors without being overheard. Neither was happy with the news about the change in the timeline. Nor were any of their Team Two comrades.

* * *

Towards eight o'clock, the lights of the Costa Brava, Spain's Mediterranean coast, came into view. An hour later, they ordered the Captain to stop the ship, then herded the entire crew into the forward cargo hold, locking the door after them.

Hiram pulled one of the collapsed inflatable boats out of his tinderbox and assembled it on the deck. He reached into his pack again, this time two net bags full of rope emerged. One of the bags spilled onto the deck and turned out to be a ladder made of a material Sarah hadn't seen before. "Nylon," he replied as she bent to touch it. "A synthetic material." The second bag contained a large coil of rope. Using a complicated-looking knot, he secured both the rope and the ladder to a bollard and threw the other end of the ladder overboard. It stretched down to the sea, then slowly swung aft as the ship drifted with the current. As Hiram passed out life vests, Sarah peered over the side of the boat. She didn't like the thought of making that descent at all.

Hiram tied the inflatable boat to one end of the rope with separate knots before tossing it overboard and climbing down. He tied a rope from the bow of the soft inflatable boat to the stern of the motorized RHIB.

Maria climbed down next, then Sarah. She made it down about ten feet when her foot slid on the nylon ladder. Unprepared, she plummeted into the cool water. The instant her head slid beneath the surface, her life vest inflated. She popped back up to the surface, thankful for Hiram's insistence on wearing one. Sarah had never been a strong swimmer and even the flotation device did not extinguish her fear as she drifted away from Hiram and the *M.V. Calais.*

The six remaining members of Team Two settled into the boats without a problem. Sarah bobbed a few feet away and tried to control her breathing as she watched. Until at last, Hiram hauled her into the RHIB.

"Thank you," she sputtered, spitting out the salty water she'd taken in from the few small waves that had caught her by surprise.

"Can't lose my only scientist."

Hiram tapped an icon on his C2ID2 while yanking on the rope and ladder. Both came tumbling down into the water. She helped him gather them up and stuff them back into their net bags.

The RHIB towed the smaller boat toward shore. Grateful to reach the rocky beach after the rough day at sea, Sarah jumped out into the shallows and fought to get the boat out of the surf and up on shore.

Hiram signaled her to take charge while he packed up the boats.

"Perform a weapons check and get formed up," she said. "We still have a couple hours' march ahead of us. But don't worry, it's all uphill." The women muttered a few curses as they adjusted their packs for another exhausting exercise. Sarah felt their pain.

They headed up the rocky slope, Hiram taking point. He led the tiny column of maids-cum-soldiers off into the darkness.

12

A temporal artifact of May 6, 2050

Hiram craved a hot cup of coffee and decided to get it from the coffeemaker in his pod. The Turkish coffee reminded him of his late Mossad spotter Jacob. He insisted on a cup first thing in the morning, unlike his parents, who had emigrated from Istanbul in the 2020s where tea had been a more prominent staple. Hiram remembered Jacob telling him about the collection of teas his father had given him before their last mission. Jacob had stored them in his pod just in case he had a hankering for "a nice feminine, flowery blend while destroying the stinking Pakistanis." Hiram smiled. Maybe his new soldiers would welcome a flowery cup of tea. Deborah probably enjoyed tea. Once he made it back to the campsite in France, to Deborah and the teams left behind, he'd retrieve the tea collection from Jacob's pod.

Hiram took another sip of his coffee. *Jacob's pod!* Why hadn't he thought of it before? He set down the small cup, unfinished. He located Jacob's pack and the portal within it. Jacob's pod was not a standard IDF-equipped pod, but rather a Mossad-equipped unit, which had been outfitted for the mission to Wah. Hiram removed Jacob's C2ID2 unit from the pack and activated Jacob's portal.

The moment Hiram began his descent into the dead man's pod, his head began to ache. The sudden pain surprised him enough that he almost lost his balance on the ladder. His feet touched the floor and he reached out to the nearest wall to stabilize himself.

He had never gone through to a second pod from within a pod. As the space around him spun, he wondered if *anyone* had tried such a thing. The familiar effects of Hagar's Curse seemed accelerated, almost ten-fold. Before the pod could do any permanent damage, Hiram reviewed the items inside. He worked as quickly as his body would allow. In less than five minutes, Hiram found a cache of state-of-the-art surveillance gear and the one item that might end the war, before the Jews now concentrated at Drancy stepped on to one of the death trains headed to the extermination camp at Auschwitz. At the far end of the pod, a Mark XII hyperbaric nuclear weapon sat nestled in a cradle.

With his weapon of choice identified, Hiram climbed out of Jacob's pod and into the one he had been assigned. His stomach roiled with relief. The intensity of pain in his head took a step back. It still felt as if he had been in the pod way too long. Without delay, Hiram climbed out of his pod and into the warm morning air.

Hiram found a place to rest in the shade of a scrubby pine tree. He slowed his breathing, tried to calm himself while his stomach settled and the pain in his head dissipated. Close by, he heard Sarah talking followed by an outburst of laughter from the others. The sound brought with it a source of comfort.

When the small words on Jacob's C2ID2 display stopped blurring, he searched for the operating manual on the Mark XII. He confirmed the weapon's permissive action lock code was stored on the device, and copied the eleven character PAL code and the manual into his own C2ID2. He wouldn't need Jacob to operate it. The only thing left – get it out of Jacob's pod.

Massing ninety kilograms, the Mark XII was designed to be carried short distances by two strong men. A pulley system came with the device that could to be used to lift the sixty by thirty-centimeter overpack up through the portal. Once he set the pulley up in his own pod, Hiram could drag the Mark XII over to a location beneath the portal and hook it up.

The link between the portal in Jacob's pack and the Mossad-equipped pod existed in a temporal artifact of 2050. Hiram couldn't be sure that the link would be maintained if he were to bring Jacob's pack out into the real world of 1942, and he wasn't sure the link could be reestablished once it was severed. Once his head and his stomach were almost back to normal, Hiram went back into his pod and then into Jacob's to extract the single Mark XII.

Twenty-three agonizing minutes later, the Mark XII and several pelican cases of advanced surveillance gear sat in Hiram's pod. Hiram closed the portal to the Mossad pod and stored Jacob's C2ID2 in a storage cabinet. He climbed out of the pod as quickly as he could, his cup of coffee forgotten.

The warm air hit him hard. He fell to his knees and expelled the contents of his stomach onto a patch of grass. Specks of red dotted the mess. The pain in his head screamed and the world around him spun. When he tried to stand, the ground seemed to fall out from under him.

* * *

0715 hours, Sunday, July 26, 1942, Catalonia, Francoist Spain

Hiram stumbled into Team Two's campsite, deep in the hills north of Canyet de Mar. His soldiers prepared breakfast in a small clearing among the tall oaks, the smell turning his stomach. Most had not slept that night. Red eyes and worn, sullen faces disclosed evidence of tears shed for family and friends. He wanted to get back to Danette and to Deborah. He wanted to hold Deborah in his arms, to feel her warmth as he explained what his meddling had done to the timeline. For a moment, he imagined running away from all of it with Deborah and Danette running alongside. Saving three lives seemed so much simpler than thirty. He shook his head in an attempt to lose such thoughts.

He found Sarah sitting next to Ester, holding the older woman's hands. When Hiram approached, Sarah patted the other woman's hands and then got up. She rushed to him. He felt her arm slide around him.

"I think I have a way to end this war quickly," he said as he leaned into her. "Walk with me."

"You aren't going anywhere. What happened?" She said.

"Nothing. It doesn't matter. I need to talk to you." He looked around at the others now standing, ready to help. "Tell them I'm fine."

Sarah said something to the others. They hesitated but seemed to fall back into their previous positions. She helped him sit down on one of the fallen logs.

"Have you ever heard of the *strong nuclear force?*"

"Of course," she said as she sat down beside him. "It's the force that holds the nucleus of an atom together."

"Right. And in a few years the Americans will discover a way to release that force. They will develop something called an *atomic bomb*, which will end the war. One bomb with the explosive power of 20,000 tons of TNT."

"That's enough to level a city!" Sarah said.

"It is," Hiram said.

Vera brought Hiram a cup of water. She said a few words to Sarah, who seemed to reassure her that Hiram was, in fact, fine.

"But how can you know this? Surely your friend the journalist wouldn't be privy to such things."

The cool water helped. "No, it's one of the few secrets the Americans actually manage to keep during this war." He held up the cup. Vera came back, refilled it. The others watched the conversation.

"So how do you know?"

"Because I lied about coming from America. I came from Israel, by way of Pakistan and India."

"Israel?" Sarah let out an awkward laugh. "Israel hasn't existed as a nation for two thousand years."

"Israel will become an independent nation again in 1948. I was born there, in the town of Nazareth, in the year 2020."

She shook her head. "Impossible." Her eyes moved back and forth across his face, searching for truth. "You're telling me you've travelled back in time? I-I don't believe it."

"I'm a soldier in the Israeli Defense Force, or at least I was," Hiram said. "I don't know how it happened, but six weeks ago I was on a mission to the city of Wah in India. I went into my pod on May 15, 2050 and came out on May 15, 1942."

"Impossible," she said again. "Time travel is impossible."

"And yet here I am. With technology from a hundred years in the future." Hiram pointed to the small cache of M22s leaning against a fallen tree trunk a few feet away. "Including the pod and all it holds."

"You mean your magic tinderbox of death and destruction. Tell me exactly what happened to you."

He sat up straighter, the pain in his head easing. "As I said, I was on a mission to destroy a weapons facility in Wah, Pakistan"

"I've never heard of Pakistan," Sarah said.

"After the war, the British will grant independence to India, however the Hindus, Sikhs, and Muslims won't be able to live in peace. After a civil war, India will split into three pieces, with Muslim Pakistan in the west, Hindu and Sikh India in the middle, and Muslim Bangladesh in the east. Pakistan and India will become bitter enemies. In my time, Pakistan falls under the control of a bunch of radical extremists called the Taliban who swear to use Pakistan's atomic weapons to destroy Israel. So, we sent a small team with our own atomic weapon to destroy their main production and storage facility."

"And you were on that team?"

Hiram nodded. "We ran into more resistance than expected, and the rest of the team was killed. I barely made it back into the pod before our bomb went off."

"And then the portal was open during detonation, when all that energy was released?"

"It makes sense. Give me a moment." Hiram checked his C2ID2, which had recorded both the countdown for the bomb, and all openings and closings of the portals in the pod. "According to my C2ID2, the portal closed within a second of the detonation." He used the display unit to show Sarah data from the two countdowns, one ticking down to the detonation, and one ticking up to record Hiram's dwell time in the pod.

"What happened next?" Sarah said.

"I tried to leave the pod through a portal that should have taken me back to Israel, but it kept returning 'destination not found'. Eventually I had to leave the pod. You can only stay in one for a few hours. So, I went back out the way I entered, only to find myself in British India, in the year 1942."

Sarah stared down at the ground. Hiram sipped some water. After a few minutes, she shifted her gaze back to him.

"Before the war, Einstein and his colleague Nathan Rosen published a paper about something called 'worm holes', shortcuts through space-time. All of the scientific speculation since has been about travelling through *space* or between *universes*, but what if they can also be used to travel through *time*, particularly when hit with a healthy dose of nuclear radiation?"

"I'm just a soldier," Hiram said. "I know how to use the thing, but I'm no expert on how it works. If it helps, I can give you a copy of the pod's manual." He handed her the C2ID2 and told her how to pull up a copy of the document.

Sarah scanned the information on the screen. "For the moment, let's say I believe you. If you're from the future, then you know what is going to happen."

"Not anymore. The timeline is changing. According to the history I know, the Jewish prisoners in F and J Blocks were shipped to the camp at Drancy in late August, not mid-July. I believe rescuing you and the others accelerated the timeline."

"Why *did* you rescue us? I assume the story about Danette's cousin is also a lie."

"My name is Hiram Jonah Halphen." Hiram looked down at his hands. "Danette is my great-great-grandmother."

"I thought I noticed some resemblance."

"My father told me Danette's story. She is the spitting image of my sister Rachel. After ending up in this time and with no way to get back, I figured I might be able to do some good. I decided I wasn't going to let her die in one of the camps. Getting the others – you included – out of there was the right thing to do."

"And the story about shipping the inmates from Drancy to Poland, is it true?"

"It's historical fact. Or at least it was. Hitler's Final Solution will nearly succeed in wiping out all the Jews in Europe." He took the C2ID2 back from her and scrolled to a history of the Holocaust, required reading for all IDF personnel. "Six million Jews die in the camps; another six million undesirables follow if we don't stop it."

"And you have a way to stop it?"

"There's a weapon in my pod similar to the atomic bomb I talked about before. It's much smaller, more efficient and more precise than the original American device. And, we can replicate it many times. It's called a Mark XII hyperbaric nuclear weapon."

"Assuming that I believe you have this powerful weapon, how do you propose to use it?"

"We'll have to drive the Nazis out of France first. Then, we force Germany to surrender."

Sarah laughed. "That's your plan? Thirty of us to destroy a force hundreds-of-thousands strong. That must be some bomb." Almost two million Nazi soldiers protected the western front. Then, add in the Vichy and Italian Fascist forces. Sarah's numbers seemed insignificant, but he doubted this was the time to correct her.

"Thirty-one if you include me."

"I don't know if we can include you in this state. What happened to you this time?"

"It's nothing. I've secured the weapon we need. Took a chance."

"Are you suffering from radiation poisoning?"

Hiram smiled. "Nothing like that. I just need a few minutes to recover."

She looked into his eyes as if she searched for a deeper truth. "Still, there are so many of them and so few of us."

"Sarah, we have an unending supply of weapons more advanced and powerful than our enemies could imagine. And yes, it *is* some bomb."

"What about the civilian casualties?"

"Hundreds of thousands. But that's nowhere near the casualties suffered during the Allied invasion. And if you consider the millions that will die in camps before the horror of the Holocaust ends, wouldn't that number be justified?"

"I don't know," she said.

"And we've got another problem."

"What's that?" She stared up at the sky.

"In my past, the Russians, the Americans, and the British met in the middle of Germany in 1945 and pretty much divided up Europe from there. Right now, the Russians are battling the Germans near Stalingrad, and the British are fighting them in North Africa. The Americans are preparing an Anglo-American invasion of Morocco and Algeria called *Operation Torch* in November, so they aren't close to invading Europe yet."

"Hiram, what are you trying to say?"

"Well, if we strike too quickly, the Red Army will overrun the Nazis, push all the way to the Atlantic Wall, and enslave the whole continent for generations to come."

"Oh, I see," Sarah said. "What can we do?"

"*You* can convince General Eisenhower to abandon *Operation Torch* and commence *Operation Overlord* as soon as we set off the first atomic bomb."

"You are joking. And, why would this General Eisenhower listen to me?"

"No, I'm not. You're the best woman for the job." Hiram pointed to the C2ID2. "You understand the technology, or at least you will."

"Say I agree to talk to this man and tell him all about this advanced technology," she said. "Why General Eisenhower?"

"He's the American general that Churchill and Roosevelt put in charge of *Operation Torch* and in two years – assuming I don't demolish the timeline – he would be in charge of *Operation Overlord*, the Allied invasion of France. He's the only American general in Europe that knows about the Manhattan Project, though it might not be called that yet." Touching the display, he continued. "You've got the manual for the Mark XII and the pod. You can read the basic nuclear science section to advance what you already know of physics. By the time you get to Eisenhower, you'll know more than enough to convince him the bomb really exists and that we have one."

Sarah paged through the open Mark XII manual and stopped at one of the schematics. "This is the contraption that's going to end this war." She stared at the screen. "And how do you propose I get to England to arrange an audience with this general?"

"Have you heard of the Spanish Maquis?"

She shook her head and looked up from the display.

"I've got a plan. It's going to be dangerous. But, as someone said, nothing worth doing is easy."

13

1730 hours, Wednesday, July 29, 1942, Perpignan, Pyrénées-Orientales Department, Vichy France

Louis Petain sat at his desk idly tossing one of the strange finned bullets from one hand to the other. *Such a small thing, and yet it could easily kill a man, or perhaps my career.*

This particular slug had been extracted from the body of a sailor killed when the good ship *M.V. Calais* was seized by a group of armed women. The small relic presented physical evidence connecting the thirty escaped maids from the internment camp to the disaster at Port Leucate, proof of his team's failure. The women roamed free with their Jew-loving dog, leaving six mangled gun emplacements and eighteen dead sailors in their wake.

No, not my team's failure. Locard's failure. Locard had enough time and every resource Petain had the authority to provide. He had spent hours in his laboratory fiddling with the damn bullets, looking at photos of mud, and drawing inaccurate conclusions. The man had nothing to show for it. Still, the criminalist was on Petain's payroll. *Authority can be delegated, but leaders can never be relieved of responsibility.* He had heard his uncle say those words once. He set the slug down on his desk. *But responsibility can be shared, and Locard has few friends in high places.*

"Sir, Monsieur Locard is here to see you," his secretary announced from the doorway. Petain swept the bullet into a desk drawer.

"Well send him in," he said. Ten seconds later Locard stood in front of Petain's desk.

"You asked to see me, sir?"

"Do have any useful information regarding the missing prisoners?" If the story told by the crew of the *M.V. Calais* held truth, a subset of his escaped prisoners had been put ashore in Catalonia, Spain along with a mysterious soldier. Petain wasn't going to tell Locard. *The fewer people that understood the connection between the two events, the better.*

"I interviewed several of the detainees that had been housed in the same barracks as the Halphen woman. They claimed she had no living relatives remaining in France, just as the records indicated."

After a pause, he added, "I would like to have questioned the women that were left behind myself."

Petain heard the criticism in Locard's voice. He wanted to rebuke the man, then reconsidered when Locard changed the subject.

"We may have another lead," Locard said. "I learned one of the other women, Rosette Bertrand, has family living in Vichy."

"Why weren't they detained with her?"

"Her husband and two children were not identified as Jews. Her husband requested that she be detained. Appears she has just enough Jewish blood to be considered by the Nazis."

"Have you had her husband brought in for questioning?"

"No Captain. If this man is involved, we might collect better results if we keep an eye on him for a while. The missing prisoners may show up. Perhaps he'll take us to them."

"You may have a point. Do you have anything else to report?"

"Nineteen days ago, a hunter from Vingrau disappeared in the woods northeast of town. His wife claims he is an experienced woodsman."

"And I'm just hearing of this now?" Petain slammed his fist on the desk.

"The hunter – Boudreaux – was reported missing by his family this morning," Locard said.

"Does Boudreaux match the description of the mysterious soldier?"

Locard considered the question. "No, sir, not at all. I'd like to send an armed patrol into that area. Perhaps our maids and their accomplice are hiding out in the vicinity."

"See to it. What about the missing guard from Camp Joffre? Any indication he was involved in the escape?"

"No reason to believe he had any involvement at this time. On the day he disappeared, guards performing a routine perimeter sweep found a recently repaired hole in the fence. The work was precise and intricate. I'm surprised the guard noticed. They neglected to report it since all of the prisoners were accounted for. But the location of the repair lined up with the direction where Boudreaux went missing."

"Well, I don't believe in coincidence. Get a patrol out tonight."

"In the dark?" Locard seemed surprised at the notion.

"It's cold in the mountains at night. Those women are frail and probably very hungry. They'll have a fire to keep warm and cook whatever food they've found. Fires are easier to spot at night," Petain said. "Now get out of my sight. You've got work to do."

Locard turned and left without another word. Petain's irritation compounded. Seven policemen dead and one missing. Eighteen shore battery sailors dead. Two civilians dead. And now another missing civilian. Six heavy guns destroyed. One ship with a full crew hijacked right from under the Navy's nose. The mystery soldier certainly was resourceful. Petain opened the drawer and pulled out the finned bullet. *And if I can get my hands on him and his weapons, I just might be able to repair the damage this whole affair has done to my career.*

* * *

0550 hours, Friday, July 31, 1942, West of Vingrau, Pyrénées-Orientales Department, Vichy France

Locard's patrol, which had been dispatched on Wednesday evening and searched for a day and a half, claimed to have discovered something of substance. Once again Louis Petain found himself in the damn woods accompanied by Lebeau, this time a half-hour before sunrise. At least it wasn't muddy, the result of a hot and dry week.

"*Bonjour*, Captain." Locard spoke with a distasteful amount of cheer for such an early hour.

"Bonjour," Petain said. "You got me out here. Now, tell me what you found."

"It appears to be an abandoned campsite for a few dozen people," Locard said. He motioned for Petain to follow him as he headed deeper into the woods. "I'm guessing either it is the missing prisoners or another group of Spanish refugees. None of the usual trash the Spaniards tend to leave behind though."

Petain looked around the site, paying particular attention to small tread impressions that weaved through a few of the trees. The tracks sank deep into the soil, left behind before the ground dried.

"The tracks bare similar characteristics to those found near the ambush site two weeks ago. I'll verify my observations when I get back to my office," Locard said.

"And where are our squatters now?" Petain said.

"Tracks lead away from the site in every direction. No way to determine where the prisoners headed. I sent for hounds about an hour ago."

Petain and Locard turned to the sound of several braying dogs approaching the former campsite.

"Ah, here they are now," Locard said.

"Send the hounds out in every direction. Call in more if these mutts fail." *Now we're getting somewhere.* The prisoners and their Jew-loving pig must not escape again.

"By the way, I heard from my contact at Drancy," Locard said as they watched the hounds sniffing around the campsite. "The Jews sent there from Camp Joffre will be relocated to a labor camp somewhere in Poland around the middle of next week. If we want to question them again, we'll have to do it soon."

"Any reason to believe they'll provide any additional *useful* information?"

"No, sir. I think I got about as much information from them as we're going to get."

"Very well, have them keep my office informed of their deportation schedule. Soon enough they'll be out of our hair."

An unfamiliar *whump* silenced the braying of the hounds. The air grew still and behind them a man screamed. His scream ended as suddenly as it had started.

"What the hell was that?" Petain said. He ducked, certain the mystery soldier planned to send a finned bullet through his chest.

"Look!" Locard pointed up the gentle slope of the hillside. Petain stood and stepped around Locard for a better look. Erupting out of a thick stand of pine trees, a ball of fire expanded quickly in the dry forest. The fire engulfed the pine trees in seconds, and, propelled by a considerable breeze, descended towards their position. His men were in danger.

"Run!" Petain yelled.

Locard moved fast. Petain followed. They headed north across the line of the fire rather than directly away from it.

"Do you know where you're going?" Petain gasped between breaths. His chest burned. The smoke grew thicker by the second.

"A wide stream about three hundred meters north," Locard yelled. "Our best chance is to get across it."

Petain didn't argue. Five minutes later they splashed across the stream and collapsed on the far bank. Other men joined them, all breathing heavily as they made their way to the shore.

"Booby trap," Lieutenant Lebeau said when he joined them. "I sent one of the men to check out that stand of trees. Then the whole thing erupted in fire. I don't think he made it out."

Petain coughed, trying to clear the building irritation in his lungs. "I'm inclined to agree with you, Lebeau," Any indication that his missing maids spent time at this campsite had been erased, along with any evidence that might lead to the next one. "Anyone else missing?"

"Not sure, sir. About half our men are here, and the other half headed back to the road. The fire seems to be burning itself out. A couple of the dogs outran the handler. He's sure they'll turn up."

"They aren't much use now anyway," Locard said. "All the scents will be gone."

14

1400 hours, Friday, July 31, 1942, Catalonia, Francoist Spain

"Hell of an ambush location," Hiram said as he took up a position next to Sarah.

"You can thank Maxime for the view," Sarah said.

Stretched out below them lay the Figures-Perpignan Highway, running north to the French border and south towards the Costa Brava. The highway was carved into the steep mountainside, with a sheer drop on the far side of the road and a hard climb up to his position, accessible via a well-hidden path one hundred meters east of the road. Hiram's vantage point provided a clear view of an easy target. Two hundred meters to the north, a team of Spanish Maquis waited to destroy the goods in an approaching convoy, unaware that Hiram and Team Two were about to pre-empt the ambush with one of their own. Up until this morning, Hiram wasn't even sure they would have the weaponry needed to accomplish the feat.

After traversing his pod into Jacob's, Hiram had suffered a nagging headache and found himself walking away from the group to excise the demon that seemed to have moved into his belly for two full days. He had avoided going back into his pod since then and only this morning decided he had the guts to climb down into his pod. He was terrified of going back into Jacob's pod and almost as scared to go into the one he had been issued. Parts of him still didn't feel quite right, but they now had the tools they needed to put on a hell of a show.

Hiram's C2ID2 displayed the long column of approaching trucks from a drone feed. The drone also captured images of each individual vehicle. The drivers appeared to be civilians. A single guard rode shotgun in each vehicle. Earlier, the drone had captured the Spanish rebels digging their rifle pits and planting an explosive charge in the roadbed. He deduced that the rebels planned to blow up the lead truck and riddle the rest of the convoy with rifle and light machine gun fire. Hiram had a better plan.

Maxime adjusted a six-shot Milkor grenade launcher, sliding the barrel through an opening in the low brush. The grenade launcher, designed in the late 20th century, was the only weapon in the pod's arsenal older than Hiram's sniper rifle. Later designs proved to be no more effective and less reliable. Although a few bells and whistles had been added, the weapon remained nearly unchanged. Eight more launchers were trained on the roadway below. Team Two awaited Hiram's order to open fire.

The trucks hauled wool destined to be fashioned into German military uniforms, probably by slave laborers. The material would not mix well with the 40mm incendiary grenades about to descend on the convoy. Destroying such a load would cause quite a headache for the poor soul responsible for clothing Hitler's minions.

Hiram waited for the last truck to enter the kill zone. "Fire!"

Around him, 40 mm grenades sailed out of the launchers in near silence. Every sixth truck in the forty-vehicle convoy exploded into flames. One of the women nearest him laughed. The sound was unnerving amidst the destruction.

A driver emerged from of one of the undamaged vehicles and examined the flames coming from the truck in front of him. He looked up the hill toward Hiram and his team as a grenade made contact with his vehicle. The explosion picked up the back end of his truck and sent his body a few more feet from the mayhem. The women worked their way through the remaining trucks, turning each one into a pyre. Within a few minutes, the fires slithered toward the woods on Hiram's side of the road. Flames climbed upward toward them, determined to engulf everything in their path.

"Time to move," Hiram called. Trailed by the nine women of Team Two, Hiram sprinted north along the deer trail, heading away from the flames. The path took them into the flank of the Maquis ambush position. As they approached, Hiram slowed and signaled the women to spread out on either side of the trail, while he, Maria and Sarah continued at a walk. The rebels waited for them, weapons at the ready.

"Hola," Maria said to the first man they saw. She had volunteered to negotiate with the rebels.

Maria said a few more words to the man. Another man stepped up to the front, his weapon slung over his shoulder. He spoke to Maria, gesturing to Hiram more than once.

"This is Jose," Maria said. "Says he'd be happy to discuss a trade if it means he'll be able to put on a show like yours."

Hiram smiled, stepped forward. "Tell him what we've got."

Maria discussed the terms of the arrangement. Hiram only picked up a few words, mostly those he'd heard in another time.

It was a simple trade. In exchange for eight Milkor grenade launchers and one hundred and sixty rounds of ammo, the Maquis would agree to transport Sarah and Maria to Gibraltar, along the same routes they ferried downed Allied pilots from Southern France. Once Hiram received word that Maria and Sarah arrived on the Rock, he would provide the Maquis with another three hundred and sixty grenades.

"He'll take us as far as Gibraltar for eight of the grenade launchers, but he wants one hundred rounds per weapon," Maria said. "Eight hundred total."

Hiram feigned reluctance. "Tell him the grenades come in crates of ninety-six. I'll agree to give him one crate per weapon when the two ladies reach Gibraltar."

Maria translated Hiram's reply to Jose. "He wants two crates now."

Hiram agreed. He shook Jose's hand, then turned and walked back down the trail to collect the six remaining grenade launchers from the rest of Team Two. He kept the more modern weapons out of sight. Advanced weapons like the nearly silent M22 rail guns would be too tempting a tool for the leftist Maquis. And if the Maquis decided to share those weapons with their good buddies in Stalin's Communist regime, the death toll would rise ever higher. When planning the trade, he feared his new business partner might share the grenade launchers with the Red Army. But Russia, in the effort to overpower her enemies with firepower, had already developed a similar weapon. The Milkor grenade launcher was a hell of a lot more accurate at longer range, but not a giant technological leap forward.

Hiram took three trips back up the trail to gather the launchers and the crates of ammo. By the third trip, the advancing flames were now only a few dozen yards away from Team Two's position. He handed the last armload over to one of Jose's men and turned towards Maria.

"You and Sarah can teach them how to use and maintain the weapons later. Right now, we need to get moving before we all burn to a crisp." Maria translated for Jose and his men. The men started heading away from the flames with their new toys in hand, leaving Jose behind.

"One more thing," Hiram said. "You two need a new call sign."

"How about Raven?" Sarah asked. "They're very clever birds, and I hear the English Crown is very fond of them."

Hiram nodded assent and said, "Raven it is."

Maria then turned and hugged Hiram, whispering a thank you in his ear.

"Go with God." Without another word, she headed off down the road, adjusting the straps of her pack as she walked. He turned to hug Sarah. "You're our best hope."

Sarah pulled away. "If I can get an audience with Eisenhower."

"You might have to convince Churchill and Roosevelt as well."

She smiled and shrugged. "It has to be easier than stomaching another of those terrible protein bars."

Hiram tried to laugh. "Hopefully, we'll see each other on the other side of this."

Sarah hugged Hiram once more and took off down the road after Maria, backpack in hand. When she caught up, Maria put an arm around her. They looked like children on their way to school, small and innocent. Jose and his men would pay a hefty price if anything happened to them.

Hiram and Jose shook hands once more. Jose followed his men back to the road. Hiram turned and headed back down the trail. He looked back once and saw Sarah hoisting her pack onto her shoulders. *God forbid that should fall into the wrong hands.* Then he shook his head. *You've taken precautions. Sarah has the self-destruct code for the C2ID2. She understands the dangers. She can be trusted.* Along with the communications interface, her pack contained a Mossad Icarus drone, which provided a secure, long distance method of communication. Once Sarah and Maria reached Gibraltar, she would use it to signal her arrival and Hiram would make good on his deal with the Maquis. *Assuming they make it to the Rock, and assuming the British let them in.*

Just then his C2ID2 chimed, indicating a radio call from Deborah. He tapped an icon and said, "Deborah?" He had managed to steal away for a few minutes to talk to Deborah every day since he left to meet Team Two. They most often spoke in the evening when he could find a quiet, secluded place to talk. Her call surprised him. "What's wrong?"

"We're all fine. But Hiram, the French police discovered our old campsite a few hours ago. We retrieved some audio from the listening device you left behind. Before the booby trap detonated, we heard a policeman say that the prisoners transferred to Drancy from Camp Joffre will be shipped east by the middle of next week."

He had covered their tracks getting to the first site, but they departed in a more carefree manner leaving obvious clues that people had been squatting in the woods. Still, the police discovery of the first campsite surprised him. Hiram pictured the policemen discovering the second campsite, coming upon his soldiers. The image led one of the men to Deborah. His heartbeat quickened. He had to get to her.

In the background, Barbara shouted, "We save the families!"

15

1830 hours, Monday, August 3, 1942, south of Périllos Pyrénées-Orientales Department, Vichy France

For three days, Hiram and the remaining seven women of Team Two hiked back in the direction of Camp Joffre. He pushed them toward the camp site south of Périllos. They kept to the woods, crossing main routes only when necessary. Drones scouted ahead. Twice the drones spotted patrols and the team was forced deeper into the woods, adding considerable distance to their trek. On day three, seven weary soldiers marched into camp. Before their packs slid off their shoulders, the welcoming party surrounded them. Danette, Barbara, Camille, Joanne, Diane, Ida, and Myriam were the first to put their arms around the weary travelers. The others joined in, all eager to greet the incoming team. Though their feet hurt and bodies ached from the kilometers traveled, they embraced their comrades and settled in to conversation, sharing the highs and lows of their journey.

As Hiram watched his troops, Deborah came to join him. "Sarah and Maria?" her words dry and distant.

"They're on their way to England," he said.

Sarah and Maria had accepted Hiram's plan, despite the fear of not being able to carry it out. Now he had to offer the same information to the other former maids, starting with Danette and Deborah.

"I'll explain, but first I need to talk to you and Danette," he said. He led the two women out of the camp. A few of the others watched them leave, though no one seemed interested enough to tag along. They walked until the voices from the camp died away. He said nothing, still trying to work up the courage to tell these two women the whole truth. They had to understand.

The three came to a gully and Hiram climbed down, signaling the two women to follow. Deborah, I need you to translate for Danette."

Deborah nodded.

Danette looked from Hiram to Deborah, confused.

"No matter what I'm about to say, you have to translate."

"Well get on with it," Deborah said.

"My name is Hiram Jonah Halphen," he said.

She hesitated, but repeated his words in French.

Danette rattled off a few words. Deborah shook her head and said something in return. Both women looked at him.

"My father was Moshi Jonah Halphen," he said.

Danette listened, struggling to understand.

"His father was Jonah Silas Halphen." Hiram waited for Deborah to translate.

"And his father was Silas Hiram Halphen," he said.

Deborah translated. Danette shook her head and said something slow and uncertain.

"She says that Silas Hiram Halphen is her son."

"He is," Hiram said.

"That doesn't make sense," Deborah said. "It must be a family name, but I didn't think you two were related. Why is this important? And why have you dragged us all the way out here to tell us about your family tree?"

Danette touched her fingers as if counting. When she finished, she looked at Hiram and spoke.

Deborah translated "Silas is her son and your great-grandfather?"

He nodded. Danette's head tilted to the side, like that damn dog trying to decipher human words.

Hiram looked at Deborah. "I'm not from America. I was born in the independent nation of Israel in the year 2020, and joined the Israeli Defense Force in 2038."

"And I'm Danette's fairy godmother," Deborah snorted, her voice dripping with sarcasm.

"Listen to me." Hiram ignored the interruption. "I was on a mission in the city of Wah, in India. Something happened with my pod. An accident I guess. Sarah seems to understand it better than I do. When I went into the pod it was the year 2050 and when I finally climbed out through the portal, I found myself in the year 1942."

Danette moved in front of Hiram, touched his face. She turned to Deborah and talked.

"She says you have his eyes."

Then, as unexpected as it was, Danette wrapped her arms around him. She started speaking again, but this time Deborah did not translate. Danette's words were vibrant, excited. Deborah's eyes, however, burrowed into him.

"You lied to us," Deborah said. "You lied to me."

"I wanted to tell you, especially you. I didn't know what to say," Hiram said. Danette released him and took a step back, giving Deborah room.

"Through this whole damn war people have been lying to us. They told us they put us in that prison to protect us, to give us our own space to be with our own people. They promised if we worked hard no harm would come to us. Then you tell us they plan to kill us. Maybe you are the one who has been lying the whole time."

"It's the truth and if we don't stop this war, the prisoners at Drancy are going to die much sooner," Hiram said. "We changed the timeline."

"And now the future's changed?" she said. "I don't believe it."

"Why would I lie?" He tried to calm himself. "It doesn't matter. I am from the future. And there is a reason I needed to tell you now."

Danette touched Deborah who returned a venomous look. Deborah talked with Danette for a minute before looking back at Hiram. "Tell us." Her eyes lightened a little.

"I have a plan to end the war." Hiram told Deborah and Danette about the nuclear weapons, though neither voiced similar concerns to Sarah's. He explained the technology as simply as he understood it, hoping they'd grasp the possible impact of using such a device. Deborah listened and translated. Danette nodded, asking a question now and then. "If we can detonate the weapons in strategic locations, we've got a hell of a chance to end this war."

"I've sent –"

"*Salaud!*" Bastard. A new voice joined the conversation. Hiram whipped around to see Barbara climbing down into the gully. She looked at Deborah, spoke as though accusing.

"She wants to know why you didn't tell us about these weapons before."

"How long have you been there?" he said to Barbara. Deborah translated. Barbara threw out a few more words.

Deborah said, "She says 'long enough. You gave us simple weapons that can kill one man at a time when you have something that can destroy an entire army with one blow.'"

Hiram looked at Deborah. "The weapons I have can destroy an entire city."

Deborah did not translate.

"We save the families," Barbara said.

Hiram said nothing.

"We save the families!" Barbara said, her eyes even more disconcerting than the night she took the hunter's life.

16

2030 hours, Monday, August 3, 1942, south of Périllos Pyrénées-Orientales Department, Vichy France

Despite exhaustion from the forced march, there was little time to rest. Everyone had been briefed on the plan and understood the timetable. The prisoners at Drancy would be shipped to Auschwitz within a matter of days. *If they were still destined for Auschwitz.*

During the long walk from Catalonia, Hiram had taken the opportunity to train Team Two on the use of the communications and surveillance equipment he extracted from Jacob's pod. Each woman operated a drone during the hike. On one three-hour leg of the journey, Agnes followed a large red deer through the woods until it met with a small herd and settled down for a mid-morning snooze. She sent the drone down into the trees when the deer stepped into a dense patch of woods. The drone stayed close, maneuvering through the trees no more than ten feet above the hilled landscape. Nora, Simone, and Ester showed similar talent flying the drones, while Vera and Charlotte picked up on the details captured by the drones. From a shallow wolf's footprint in the mud, to a French soldier's hideout camouflaged as a hunting cabin, they picked up on the little details needed to keep the group safe. Hiram had use for their skills.

Now, the time had come to reorganize the women into smaller teams, assigning one newly trained communications specialist to each team. As they sat down to enjoy a well-earned rest and a not so delicious meal, Hiram called for everyone's attention.

"We are all so thankful to be reunited today. It's been a long journey. But, it's not over."

Deborah translated.

"We should leave tonight," Barbara said, Deborah translating. "We should all go to Drancy with your *nuclear weapons* and destroy everything in our path, starting with the Vichy government."

"We can't do that," Hiram said. "The weapons leave residual contamination. We can't move through the area where we detonate one of the weapons. And, we intend to minimize civilian deaths as much as possible." Deborah translated his words, which prompted an immediate outburst from Barbara and several other women.

"They want to know why we should care about the French Gentiles – they do not care about us?" Deborah said.

Hiram shook his head. "If we kill off innocent people, no matter their beliefs, we are no better than these Nazi sympathizers."

"Fuck the French. We save the families," Barbara shouted. She'd learned that much Hebrew along the way.

"You want to kill millions of people to save our families?" Danette retorted in French, Deborah once again translating for Hiram's sake. The discussion degenerated quickly into a shouting match.

Rosette, who hadn't expressed an opinion on any topic since the rescue, began yelling at Barbara. She charged the smaller woman, knocking her to ground.

Both women yelled and cursed as they struggled. Rosette gained the upper hand, slamming a fist into the smaller woman's ribs. On the third strike, Barbara reached for a bayonet in its sheath at her waist. Hiram drew his Taser and let the twin darts fly. He hit Barbara in the ribcage. The two women were so closely locked together that they both collapsed in spasms until he released the trigger. Danette disarmed Barbara and Deborah pulled Rosette more than an arm's length away. Both women lay on the ground in a stupor.

"What the hell was that all about?" Hiram asked Deborah when she straightened up.

"Rosette's family lives outside Vichy. Her husband and children were not taken as part of the roundup. She told me a few days ago that she's only one-eighth Jewish and her husband is all Gentile. One of her great-grandmothers was Jewish, the rest Catholics. She never even thought of herself as a Jew until the roundups began."

"Her family is worth saving too," he said. "We will not massacre the French people. Keep those two apart."

Hiram gave the group a few minutes to calm down. Barbara, red-faced and irritated, stormed away from the group. Rosette wiped a smear of blood from her lip on to her pants leg. The others stood around waiting for further direction.

He looked back at each of his soldiers. The road had been hard for all of them. This most recent leg of the journey from Catalonia had taken its toll on him. Tomorrow, the road would lead them back to their families, hundreds of kilometers from the concealed safety of the forest. "No more arguing. Tonight we rest."

Nora, the silent soldier who had traveled so far on foot with him, let out a sigh. "Barux Hashem!" *Thank God!*

* * *

0650 hours, Tuesday, August 4, 1942, south of Périllos Pyrénées-Orientales Department, Vichy France

"We've got a surprise for you," Deborah said as Hiram finished his welcome but unappetizing breakfast of pod-food. Even *pseudo-turkey medallions with gravy* was preferable to another of the protein bars he'd been eating for the last several days.

"I don't like surprises in the field," he said. "They tend to get people killed."

"You'll like this one." Deborah took his hand, led him over to the location of a parked sidecar motorcycle. Justine and Emma followed them. "Remember the French soldiers we ran into on our way from Vingrau? Emma and Justine went back for the motorcycle a few nights after we arrived here. They snuck off in the night and wheeled the thing back into camp without anyone noticing." The German-made BMW R75 was a very capable on and off-road machine and it had been altered. And then he saw pieces of one of the combat robots on the ground near the bike.

"What have you done?"

"It was Emma and Justine's idea. Emma noticed that the wheelbase of the bike's rear axle is almost identical to standard gauge railroad tracks here in France. She wondered if we could adapt the bike to run on the tracks. There'd be far fewer checkpoints to bypass if we took the railways instead of the roads, travelling at night. And, the rail lines are more direct."

Hiram scratched the back of his head, still considering the demolished robot. "I can't argue with that."

"Justine figured out we could adapt the robot's wheels into rail guides." She pointed to the small wheels mounted beneath the bike, parallel to but offset from the bike's native tires. "They can be retracted to allow the bike to run on the road." She pressed one of the hand controls on the bike and the rail guides folded up and out of sight. "The guides will keep the bike's tires centered on the rails, and if we slightly underinflate the tires, they'll get a good enough grip to propel the bike."

"That's brilliant," Hiram said. Justine and Emma beamed. "But what did you do with the robot's drive system?"

"Take a look inside the sidecar."

Hiram did as instructed. The drive had been connected to the rear axle of the bike.

"The solid rear axle is uncommon among sidecar motorcycles," Justine said by way of Deborah's translation. "Lucky those soldiers had *this* bike."

"Where'd you get the gears?"

Emma made a few dramatic hand movements as she spoke. "Ida was flying the recon drone around and spotted an abandoned tractor a few kilometers away," Deborah translated. "A few of us went and removed the transmission, then carried it back here. We used the tools in the robot repair kit you left out."

Hiram liked the initiative and resourcefulness of the women in his absence. *Yahweh knows they're going to need it, since I have to split them up again.*

"I wish we had a half-dozen more of them," Deborah said, bringing him back to the present.

"That's one wish I can grant. We need to disassemble the whole thing, lower it into my pod." His stomach turned at he said the words. Even now, after days without accessing either pod, his stomach continued to remind him of his trip into Jacob's pod. "I should be able to enter the pod multiple times until we have all the parts we need for seven bikes."

"If you say so." Deborah relayed his direction to Justine and Emma who jumped in to help. Within twenty minutes they had disassembled the motorbike into small enough pieces. They lowered the disassembled motorbike through a portal. An hour later, the components for seven modified bikes lay out before them.

"How long to put them all back together?" Hiram said.

"An hour, maybe two per device," Emma said, Deborah translating. "It's harder than taking them apart."

"She thinks they can get it done in about ten hours," Deborah said.

"I'll help," Hiram said as he stooped down beside one of the sets of parts. Emma said a few words to Deborah.

Deborah laughed. "She says this is woman's work. You have an attack to plan."

Hiram looked around at the six women now surrounding the copied bike and robot parts. He dared not doubt their ability to complete this task after all they'd been through. Besides, he needed to get rid of his headache. "So be it. We leave tonight," he said.

17

0915 hours, Tuesday, August 4, 1942, south of Périllos Pyrénées-Orientales Department, Vichy France

"Rosette's gone," Deborah said. Hiram looked up from the map he studied on the C2ID2.

"You're sure?" he asked.

"She didn't show up for breakfast. When Simone went to look for her she found her C2ID2 attached to a log, so we can't track her electronically. She probably left right after her watch at three o'clock this morning. Looks like she took an M22 and a pair of night vision goggles. Should we send a drone looking for her?"

"We need to get the M22 and NVGs back before they end up in French hands. Put Agnes on it. She's the best drone operator we've got. Any ideas where she's headed?"

Deborah was already walking away. She called back, "Towards Vichy. Back to her family."

Hiram tried to turn his attention back to his C2ID2. Barbara and another of the women – Isadore by the sound of it – argued behind him. He guessed Isadore blamed Barbara for Rosette's departure. Barbara's "kill them all" mentality had set most of them on edge last night. Most of these women once lived among the French Gentiles. They shared afternoon tea with the neighbors, watched as their children played together in the yard. Even after all the French had done to them, they did not wish death on their estranged friends.

He set down the C2ID2 and headed toward the commotion. Deborah, on her way back with news, said a few loud words to the group, then kept walking. They quieted and headed toward Agnes, all eager to find their missing comrade.

"Agnes launched a drone." Hiram returned to his seat and picked up the C2ID2 auxiliary display. Deborah sat down beside him, close enough that her shoulder pressed against him, ensuring a good view of the monitor. "What are you up to anyway?"

"Trying to figure out the safest route to Saarbrücken, or as close as we can get," he said. "I thought the road maps were bad. Look at these rail maps." The drawing showed huge gaps in the tracks. The tracks either remained unfinished or the map reflected an incomplete picture.

Deborah traced the railway with her finger from the flagged location of their camp all the way to Saarbrücken. "Why Saarbrücken?"

"From what I remember of my father's research, all the Holocaust trains from Drancy pass over the Saar River and through the major rail junction in Saarbrücken on their way to Auschwitz. It's also a major transit point for German supplies."

Deborah looked at him, hopeful. "You think detonating one of your nuclear bombs in the area will stop the trains leaving Drancy?"

"I hope so. The loss of the Saarbrücken railhead puts more pressure on the other major crossings into France. With any luck, the prisoners at Drancy will be a low enough priority that they'll get pushed way down the cargo lists."

"Saarbrücken is a long way from here."

"I think we can handle it, thanks to Emma and Justine's ingenuity."

"And when you say 'we'" Deborah looked at him sideways as if expecting him to finish.

"Me, you, Danette, and Vera."

"Vera?"

"Have you seen her operate a drone?" Hiram said. "Almost as good as Agnes, whom I have other plans for."

"I should have expected that. What about the others?"

"To stop the war, multiple targets need to be eliminated near Hitler's Atlantic Wall. The quickest way to carry out those attacks is to split up into smaller groups. Seven teams should be sufficient. The bikes have two seats. And, we can squeeze two into the sidecar. Up to four in each team. Call them Alpha, Bravo, Charlie, Delta, Echo, Foxtrot, Golf, and Hotel."

"I'll assume we belong to team Alpha."

"I need you with me to translate radio calls since not all the teams have English or Hebrew speakers, Vera can focus on interpreting the drone data and—"

"And you don't want to leave Danette behind," she finished for him.

Hiram said, "You got it."

"Where are we sending the others?"

"Towards the coast. Somewhere along the Loire River near Tours should do until we hear Sarah and Maria have made it to England. We need to keep them on this side of the demarcation line from occupied France. Everything depends on Sarah talking to General Eisenhower."

* * *

"Agnes found Rosette, about 20 kilometers west of here, near Padern," Deborah said, Agnes and Nora standing by her side. "I'm not sure why she's going west. Maybe because we expected her to head north."

"So much for scooping her up on the way. We can't waste the night chasing her down. Agnes — keep her in view and switch out with Nora if you need a break." Hiram waited for Deborah to translate.

Agnes nodded in acceptance of the task. Nora stood by her side ready to assist.

"We leave at full dark. We don't have a lot of time to spare."

* * *

2015 hours, Tuesday, August 4, 1942, southeast of Orange, Vaucluse Department, Vichy France

The train rolled down the tracks thirty meters ahead. Hiram watched through his NVGs, alert for any signs of slowing. They made good time, almost eighty kilometers per hour, but it was still a long way to Saarbrücken. He enjoyed the feel of Deborah's arms wrapped around him from behind, her helmet resting against his back. His goggles flared when he looked to his right. Vera, seated in front of Danette in the sidecar, focused on the C2ID2 screen. The sensitive goggles reacted to the light from the display. He reminded himself the light was barely visible beyond the sidecar to anyone not wearing NVGs. Still, it made him nervous.

The train ahead *clack-clacked* as it rattled over the rail junctions, audible over the railbike's quiet electric engine. The BMW's previous internal combustion engine had been powerful, but too noisy to carry Alpha team this close to a train. Cannibalizing the combat robot had been a stroke of genius.

A sudden, piercing whistle cut through the night, the sound familiar and unforgettable. He cut the engine's power and slammed on the bike's brakes, the rubber tires squealing along the rails as the bike came to a halt.

Danette and Vera scrambled out of the sidecar and disappeared over the opposite side of the tracks as Hiram and Deborah dove off the railbike. Hiram and Deborah fell to the ground and rolled down the slight embankment, stopping in a muddy puddle as the first bomb detonated further up the line. Ten seconds later the ground shook as a second bomb hit much closer.

"Incline Thine ear, O HaShem, and answer me; for I am poor and needy." Hiram had not heard Deborah pray before. It took him a verse to remember the psalm, but he soon joined in.

"Be gracious unto me, O Lord; for unto Thee do I cry all the day." Deborah opened her eyes and tried to smile, the effort thwarted by her fear. She squeezed them shut again and resumed praying as a plane roared overhead spitting cannon fire at the train. After another verse, a second plane crossed the sky, firing again at the train. Hiram guessed the planes were British or American fighter-bombers, armed with bombs and 20 mm canons.

One of the shots hit something volatile. The train erupted in a cascade of explosions. *I guess they bombed a train full of bombs,* Hiram thought as the shock waves rolled over them. Isolated explosions continued for the next few minutes, then silence.

He checked himself – no damage. Beside him, Deborah smiled with relief. He reached out and touched her. She shook her head and pointed back toward the tracks, mouthing Danette's name. Hiram raised his head to shout across to the other side of the embankment. "Danette, are you okay," but he couldn't hear his own voice. "Vera!" That's when he noticed the ringing in his ears. He turned his head to look down at Deborah and saw her mouth moving again. He heard nothing.

"Can you hear me?" he said. Deborah looked at him for a moment, then shook her head. Hiram got up on his knees and took a quick look around. The NVGs rested on the ground an arm's length away. Once he had them settled in place, he took another look around before scrambling over the tracks to find Danette and Vera.

He found Vera lying on her stomach at the bottom of the embankment, eyes fixed and unmoving, her head contorted at an impossible angle, her neck torn open. A twisted shard of metal stuck out of the wound. He looked around wildly for Danette.

To his surprise she lay a few feet away on the ground in a perfect prone firing position, sighting her M22 up the tracks. He glanced in that direction but saw no threats. He tapped her on the shoulder to get her attention. He pointed to his ear and shook his head. She nodded in agreement. They were all deaf.

Danette resumed her firing position. Deborah who had observed Danette's calm professionalism, took up a similar position, looking in the opposite direction. Hiram went to examine the railbike, which had slipped off the tracks. The bottom of the front wheel bent inward. Otherwise the bike seemed fully functional. He retracted the guide wheels that had kept the railbike on the track, then swapped the damaged wheel with the spare his mechanics had insisted each group take with them.

Twenty minutes later he signaled Danette and Deborah to climb aboard. He loaded Vera's body into the sidecar with Danette. Danette held the dead woman like a child, supporting her head as her neck no longer would. Tears streamed down Danette's cheeks as she turned to face him.

"We need to take her where she won't be found," he said. He spoke loud, unable to hear his own words above the ringing in his ears.

Deborah and Danette seemed to understand him, although it was likely their hearing hadn't returned either. Hiram climbed on to the bike.

Farther down the tracks, local firemen approached the burning train, black silhouettes against the flames. They'd have to find a way around the wrecked train and the response forces streaming towards it. More delays. More time wasted. Time the families in Drancy could not afford.

18

1300 hours, Tuesday, August 4, 1942, Marbella, Costa del Sol, Francoist Spain

Sarah was quite sure she would never eat another orange as long as she lived. For three days she'd hidden along with Maria in the back of an ancient flatbed truck, occupying a small space between dozens of crates packed with fragrant oranges.

Since Sunday night, they'd shared the cramped space with Flight Lieutenant Anthony "Tony" Farley of the Royal Air Force's 138th Squadron. Tony had bailed out of his Westland Lysander over southeastern France a week earlier, his aircraft falling victim to a German fighter plane. He'd been lucky to survive the night jump into a forest, but his lone passenger, a British SAS officer, had perished when he snapped his neck on an unseen branch.

Hiram had instructed Sarah and Maria not to reveal their true mission to anyone until they spoke to an American officer, either on the Rock or in Britain. Tony's questions went unanswered, so he had resorted to flirting. Sarah wasn't in the mood, but she knew Tony could help them get ashore at Gibraltar. She tried to be polite. Tony judged her lack of interest, and focused his attention on Maria, the two of them verbally fencing as the truck rolled down the road.

The truck came to a halt and the stacks of orange crates began to disappear, allowing them to crawl out into the light, shading their eyes at the sudden brilliance of the Costa del Sol. The truck had stopped at a small vineyard located below a high ridge. Sarah saw the Mediterranean Sea a few kilometers to the south, beyond a fishing village on the coast below them.

Maria asked the driver, Ricardo, the name of the town. He was a short, swarthy man with considerable body odor and worse breath. Still, it was preferable to oranges.

"Marbella, *mi señora*." Ricardo pointed down toward the town and said a few more words to Maria.

"He says we'll be boarding one of the boats down there for the trip to the Rock. About 70 kilometers by sea. But first," Maria smiled "we eat!"

Sarah hoisted her backpack onto her shoulder and thanked him, Maria translating, then asked for directions to the toilet. Sarah left Maria and Ricardo and headed for the privy. As she made her way around the ramshackle house, she wondered why Ricardo had once referred to Tony as a spy during their trip south.

She nearly collided with Tony as she turned a corner. "Pardon me, madam," he said in his clipped English accent. He stepped aside, allowing her to pass.

"Entirely my fault." She smiled and continued on her way. Tony was one of those Brits you could pick out of a crowd instantly. Fair-skinned, square-shouldered, and possessing a ramrod-straight posture, he radiated English aristocracy, even dressed as he was in peasant rags and leather sandals. *That man would make an awful spy*. He spoke terrible Spanish and poor French. Maria had been translating for him since they met.

Sarah breathed in the open air, glad to be free of the stuffy truck and the acidity of the orange-tainted air she'd endured along the way. The scent of oranges lingered and she wondered how long it intended to stick with her.

The familiar pop of a gunshot sent her ducking behind the outhouse that had been her destination. After a second shot, she took off running in the other direction. She plunged into a thick copse of juniper bushes at the edge of the woods. Moments later, two Spanish policemen rounded the corner of the building, guns drawn. They advanced on the outhouse, then yelled for her to come out. When she didn't respond, they yanked the door open.

Moving slow and quiet, Sarah reached into her pack and withdrew the handgun Hiram had provided her for self-defense. She kept an eye on the policemen, who searched a jumble of discarded farm equipment near the privy. With the silencer screwed on tight and a full ten round magazine she waited.

The policemen moved their search into the house while Sarah crawled deeper into the woods. She rose to a crouch, circled around to the front of the dwelling, and took up a position under a broken-down wagon at the edge of the woods. Tony, Ricardo and another man, along with a middle-aged woman, sat on the ground in front of the house with their hands on their heads. Three policemen stood guard over them, one with sergeant's stripes on his sleeve. Maria lay sprawled on the ground nearby. She wasn't moving.

Sarah put her head down and tried to calm herself. She had left Maria alone for no more than ten minutes and now she lay dead at the feet of those bastards. *Strong, brave Maria.* If she hadn't taken the time to relieve herself, she may have been right there on the ground beside her, just as silent and still. *You've still got a job to do.* Sarah took in one deep breath, letting out all the fear and sadness along with it. *These bastards deserve to die!* She returned her focus to the scene, drawing on the long hours of training Hiram had put them through.

The sergeant was armed with a pistol, holstered at his hip. The other two men had rifles. She longed for an M22 assault rifle, but the handgun would have to do.

The two men searching the house emerged onto the front porch and all three of the policemen in the yard turned in that direction. Sarah fired.

From a distance of almost twenty meters, she aimed for center of mass, hitting the policemen nearest Tony in the back. He screamed as he crumpled to the ground. Sarah shifted her aim to the second rifleman and fired again. The heavy slug caught him in the shoulder, spinning him around as he fell. His spin revealed more information on her hiding place than the nearly silent shots she'd fired. The policemen on the porch fired in her general direction and she scrambled farther under the wagon. She lifted her head in time to see Ricardo lunge at the sergeant, knocking him to the ground. Both men wrestled for control of his pistol. Without a clear shot, she shifted her fire to the men on the porch.

Tony grabbed the nearest fallen policeman's rifle and aimed toward the two surviving officers, adding his fire to Sarah's. One man was hit and the other dove for cover. Sarah returned her attention to the struggle between Ricardo and the police sergeant. Ricardo had lost, he lay dying in the dirt. The sergeant pointed his pistol at Tony. Tony faced the porch, rifle still pointing toward the falling policeman on the porch. Sarah and the sergeant fired at almost the same instant.

19

1410 hours, Tuesday, August 4, 1942, southwest of Monda, Costa del Sol, Francoist Spain

Pasqual drove too fast for the dirt track, but not fast enough for Sarah's liking. Tony groaned as the truck hit another bump in the mountain road. Every little movement aggravated the bullet buried deep in Tony's shoulder, and while the magical foam in her medical kit had stopped the bleeding, he needed expert medical care, and needed it soon. She'd given him as much pain killer as she dared, fearful of a fatal overdose. The stout vineyard owner, Pasqual, had directed them to a trustworthy doctor in the town of Monda. But Monda waited fifteen kilometers in the wrong direction, away from the sea and the boat that would carry them to Gibraltar, along a route riddled with police patrols and roadblocks. Sarah regretted not taking the time to bury Maria, but Tony still had a chance and she feared he might die of shock or infection without help.

Peeking between the crates, she could see Pasqual's wife Josefa following them in another truck, that one carrying most of the family's possessions. Pasqual and Josefa planned to flee into the mountains after finding the doctor, their cover compromised. The family vineyard would likely be confiscated by the government.

"Bloody hell," Tony said as the truck jostled around another sharp turn.

"How are you feeling?" Sarah said.

"How much farther?" he asked, ignoring her question.

"I don't know. Not far." *I hope.* The truck eventually slowed, and Sarah stole another glance between the orange crates. They had entered a village. Two more quick turns, and the trucks came to a halt. Between the three of them, they managed to carry Tony through the backdoor of what she presumed to be the doctor's office. She was disappointed to see they had entered a storeroom instead. At least there was a cot, and they laid Tony down on it.

"Wait here, I bring doctor," Pasqual said, then turned and left via the room's front door.

"And I watch trucks," Josefa said. "Street urchins steal everything." She left through the door they had entered, leaving Sarah alone with Tony.

"Do you think he'll come back with the doctor?" Tony clutched his wounded arm.

"Yes. If they wanted to abandon us, they'd have done it at the vineyard," she said. The heat in the small storeroom seemed to grow more intense as they waited. Sweat beaded on Tony's forehead. Sarah wet her kerchief with her canteen and mopped his brow, letting a little of the cool water trickle into his hair. Tony relaxed a little despite his suffering.

They waited about fifteen minutes, an eternity in the closed-in space. Pasqual returned with the doctor, a plump middle-aged man a head shorter than Sarah. As the medic bent to examine Tony, Pasqual turned to her and said, "We leave now. The *Policía* look for the trucks. *Ve con Dios.*" Go with God – a sentiment she learned from Maria. He left before she could reply.

Tony winced as the doctor pulled the bandages back from his shoulder. The doctor talked to Sarah, but she couldn't understand the blur of Spanish that came out of him. He pointed at the wound, touched the foam that had bubbled up out of the hole in Tony's shoulder.

"Clotting foam," she replied.

Tony took hold of the doctor's hand and said something back to him. His version of Spanish barely resembled the doctor's language. The short man winced as Tony talked, as if struggling to understand. The doctor looked at the wound again and then back at Sarah.

"Wait outside," Tony said right before he moaned in agony. "Go," he hissed.

Sarah reached for her pack on the floor next to Tony's cot, except it wasn't there. She looked around the small room, bent and peered under the cot. Not there. *Where the hell is my pack?*

"It's on the truck!" Sarah sprinted out the back door where they had come in. The trucks had pulled away. Her backpack, medical kit, handgun, and Icarus drone were gone.

She ran down the road in pursuit. "Pasqual!" She cried. "Josefa!" The trucks kept moving. For a few minutes she watched them, not sure what to do.

Cursing, she ran back to the storeroom. Inside, Tony lay still on the cot with his eyes closed. The doctor's fingers explored his shoulder determining the extent of the damage. *"Dormido, no muerta."* Tony let out a breath.

Sarah sat down on a crate next to the door. She pulled up the sleeve of her shirt, revealing the C2ID2 strapped to her forearm. She tapped a few icons and cursed again. Pasqual's truck, and her backpack, were six kilometers away and travelling at nearly fifty kilometers per hour. Soon it would be out of the C2ID2's range. She activated the self-destruct menu, entered the code Hiram made her memorize on the walk to Catalonia. *Sorry Pasqual. I hope you and Josefa survive this.* She tapped the activation icon. The sound of the explosion disrupted the doctor at work. He looked at Sarah and shook his head. After a few heated words, all unfamiliar to Sarah, he returned his attention to Tony's wound.

The doctor removed the bullet from Tony's shoulder, along with a small patch of clothing carried into the wound by the bullet. The cloth and the bullet sat on the cot next to Tony's limp body. He doused the wound with sulfa, packed it with a poultice soaked in honey, bandaged the wound, and then placed Tony's right arm in a makeshift sling. Tony had passed out sometime during the process. The pain killers Sarah had given the pilot had worked well enough to get him here, but the pain induced by the doctor's poking and prodding had been too much. She doubted he'd wake any time soon.

The doctor cleaned his hands with a rag he pulled from his worn bag. He seemed to assess his work, then headed for the door.

Sarah followed him, but he stopped her from leaving the storeroom. "No," he said. He took her arm and guided her back to the cot. He pointed to her and then to Tony.

"I don't know what you want me to do."

He said a few more words to her and then headed for the door again. As he closed the door behind him, he held up his hand palm out in the way one would command a dog to stay. She nodded. The doctor closed the door and left her behind with the injured pilot.

She sat down on the foot of the cot, leaned against the wall, and waited. She needed Maria. Maria would know what to do. Maria would have understood the doctor. But Maria was gone. Her body lay sprawled on the front lawn of the vineyard, abandoned. Sarah cried.

* * *

"Sarah," a hushed voice called. "Wake up."

She opened her eyes, tried to adjust to the darkness of the room. Night had fallen. Inside the storeroom, she could see nothing.

"Someone's out there," Tony said – a weak, but alive Tony. They heard talking outside. After a few seconds, light crept in under the door, interrupted by shadows as people moved around outside.

Sarah looked around the room, searching for a place to hide. A few stacks of crates, most filled with sacks of flour and cans of food, were pressed against the outside walls. If she tried to move them, the people outside would hear. Besides, she had no time to hide Tony.

The people outside grew quiet, and the door started to open. Sarah felt around the room, searching for a weapon. She grabbed a can out of the crate nearest her. As the man's head popped in, she threw the can as hard as she could – and missed.

The man rushed in and took hold of her, pinning her arms to her body in a bear hug. Two more men came in and eased Tony up off the cot.

"Don't move him!" she yelled. "Let him be. He's hurt."

The man who held her said something to her.

"Please," she said.

"Sarah, don't fight them," Tony said.

"Who are they?"

Tony went out the door, the two men supporting his weight. "I don't know."

The man holding Sarah relaxed a little. Her arms slipped down his body and she felt the hilt of a knife on his waist. She grabbed the weapon and moved out of arms reach. She turned on the stranger and waved the knife at him. He put his arms up as if defeated and backed out of the room.

Sarah ran out after Tony, the knife out in front of her. She was met with blinding headlights of a large truck. With one arm blocking the light and the other wielding the knife, she searched for Tony.

Two men walked toward her, hands in the air. The man on the left had earlier restrained her in the storeroom. He said something in Spanish, the same thing he had said when he let her go.

"Where is he?" she asked.

The man spoke again.

Tony emerged from behind the truck. A man supporting him as he moved toward her. "Our good friend the doctor sent these strong young men. Now come on, we've got to get out of here. The police are searching for us."

The man on the left motioned for her to come along. She looked at Tony and back at the others. The four young men bore quite a resemblance to the doctor, though they were fortunate to have picked up a few more inches in height. She headed towards the back of the truck.

As she passed the man on the left, she tried to hand the knife back to him. He shook his head. She hesitated, said "*gracias*." The big man put a hand on her back and guided her to the truck.

Once Tony settled onto a pile of blankets on the floor, the men helped Sarah up into the open back truck. She sat on the floor beside the pilot.

"Where are we going?" Sarah asked.

He pointed to the smallest man in the truck. "This is Luis. The doctor's nephew. He'll be escorting us to the docks."

20

2300 hours, Tuesday, August 4, 1942, Mediterranean Sea, south of the Costa del Sol, Francoist Spain

"Bloody fucking sea," Tony grumbled as the rowboat rose and fell with the waves. "If I wanted to be a sailor, I'd have damn well joined the Navy, not the RAF."

Luis huffed as he fought to make his way out into open water.

Tony put his hand against the bandages on his shoulder. "Why in hell did we have to take this boat?"

They had intended to board a fishing boat at the docks. Luis had known one of the locals and promised safe passage. But a roadblock a few kilometers into their journey sent them on a less well-known road. They pulled into a small fishing village just past Marbella. Now, Luis, Sarah, and Tony rode in Luis' family's little boat with no motor and no lights headed out from the shore with only the dull glow of the quarter moon to guide their way.

"Try to focus on the horizon," Sarah said. "Throwing up would not be a good thing for a man in your condition. You're already dehydrated."

He said a few words under his breath and looked away.

"When we were back at the vineyard, Ricardo called you a spy. Why?" Sarah tried to take his mind off the waves, and her own off Maria's death.

"The 138th Squadron is a 'special' squadron. We support the British Special Air Service, the SAS, flying them in and out of France, dropping supplies, and carrying messages too sensitive to transmit by radio. And now that I've shared my spy secret with you, I don't suppose you'll tell me why you are going to the Rock." He did not take his eyes off of her. As a wave hit the small boat, he winced. Still, he didn't look away. The longer he looked at her, the more she wanted to tell him the whole story. She wondered if this was one of his spy tricks.

She supposed he deserved an answer. Tony might be her only chance to make it to Gibraltar. They fought on the same side. "I'm on my way to see General Eisenhower," she said.

"Eisenhower? What business could you have with him?"

"Well, first I'm going to tell him to keep an eye on Saarbrücken, Germany. I'd hoped to tell him exactly *when* to keep an eye out, but I lost my radio. It won't be long though," she said.

"What would he be watching for?"

"For a very large explosion."

Tony smiled. "Your comrades are planning to blow up something in the city?"

"More like, they're going to blow up a large portion of the city," Sarah looked down at her hands.

"How?"

"That's a secret I can only tell the General, I'm afraid. For American ears only."

"You're not American," Tony said.

"Nope. French Jew. Spent time in America as a post-doctoral student, then returned to France. I got stuck in an internment camp when the Nazis put the Vichy in charge. Escaped with the help of a friend's grandson. He's American, or at least his father was. Anyway, once Eisenhower sees the explosion, I'm sure he'll be interested in discussing further applications." She'd skipped over a couple of generations between Danette and Hiram. He'd never believe the truth. She hardly believed it herself.

Sarah said all she intended to say. Tony wanted more. Not wanting to feel the urge to tell him everything, she turned to the sea, anxious for any sign of the expected fishing boat.

"*Donde* bloody *barco?*" Tony said, his terrible Spanish accentuated by his irritation, which rose with the waves.

Luis shook his head and spoke to Tony.

"We are right where he was told to wait," the pilot said. Even in the moonlight, Sarah could see for quite a distance. Not a single ship waited nearby.

One of Luis' brothers had gone back to the docks to notify his contact of the change in plans. She hoped he had made it. Sarah was running out of time.

A few moments later, the water a few meters away stirred.

"What is that?" Sarah said.

"That, my dear, is our ride." Tony said. "Word of my injury probably prompted a change of plan."

A dark shape rose up out of the water. *A submarine!* The small boat rocked in the wake.

She heard a deep bang, saw the silhouette of a man climb out. A voice called out, "Lieutenant Farley, I presume?"

"Ho!" Tony yelled. "About damn time."

A flurry of movement erupted from the opening in the submarine as others climbed out to assist. A man on the sub tossed a rope toward them. Sarah caught the line and reeled them in.

"We'll need help getting him aboard," she said. "He's injured." Two sailors clambered down a rope ladder into the rowboat to assist Tony. Sarah shuddered at the sight of the rope ladder, remembering her experience disembarking from the *M.V. Calais*.

Once Tony had been hoisted up to the sub's deck, she turned back to Luis who waited, his face betraying nothing. She took one of his hands. "I don't know how we'll ever repay you and your uncle. Thank you."

He nodded as if he understood.

When she started to climb up the ladder, a sailor held up his hand. "Sorry, miss. Only the Lieutenant."

"Let her aboard," Tony yelled from above. "We don't want her to end up in the wrong hands."

21

2020 hours, Tuesday, August 4, 1942, Vichy, Allier Department, Vichy France

Rosette stepped off a train in Vichy, wearing a faded gray frock she had stolen from a clothes line back near Perillos and a pair of women's oxfords left to air out on a porch a few doors down. The M22 and night vision goggles had been hidden beneath an old broken-down tractor on an abandoned farm, wrapped in the uniform she had to leave behind. She had felt naked without the weapon at first.

Although the new ensemble did little to announce her sense of style, the plain clothes provided a more suitable costume on the train than the adaptive camouflage uniform and heavy boots she had worn back at Hiram's camp. As she walked down the packed dirt road towards her home in Brugheas with her lower legs showing, hips accentuated by the shape of the frock, and hair pinned back on the top with an inward curl resting on her shoulders, she remembered what it felt like to be a woman. *Not my best, but at least I won't scare Garon or the children.*

The oversized shoes rubbed the back of her heel raw as she walked. She refused to slow down. Her family waited. She could not wait to feel Garon's arms around her or Sophia's warm breath on her neck as she held her tight. And Leverette, who looked so much like his father, would rattle on about everything that had happened in her absence. She predicted a short stay, considering the number of policemen on the lookout for the missing maids. Any time she could have with her family, she would take. She walked faster.

As she approached her home, she noticed candle light flickering through a neighbor's curtains. *All the lights should be out at night. I will be sure the Dumont's are reminded, but not until I see my little ones.*

Rosette slipped through a break in the houses and headed around back. The back door always stayed unlocked. Careful not to step too close to the Dumont's house and set off their old, blind, and almost deaf hunting dog, she walked wide around their back door. She took hold of the door handle, released the catch, took a deep breath as the door swung open, and tiptoed into her home.

After taking off the Oxfords, she ascended the stairs with light steps hoping not to wake the children. *Not yet. I want to see them sleeping snug in their beds, oblivious to the dark turn of the world around them.*

She stepped into the quiet nursery but found Leverette's bed empty. The quilt she had stitched for him spread out over the made bed, not a ripple in sight. For a moment, Rosette panicked but then thought the child may have taken refuge with his father. The boy had been known to have nightmares on occasion. She walked over to Sophia's crib, but the foot board shadowed the sleeping area making it impossible to see anything inside. Rosette reached into the crib and ran her hand across the cool fabric searching for her little girl. The crib was empty. She closed her eyes and took a breath before heading to the master bedroom.

As she passed the stairs, she heard a voice from the main floor. She moved down the stairs, no longer worrying about waking anyone. Garon stood in the doorway of the kitchen, silhouetted by the candle burning on the table.

"Rosette?"

She ran to him, wrapped her arms around his thin body. "It's me!"

He hugged her loosely for a moment, then pushed her away. "You-you shouldn't have come here," he said.

"I missed you all terribly. I know I won't be able to stay long. Where are the children? Have you left them with Mabel? I was hoping to see them before I had to leave."

"The children are with my sister," he said. "Where it's safe."

His sister lived on a farm, far from the towns that had been targeted by attacks from the enemies of those who occupied France. Hiram had told her of the destruction brought about by the war, after all that was why she was here. "I suppose that is best for now. But you will need to get away from here, out of France if you can help it. Get the children and go as far away as you can."

"I am in no danger here."

"You don't understand. The whole area, all of Occupied France, is under attack. Not just from the Germans you see. The Allies are preparing to destroy all those who support them. Everyone is in danger. You need to leave."

"Impossible," he said. "I have nothing to fear from the Allies. Vichy will protect us."

"Think about the children, Garon. Your sister is less than one hundred kilometers from here. Not far enough away from what's coming."

"You should get back to the work camp. Someone will know you are here. If you really wanted to protect me, you wouldn't have come here."

"I cannot go back to the work camp. They were going to kill us, all of us."

"A little hard work isn't going to kill you."

"It's not the work that is going to kill us. They are going to gas everyone. Everyone at the camps is being shipped to Auschwitz. Hiram called it an extermination camp."

"Hiram?" Garon said.

"He helped us to escape."

"There are more of you?"

"Yes, but they are safe. Garon, I need you to listen to me. Get the children and get away."

Garon stood and made his way over to the stove. "I understand. Why don't we sit, have a cup of coffee? You can go with me to get the children and we will get out of France together – as a family."

She nodded, relieved. "What about the check points? The police are everywhere."

He approached the stove, loaded a small amount of coal inside, and struck a match to set it ablaze. "You let me worry about the police. Sit down and relax your weary feet."

Rosette sat, watching the man she loved work the kitchen. He should not know how to do these things so well. She had been gone too long. Months had passed with this hard-working man caring for himself. Yet, she did not jump to help him.

"We should take a change of clothes with us. Some for the children, don't you think?"

"Coffee first," he said.

She sat in silence, taking in the room she thought had been forgotten. A few hours here and she could make a delightful meal for the family, maybe one of Leverette's favorites – a cheese soufflé. The rations provided enough for a small dish. How she longed for a delicious home cooked meal. After weeks of eating Hiram's packs of food, she thought she might kill for a decent dish.

Garon ran coffee beans through the grinder, the familiar crunch announcing the rich scent to follow. She missed real coffee.

"Where did you get coffee? I don't remember it being on the ration card."

"I-" a sound outside interrupted Garon's words. He set down the sack towel. "Stay here. I'll see what is going on."

"I saw a light on in the neighbor's house. Maybe something happened to them."

"Perhaps." The light of a torch passed by the front window. Garon slipped out the door, closing it behind him.

Rosette waited as instructed, the kettle on the stove beginning to moan as the water came to a boil. When the front door opened, it was not Garon who stepped inside. A policeman entered the house. Her heart sunk. She had made it so close to escaping.

"No, I'm not even Jewish," Rosette said. Her voice riddled with desperation. She backed away from the man. "They are going to kill all of us. I can't go back there. I know what you are doing to those people. I'm part of it because my great-great-grandmother fell in love with a man who was born Jewish. I'm Catholic!"

"Rosette, I am Emile Locard. We need to get you out of here," the policeman said.

"It doesn't matter who you are. I'm not going back to one of those camps. You'll have to shoot me. Please. One shot," Rosette said.

"I do not want to hurt you," he said. "I think we need to talk."

She searched for a way out of the kitchen. If she could slide past the policeman, she could run outside. Garon would be waiting to get them out together, just like he planned.

The policeman stepped farther into the kitchen. "Come with me," he said. "I can keep you safe."

"You are one of them," Rosette said. "How can I trust you?"

"You think you can trust your husband?" Locard said.

"Of course. I needed to go away for the children. We both thought it would be better for them."

"And where are your children now?"

"With family. Garon can't hold his job with the responsibility of the children. He is an important man you know."

Locard's voice grew harder. "He turned your children in too, Madame."

"No. Can't be. He loves them."

"He loves himself more. I read the report. He turned your kids over to the police. Said they might turn on him. He is protecting himself."

"He wouldn't do it," Rosette said, her voice soft, disbelieving.

"Who do you think called the police?" Locard paused, waited for her response, but she said nothing. "Come with me, quietly. I know of a place where you will be safe."

"The children – can you help me find them?" Rosette said.

"I don't know where the children have been taken," Locard said.

"Please," she begged. "Sophie is so little. She'll never survive. Please."

"I can try. Will you come with me?"

Rosette looked at Locard, then back to the door. "Promise you'll help me find them."

"I'll help." He looked back to the door, as if waiting for Garon to come back in as well. "Now, come with me. We don't have much time to get you out of here. If I am gone too long my superior will suspect."

Rosette walked toward the man. He grabbed her arm and squeezed. "Walk with me, and don't say anything."

She nodded and followed his instructions.

As they approached the policeman's car, Garon approached her. He walked with purpose, as if he intended to take down the policeman. At that moment, she knew they were getting out of this place, out of France. Rosette played out her part in her head. She would grab Locard's pistol as she tried to set him off balance. Then she could get him to the ground.

Garon closed in on her position. Rosette turned as if she wanted to say goodbye to her husband, setting her in the perfect position to take down the policeman.

But the man she had been married to for eight years wanted to clear his own name with the policeman named Locard. "I wasn't hiding her," he said. "She just showed up. I called you as soon as she walked in the door." Rosette's world fell apart.

"You took the appropriate action. We'll make sure her actions are punished," the officer said as he opened the door for Rosette. She climbed in, her action's mechanical, tears streaming down her face. He closed her door and climbed in himself.

As the car's engine started, Garon yelled "filthy Jew" at the car and spit on ground.

22

0715 hours, Wednesday, August 5, 1942, Perpignan, Pyrénées-Orientales Department, Vichy France

Captain Louis Petain arrived at the office early. His assistant had reported a call about a Jewish woman breaking into a home in Brugheas. All of the Jewish people in the town had been rounded up back in June. He heard of no exceptions in the area. With a small army of his men living and patrolling in the town, Petain doubted they missed a single woman. The French families in the area knew better than to hide the Jews in their homes or on their property. He had seized more property in the last three months than the office had in the previous ten years for such intolerable behavior. Perhaps one of his men had become soft.

He had decided to send an officer out to the site anyway.

The call had come in before dawn. Petain recalled few details. Perhaps he had not paid enough attention. He had been so distracted by the mess caused by this mysterious Jew-loving soldier that his interest in the mundane day-to-day operations of running this office dwindled. Of course, he remained skeptical of his direct reports ensuring things ran well without him.

"*Bonjour Capitaine Petain,*" his assistant Rubi said as he approached her desk. Her energy escalated his unpleasant mood. She worked harder than the assistants he hired in the past and she made one hell of an espresso. Both warranted keeping her around. Her willingness to share information – gossip as she called it – deemed her an ally. "Espresso this morning, sir?"

"Yes," he said and then headed to his office, almost forgetting the break-in. "Was the suspect in this morning's break-in apprehended?"

"Thibult was going to go, but then the assignment was taken over by Monsieur Locard. I have no confirmation on the outcome, sir."

"Locard? Why would Locard be making house calls?"

The assistant looked at him for a moment, unsure how to address his question. "I-"

Just then Petain saw Thibult step into the office area.

"Perhaps Officer Thibult will be able to provide an explanation as to why a criminalist's time was spent apprehending a break-in suspect." Petain spoke loud enough for Thibult to hear him. Two other officers in the office looked from Petain to Thibult.

Thibult quickened his pace to join Petain. "Sir, Locard believed the call was related to another case he was working on. He had asked to be informed if any calls to the police were made concerning that location. Said you would prefer that he address the situation."

"And you allowed Emile Locard to address the situation alone?"

"It was one girl, sir. He said he could handle it."

"And where is Locard now?"

"Sir?"

Petain's impatience magnified. "Where is Locard?"

"I don't believe he has returned," Thibult said.

"Well get out there and find him!"

Thibult said, "Sir, he borrowed the squad car."

Petain took a deep breath, fearing he'd shoot the man standing in front of him if he did not take a moment. "If anything has happened to the criminalist, the payment will be cut from your hide. Are you off in the head, Thibult?"

"Sir?"

Petain addressed the two officers sipping espresso and seeming to enjoy the show. "Go find Locard!" He looked back at Thibult. "Give them the damned address."

Thibult headed towards the two officers who had set down their drinks.

Then, as if on cue, the door opened and Emile Locard stepped in with his suit coat draped over his shoulder.

"Perhaps Monsieur Locard is more competent than Officer Thibult after all. Locard, will you join me in my office?"

Petain entered his office and Locard followed. "The door, if you don't mind, and have a seat."

The Police Captain sat down in his chair, a comforting experience that eased a small portion of his irritation. He found that Locard's safety added to this light improvement of his mood.

"Officer Thibult should have accompanied you to the scene this morning," Petain said.

"The original report stated that the woman breaking into the home was believed to be Rosette Bertrand."

"Bertrand?"

"One of the thirty missing maids."

"I see. And have you secured this woman for questioning?"

"No sir. Turns out the report was from a neighbor. Rosette's husband Garon Bertrand had invited over his mistress with instructions to come to the back door."

"The day appears to be littered with the actions of the feeble-minded," Petain said. Any man considering involvement with a mistress should know better. They are things to be played with away from the family home. His own experience taught him the neighbors were the most likely to question one's actions. Though he supposed a man who married a Jew could not be considered an adulterer. "Any other news to report on our missing maids?"

"No sir. The incident provided me access to this woman's family home. No indications of Madame Bertrand's presence or any of the others."

"Do you think Monsieur Bertrand is hiding anything?"

"No sir. The man even turned over his children to the police. Said he thought they had been corrupted by their mother's blood."

"Mongrels. It's probably best."

Rubi brought in his espresso and a cup of tea for the criminalist. "Anything else I can do for you sir?"

"The train?" Petain sipped his espresso.

"Yes sir. Telegraph arrived a few minutes ago. The train is scheduled to depart Drancy tomorrow morning."

"That should put them out of France by tomorrow night. Thank you."

Rubi left, closing the door behind her.

"And the thirty missing prisoners?" Locard asked.

"They are a threat to our people Locard. The sooner we find them the better." *The sooner I get my hands around their little necks, the sooner I can end the headache they've caused me.*

23

0530 hours, Wednesday, August 5, 1942, Gibraltar, United Kingdom

Soon after disembarking from the *HMS Talisman,* Sarah was escorted into the spartan office of Royal Air Force Wing Commander Michael Brigadoon.

"Good morning, Miss Mendelson." Brigadoon rose from his chair and came around the desk to take her hand.

"Good morning, sir," she said. "Thank you for seeing me."

"I should thank you for saving Flight Lieutenant Farley's life. He tells me you are very handy with a pistol. And the medics tell me you worked a miracle keeping him from bleeding out until you got him to a doctor."

"Well, I had a lot of help from our Spanish friends in that regard. And I lost a good friend during the fight."

He held her hand in both of his for a moment. "I'm sorry to hear about your loss. A lot of good friends have been lost in this war." Brigadoon released her hand and returned to the seat behind his desk. "Please, have a seat."

"Thank you, sir." Sarah seated herself in the straight-backed chair facing him.

"Now, how may I be of service?"

"I'd like you to get a message to American General Dwight Eisenhower in England, please."

"I see. Can I assume this message has something to do with the impending attack on Saarbrücken?" He paused a moment. "Lieutenant Farley informed me of what you told him."

"Yes, sir. And I assume he also told you that the message was for American ears only?"

"He did. You know we are allies with the Americans? There are no secrets between us."

Sarah only smiled at him.

After a moment, he sighed. "As it happens, there are several senior members of Ike's staff here on the Rock today. Let's see if we can't get a few moments with one of them."

Directing his voice at the closed door, Brigadoon called to his aide, who soon stuck his head into the room through a half-open door. "Yes sir?"

"Captain Weathersby, please find out who is managing Major General Smith's schedule and find us a few minutes to meet with him today. It's an urgent matter. And send in some tea."

"Very good, sir." The aide disappeared, quietly closing the door. Moments later a corporal knocked before entering the room with a tea service for two.

"Who is General Smith?" Sarah said when the orderly had left.

"Major General Bedell Smith has recently been appointed as Ike's chief of staff. He stopped here on his way to England to take a tour of the Rock."

"To set up the headquarters for Operation Torch?" she asked.

Brigadoon grinned. "You are well informed. How did you come by that information?"

"Doesn't matter. Once I've spoken to General Eisenhower, Operation Torch will be cancelled," she said with assurance. "And I'm afraid I can't say more than that."

Brigadoon gaped at her.

Sarah and the Wing Commander passed the next few minutes chatting about conditions in Southern France, particularly with regard to the roundup of Jews.

"Excuse me, sir." The aide's head had reappeared at the door. "General Smith's assistant says he is touring the central tunnels. You can join him now or schedule an appointment for Friday."

"I think it's best we join him underground. Thanks Weathersby." Brigadoon stood. "Miss Mendelson, please follow me."

They walked for what seemed like miles through the dimly-lit limestone caves of Gibraltar, Brigadoon stopping to show his credentials and sign Sarah into visitor's logs at three different checkpoints. Finally, they caught up to General Smith's tour group.

"Good morning, Wing Commander. I'm told you wished a word," Smith said before Brigadoon snapped off a salute.

"Sir, it's this young lady that would like a word." Brigadoon turned to Sarah. "May I introduce Miss Sarah Mendelson? She has a message for General Eisenhower. I believe you should give her a moment. She seems to know a lot of things she shouldn't."

"Pleased to meet you, Miss Mendelson." Smith extended his hand and Sarah shook it.

"Likewise, sir," Sarah replied. "May we talk in private? It won't take long."

"Very well." Smith turned to an aide, who indicated the way to a nearby empty office. An armed man stood guard outside the office, falling in to position as if he'd been handed this assignment many times. Once alone inside the room, Smith smiled and pulled a small notebook from his pocket. "Okay, miss. What's the message?"

"Tell the general that Professor Conant's flowers are about to bloom in Europe, the first in Saarbrücken, with others to follow soon thereafter."

Smith stopped scribbling at "bloom." He looked at Sarah, mouth hanging open, eyes wide. "Not possible," he said.

"I assure you it's going to happen," Sarah said. "Probably in the next day or two." *I guess Eisenhower isn't the only American in Europe with knowledge of the atomic bomb project.*

Smith walked to the door and yanked it open. "Commander Birley, this woman, Wing Commander Brigadoon, and anyone she has had contact with since her arrival, are to be placed in isolation, under guard, immediately. And no communications with anyone until I say so. Is that clear?"

"Yes, sir," Birley said. Sarah had learned the British naval officer was the base commander. "Sir, the lady and Lieutenant Farley were brought in on the *HMS Talisman*. Should they be isolated as well?"

"Is the sub still in port?" Smith asked.

"Aye, sir," Birley answered.

"Then confine all personnel to the ship for the time being. But disable their radio. No mail in or out."

Wing Commander Brigadoon offered no protest. Instead, he glowered at Sarah as Birley led them away.

* * *

Eisenhower arrived shortly after sunset, travelling from RAF Uxbridge aboard an American A-20 Havoc bomber escorted by a flock of British

Spitfires. Colonel Watson, a member of General Eisenhower's staff, informed Sarah of his arrival. Accompanied by two American military policemen, he escorted her from her cell to an office deep in the Rock. They walked in silence.

Watson stopped in front of a door set into the rock wall of the tunnel and knocked.

"Enter," said a voice from beyond the door. Bedell "Beetle" Smith waited while Watson ushered her into the room. He indicated she should sit in one of the vacant chairs arrayed around a small conference table sitting in front of Smith's desk. "General Eisenhower will be here in a moment." Turning to the colonel, he said, "That'll be all Colonel. Please see that we are not disturbed once the General arrives."

Watson saluted and left the room. A few minutes later General Eisenhower entered the room. He looked much younger than the photos Hiram had shown Sarah, the stress of leading the Allied invasions of Africa and Europe not yet showing on his face. Sarah started to rise when Eisenhower waved her back into her seat. He took a chair opposite her at the table.

"Miss Mendelson, you wanted to get my attention, and now you've certainly got it. What is this all about?" Eisenhower asked.

"The atomic bomb, of course," Sarah said.

"And what do you think you know about atomic bombs?" Smith kept his eyes on Sarah.

"Actually, quite a bit. I know the American scientists, under auspices of the S1 Executive Committee of the National Defense Research Committee, are working to build two different types of atomic bombs based on nuclear fission. The weapons design work is led by Professor J. Robert Oppenheimer of the University of California at Berkeley, although many other research facilities are involved. One is a gun-type device using highly enriched uranium and the other is an implosion device using plutonium." From the looks on their faces, Sarah guessed that even they had not been privy to that last bit of detail.

"Dr. Edward Teller has proposed an even more powerful device called a hydrogen bomb, based on nuclear fusion, the same force that powers the Sun. The next step beyond the hydrogen bomb is the thermonuclear bomb, which uses nuclear fusion to trigger a much larger nuclear fission event. As much as a thousand times larger than Oppenheimer's bomb in fact, although the one that is about to go off in Saarbrücken, Germany is only about fifteen times larger."

"I don't believe it," said Smith. "You're making this up based on some bits and pieces of leaked data."

"It isn't necessary for you to believe me now," Sarah said. "It's only necessary that you watch Saarbrücken for the next few days and see for yourselves."

They sat quietly for a few minutes, Eisenhower thinking while Smith made some notes.

Smith looked up from his notebook. "Who made the bombs, and how did you get them?"

"Call it the Jewish Defense League, if it helps to have a label. While I have a basic understanding of the physics – did I mention I'm a professor of physics at the University in Lyon? Or at least I was before the war." She paused a moment to regain her train of thought. "Hiram, that's our leader, brought seven of them with him when he rescued me and twenty-nine other women from Camp Joffre. How he got them, I can't say."

"Can't? Or won't?" Smith said.

"Both." Sarah offered no more on that subject.

"Well, then Miss Mendelson, can you tell me why Saarbrücken was chosen as the target?" Eisenhower said.

"I'm sure you're aware that Saarbrücken is a major rail hub and river crossing for trains travelling between France and Germany." Both men nodded. "Among the cargo being transported eastward are thousands of Jews destined for the Nazi extermination camps in Poland. We intend to put an end to it."

"There are other train routes," Smith said, without acknowledging the existence of the extermination camps. The omission angered Sarah.

"And we have more bombs," she said.

"I understand," Eisenhower said, leaning across the table. "We've heard rumors of Hitler's Final Solution but found no concrete evidence."

"I spent time in a Vichy internment camp at Rivesaltes before I escaped. The families of my friends have since been shipped to a concentration camp in Drancy, near Paris. From there it's on to Auschwitz in Poland. It isn't a rumor, sir. It's a determined attempt to kill off all the Jews, and the French in Vichy are helping."

"We'll look into it Miss Mendelson. Beetle, put the G-2 on it right away."

"Yes sir." Smith made a few more notes.

Eisenhower returned his attention to Sarah. "You said you have more bombs."

"We do. At least six more."

"I can think of better uses for those bombs than blowing up rail crossings," Smith said.

"Hiram believes that as well. He recommends you abandon Operation Torch and refocus on an immediate cross-channel invasion of France, using these bombs to breech Hitler's Atlantic Wall."

"Tens of thousands of Frenchmen will die," Eisenhower said. "Maybe hundreds of thousands."

"Millions are going to die in the camps if you don't." Her voice cracked, the fear and sadness spilling out in her words.

"I'm not saying I believe her," Smith said, "but if her people can really eliminate a half-dozen or more Panzer divisions, it would save a lot of British and American lives."

"You'll have to move fast, occupy Western Europe before the Eastern German Front collapses and the Soviets push all the way to the Rhine."

Eisenhower sat back, his face draped in disbelief. "The Russians are our allies."

"It won't last," she said. "Hiram believes you should listen to General Patton."

"Patton?" Smith smirked, clearly not a fan of Patton's.

Eisenhower ignored Smith's comment. "Well Miss Mendelson, you're either a well-informed lunatic, or you and your friends are a Godsend. For security reasons you'll have to remain in isolation until Saarbrücken disappears, at which time we'll talk again. Or until the end of the war if it doesn't. I guess we'll know in a couple of days."

24

2030 hours, Thursday, August 6, 1942, Spicheren, Occupied France

On his C2ID2 display, Hiram tracked an Icarus drone as it drifted over Saarbrücken. With the drone's engines shut down and the balloon inflated, it allowed him to calculate wind speed based on the drone's horizontal and vertical movements. Hiram leaned against a tree on the ridgeline one kilometer west of the French-German border. At ground level, gentle winds rolled in from the west. The balloon's rough ascent revealed that the winds aloft grew stronger, moving in from the north with increasing altitude. The dangling radiosonde danced as the breeze pushed upward.

Deborah sat on the ground a few meters away manning the remote control for the smaller drone. She trailed the border between Occupied France and Germany, searching for a safe way in. Hiram had hoped for a lightly guarded border. No luck. Heavy concentrations of armed men, barbed wire fencing, and diligent checkpoints on the main road prevented passage by land. Any attempt at crossing the border into Germany would start a firefight that Hiram refused to chance. The train attack that had cost Vera her life, had made Hiram more cautious. He refused to sacrifice Danette or Deborah.

Deborah looked up at him. "How do we get in?"

"Same way I got in to Camp Joffre. I'll jump through the pod's aerial portal, fly across the border, setup the bomb, and start the timer. Then I'll use the portal in my backpack to leave." *Like in Wah. Of course, that hadn't gone as planned. Nothing on that mission had gone as planned.* This time he planned to

STEVEN LANDRY & KATIE RAE SANK

jump through the portal well-before the bomb detonated. This time he wouldn't forget to deactivate the portal.

"Alone?" Deborah said.

He nodded. "I can get in, set the bomb, and get out. I'll have to wait in the pod for a few hours until the radiation dissipates. Not looking forward to it. When it's clear, I can use the aerial portal to jump back across the border. It'll still be dark and there'll be a lot of confusion on the ground I can use to my advantage." But it wouldn't be that simple. First, he needed to haul the bomb up through the portal. The time necessary to complete the task increased his vulnerability to detection. The uncooperative winds aloft ensured difficulty hitting his original target - the wooded area northwest of Saarbrücken. Based on his current position, the ideal landing zone, a park along the riverbank, sat almost three kilometers from the bridge and rail junction they needed to destroy. Given the distance between the park and the ridge, his calculations suggested a steep dive angle, which meant more speed, and ended in a harder landing. Landing at the park increased his distance from the intended target by almost five-fold. To ensure the explosion reached the rail line, the bomb's required size grew. The larger bomb radius sent the number of anticipated civilian casualties soaring.

"If you don't remember, we were with you at Camp Joffre, waiting to back you up. You flew into an empty camp and dealt with a single policeman. I thank Hashem nothing happened to you then. This time you are flying into enemy territory – alone. The area is overflowing with soldiers. Every German citizen is on the lookout for suspicious activity every hour of the day. You are planning to set a bomb up in plain view of those citizens. If anything happens to you-" she turned away.

"I don't see another option." He sat down beside her on the ground, put his arm around her shoulders, and pulled her close. She had grown stronger since they first met. He remembered a scrawny woman with unkempt hair. Now, he felt the muscular definition of her arms through the thick fabric of her uniform. A wisp of hair had escaped the pins holding the rest in place, a gentle reminder of her defiance. She had been strong-willed then. Now, he sensed fear muted her strength. "This is our best chance to stop the train – all trains – from getting into Germany."

Danette, who had been standing watch a few yards away, joined them, her assault rifle still in position to fend off any incoming attack. She spoke without taking her eyes off the landscape.

"She wants to know the plan," Deborah said.

Hiram stood and helped Deborah up. He said, "We have to move. I can't reach the target from this location."

"Where should we go?" Deborah said.

"North. Up near Schoeneck."

"The whole area between here and there is heavily populated and patrolled." Deborah didn't look up from the C2ID2 display as she spoke.

Danette spoke to Deborah, her frustration apparent. "And, it will set us back at least a day or two."

"I know, but-"

Deborah cut him off before he could finish. "There's a train." She pointed to the location on the display. "Crossing the river near Chapey-sur-Moselle. About seventy kilometers west of here as the crow flies. Maybe an hour until they reach the Saar River crossing."

Hiram took the display from her and studied it for a minute. *Kak. That sure looks like a Holocaust train.* He directed the drone to move in closer. "There," he said pointing at the display. "See the hands sticking out through the slats in the cars. That train's hauling human cargo."

Danette put her hands up in the air and growled a few frustrated words.

Deborah watched her, even as she spoke to Hiram. "What are we going to do?"

"What we came here to do," Hiram said. *And the folks in the Saarland are about to pay a very steep price for voting to return to the Reich in 1933.*

"I want you two down in the shadow of this ridge as soon as possible. The last farmhouse we passed – see if it has a basement or a storm cellar. Take the family with you if they'll go." Hiram touched Deborah on the cheek, kissed her. "After the explosion, I'll launch another drone – the two we have up now will be destroyed. I'll have to fly south with the wind when I leave. Head to the rendezvous point as soon as it's safe to move. I'll meet you there." He opened his pack, activated the portal, and disappeared.

* * *

Coming in hot, Hiram touched down hard. Pain shot through his left ankle and he lost his balance. He bounced once and landed in a heap. He tried to stand, the pain in his ankle too much to support his weight. He went down on his knees. He peered into the surrounding darkness as he wrestled his M22 assault rifle from its sheath. *Where are they?* On his way down, he saw two guards south of his landing spot, immediate threats he needed to neutralize. Two shadows advanced from his left, running along a brick path with weapons high, swinging from side to side. He raised the rifle and fired. The heavy slug crashed into the torso of the leftmost target in silence. The second man pivoted, fired at Hiram, and missed, the shot going wide to his left. The sound of gunfire would draw more guards from the post further up river. Hiram fired again before the man chambered another round in his bolt action rifle. The second guard fell. Hiram got to his feet and started to move. As he put weight on his bad ankle, he almost went back down again. He moved as fast as possible, half limping, half hopping.

A few minutes later he located and donned his goggles, removed his wingsuit, and erected a small, camouflaged blackout tent. He crawled inside the tent and sealed the flap behind him concealing his location in the darkness from incoming guards. After removing the night vision goggles, he opened his backpack and activated the portal. The soft white glow from the portal illuminated the inside of the tent. He hoped the blackout material contained the glow but had never tested his theory.

Hiram reached into the pod and untied a rope from the top rung of the ladder, then used it to pull up the tripod and pulley system designed to support the Mark XII hyperbaric nuclear weapon he had stored in his pod well over a week ago. He slid down the ladder into the pod, landing on his good foot. Handholds around the pod made it easy for Hiram to maneuver through the space. Hiram opened the first aid cabinet, took two pain killers, and wrapped a moldable cast around his lower left leg to protect the ankle from further injury. The cast grabbed hold of his boot and applied pressure as it expanded and solidified.

Massing ninety kilograms, the Mark XII was designed to be carried short distances by two strong men, not one man with a bum ankle. He secured the harness around the device, attached the pulley chain to the harness, and detached the sixty centimeter by thirty centimeter overpacked bomb from the cargo clamps in the pod. The weapon swung out of position and crashed into the opposite wall. Hiram drew a sharp breath, fearing the low velocity impact might set the bomb off. Nothing happened. The device swung a few more times before settling centered beneath the tripod.

Hiram climbed out of the portal and hauled the bomb out of the pod. He pulled until the bomb rested inside the dome tent.

Hobbled by his injury, the whole process took him about half an hour. Hiram sat on the ground beside the device, panting, sweating, and in pain.

"The weapon is in place," he whispered into the C2ID2.

"Hurry Hiram, please hurry!" Deborah's voice in near panic. "The train is approaching Forbath."

Any farther than Forbath, the last junction in France before the border, and they took the chance of destroying not only Saarbrücken, but also the train.

"Ten minutes." He wasted another minute searching for the proper PAL code on his C2ID2. He dialed in a 500 kilotons TNT-equivalent yield on the weapon. If it worked, everything within four kilometers would be turned to rubble, including the railroad bridges over the Saar River.

"Setting the timers now," he said. The first timer started the detonation sequence on the Mark XII in exactly five minutes. The second set off a ten kilo C4 demolition charge in six minutes. It would destroy both the Mark XII and the backpack he'd have to leave behind, along with the portal, should the Mark XII fail to detonate.

Outside the tent, men approached. They called back and forth in German. "I've got company."

"Fifty meters south of you and moving fast. They have flashlights." Deborah said, her voice calm through his earpiece.

"How many?" He asked.

"Three."

Hiram closed a flap of the backpack over the portal without deactivating it. He unsealed the tent flap and peered in the direction Deborah indicated. He put the googles on, adjusting them to address the light of the men's flashlights. The goggles flared, then settled into the correct saturation, revealing three men sweeping the area, swinging flashlights from side to side, searching for their comrades.

Hiram fired a round at each target. The quick shots from the rail gun brought the men down in near silence. The timers continued to count down.

"Anyone else?" he said over the radio.

"No one else in the park," Deborah said. "Four more on the main road appear to be making their way toward you. You better get out of there."

Hiram ducked back into the tent and saw the Mark XII timer roll over from one minute down to fifty-nine seconds. *Not again!* He pulled up the backpack flap and dove through the portal, landing hard on the mat at the bottom. He slapped at his C2ID2 and the portal snapped shut above him.

113

25

2052 hours, Thursday, August 6, 1942, Spicheren, Occupied France

The ground shook and the thunderous sound of the explosion grew. As the blast wave rolled over the farmhouse, everyone screamed. The house above them creaked and grumbled, furniture slid across the wood floor over their heads. Within seconds, the structure above collapsed and the blast wave carried the pieces away. Debris rained down into the dark cellar, falling through the gaps in the floor above them.

Danette curled into a tighter ball, hands over her ears. Her mask-covered mouth remained wide open as Hiram had instructed. Something heavy crashed down through floorboards, landing between Danette and Deborah. Whatever it was, it was hot. Danette rolled away from it.

"Deborah," Danette yelled. "Are you hurt?"

After an uncomfortable delay, Deborah coughed. "I'm fine. You?"

"Still here." After a few seconds, the initial wave had passed and debris stopped falling. A cloud of unsettled dust filled the room.

The farmer coughed, one of the little ones followed. Through the haze, the farmer and his wife started to get up. "Stay down! It's not over yet."

Outside the world grew silent. And then, as Hiram had warned, air rushed back toward ground zero. The negative pressure wave rocked the timbers above them once more and showered them with dirt and broken pieces of the homestead. Several of the floorboards above them wriggled loose and disappeared.

Danette ducked her head between her knees and covered her head with her arms. *My God, the blast was four kilometers away. What must have happened closer in?*

"*Merde!*" Deborah gasped.

"What's the matter?" Danette turned to face her dusty companion.

Deborah kneeled beside the upended cast-iron stove between them. She held on to one of the backpack straps. The pack sat beneath the stove, the fabric smoldering. Danette looked around her, pushing away debris, searching for the other pack.

Deborah reached out and touched Danette on the shoulder. "The packs were next to each other. We lost them both."

PART II

26

0545 hours, Friday, August 7, 1942, Spicheren, Occupied France

Danette spent the rest of the night in the root cellar with Deborah and the farmer's family. They extracted the two backpacks from beneath the fallen stove once it cooled. Both were heavily damaged. The flexible ring that constituted the portal perimeter in each pack had been broken and burned, as had much of the equipment in the proper portion of the backpacks. The C2ID2s had been inside where the pack's shielding would protect them from an electro-magnetic pulse when the weapon detonated. Several ammo magazines for the M22s remained in working order, but little else. God only knew what was happening in Saarbrücken.

With both communication devices destroyed, Deborah and Danette had no way to contact Hiram. They would meet him at the rendezvous point. Danette refused to think about the alternatives.

The farmer and his family grew restless. One of the children, a young boy of about five, pulled at the surgical mask Danette had given him. She sympathized with him. The mask she'd been wearing since the previous night irritated her more every minute. She scratched the side of her head where the tie rested.

Deborah touched the boy's hand and shook her head. "You need to keep it on a while longer. The dust might make you sick." Her gentle words earned a nod in response and he settled the mask back in place.

"Can you make sure your brother and sister keep them on as well?"

He nodded and turned to his siblings. His sister rolled her eyes at the idea of taking direction from her little brother.

Danette explained that they needed to keep them on for a few days. She offered the farmer a package containing enough masks for the family for that amount of time. "Replace everyone's mask a couple times throughout the day." The farmer agreed and waved the kids toward him. They all settled in close. He hugged his family tight, thankful they had all survived.

Hiram had explained that the fallout from a hyperbaric nuclear device was minimal compared to the atomic bomb under development by the Americans. He expected the danger here to dissipate after a few days. Danette prayed for the accuracy of Hiram's assessment.

"I think it's time we get out of here," Deborah said. They climbed out of the root cellar into a wasteland. With the exception of a few timbers and bottommost structure of the fireplace, the blast demolished the farmhouse. The wooden structure of the barn had been replaced with foreign debris, including an upended car carried in from one of the main roadways. A pall of dust hovered like fog above the farmer's decimated wheat field.

They found the railbike entangled in the branches of a fallen tree. Deborah struggled to part the bike from the thick limbs, careful not to inflict additional damage. Fifteen minutes later, Danette made her stop. With a broken axle, crushed controls, and an oozing power core, they deemed the bike a total loss.

"What do we do now?" Deborah said. "We can't leave it here like this."

"You're right." The bike's improvised drivetrain might not have been as advanced as Hiram's portals and nuclear weapons, but they couldn't take the chance of the technology falling into the wrong hands. Danette unclipped a hand grenade from her combat vest, pulled the pin, checked to make sure the farmer and his family remained in the cellar, and dropped the grenade into the center of the broken power supply. Both women turned and ran, diving into a drainage ditch three seconds later, a full second before the grenade detonated.

Danette and Deborah headed south with their M22 rifles and four and a half magazines worth of ammo. They walked in silence. Danette searched for danger. Deborah searched for Hiram.

The earth around them had been abused by the blast. Crops that had yet to be reaped had been ripped out of the ground. Most of the nearby structures – mainly houses and barns – had been battered. Roof shingles and broken glass littered the ground in every direction. A few automobiles settled upside down in a field near a main roadway. A once beautiful writing desk had fallen in the middle of a dirt road, two legs reaching for the sky, nubs where the two others had been. A layer of dust coated everything from the leaves of the trees to the walls of the broken buildings they passed. She dared not imagine the severity of damage closer to ground zero.

They walked south in the direction of the Vosges Mountains, toward the rendezvous point Hiram had designated on their trip north. On foot, the fifty-kilometer journey would take days. The forest provided cover where possible. For a stretch of the journey, they passed through the town of Rouhling. As they hid behind a small feed store, a convoy of military vehicles raced through the town. French policemen, a handful of German soldiers, and civilian drivers filled every truck. The driver of one of the smaller vehicles at the front of the line came close to running over a little girl. Her father pulled her out of the way just in time. The driver did not slow. From their vantage point, Danette saw the man laughing as he passed. The convoy had been in a hurry, headed back toward Saarbrücken, she guessed.

27

1215 hours, Friday, Midday August 7, 1942, Gibraltar, United Kingdom

"Holy Mother of God," whispered Beetle Smith. He stood next to Sarah at the map table in his subterranean office on Gibraltar. She'd been summoned from her isolation cell in the middle of lunch.

Sarah peered down at the aerial photos lined up on the table. At first, the images appeared to contain debris, piles and piles of it. A line of water cut through the mess. *The Saar?* She looked at photo after photo, the extent of the damage growing clearer. A crater had been punched into the city. A single building stood near the center, a mere shell. Spreading out from the impact zone, the destruction continued. Some buildings had fallen, some disintegrated, leaving behind rectangular stone and brick foundations etched into the earth. The damage reached out away from the crater for kilometers. Outside the city, the impact wave knocked down trees and blew away small homes, leaving discolored patches where they once rested. One shot captured a bull impaled by a wooden post near a farmhouse. Sarah's hands shook and the images began to spin.

Smith took a pair of calipers from a drawer beneath the table and measured the width of the dark gray area in the center of one of the photos. He then measured the distance between the two points on the calipers with a ruler and whistled.

"The crater's over a mile wide," he said, looking at Sarah. "The radius of destruction extends almost three miles from ground zero. I guess you weren't full of shit after all. My apologies, madam."

Sarah wasn't sure whether he was apologizing for his language or his earlier skepticism. But she thanked him anyway.

"And you say your comrades have six more?" Smith said, leaning over the table.

"Yes." Her voice wavered and bile bubbled up into her throat. "I have to reestablish communications with my team."

"Do you have any idea how to communicate with them?"

"I'll need my C2ID2." The device had been confiscated when she'd first come ashore.

Smith didn't seem to understand.

"The communications device I had strapped to my forearm when I disembarked from the *HMS Talisman.*"

Smith still looked confused.

"I guess the British didn't think you needed to know."

"Wait here," Smith said, and stormed out of the office.

Sarah looked at the pictures once more. Nothing prepared her for the level of destruction Hiram's bomb inflicted. Horror crept up inside her, mingling with the bile in her throat. The whole city lay in ruins. *How many people had they killed? Tens of thousands? More?* The device was supposed to go off closer to the railroad bridges and junction, with a much smaller blast area. From the photos, the zone of destruction extended well past Saarbrücken, across the French border near Spicheren. *Something must have forced Hiram's hand, but what?*

She looked at the wider-angle photos more carefully. One showed a train stopped on the tracks near Forbach, west of Spicheren. A few seconds later she found a magnifying glass in one of Smith's drawers and took a closer look at the train. A line of boxcars. *A Holocaust train, maybe. Is that what forced the change in plans?*

Smith strode back into the office. "Your device... What did you call it?"

"Combat communication and information digital device. C2ID2 for short."

"Your C2ID2 is at a lab in London. Hopefully the scientists haven't started their dissection. Ike promises it'll be waiting for us when we arrive at Camp Griffiss. We're leaving as soon as adequate transportation and a fighter escort can be arranged. Have you eaten?"

"I don't think I could keep anything down," she said. "Perhaps some water or tea?"

THE MAIDS OF CHATEAU VERNET

* * *

1910 hours, Friday, August 7, 1942, London, England, United Kingdom

Sarah climbed down the ladder leading from the cargo plane's rear door to the tarmac. The cool, overcast day brought about a shiver. A young uniformed man offered her a jacket, then directed her to a waiting car.

"APO 887," Smith told the driver as he settled into the rear seat beside her. As the car pulled away, Smith clarified their destination for Sarah's benefit. "Headquarters, European Theater of Operations, United States Army. It's Ike's headquarters at Camp Griffiss in the London Borough of Richmond upon Thames."

Sarah, escorted by Smith, passed through several security checkpoints before being admitted to a nondescript conference room on the first floor of a nondescript building. In addition to General Eisenhower, four men waited in the room, only one of whom she recognized.

"Pleased to meet you, indeed." Sir Winston Churchill smiled after Smith's introduction. Beside him, stood Vice Admiral Lord Louis Francis Albert Victor Nicholas Mountbatten – a name Sarah would never remember – British Chief of Combined Operations.

Lord Mountbatten introduced her to the next man in line. "And this fellow is Colonel Donovan, head of the American Office of Strategic Services." Donovan wore civilian clothes despite his rank.

With introductions complete, everyone found a seat at a rectangular conference table. Sarah sat between Donovan and Eisenhower. Churchill and Mountbatten sat opposite them. A movie projector on the table between them blocked her view of the men on the other side. Smith switched off the lights and started the machine.

"This footage was captured four hours ago by a Westland Lysander of the Royal Air Force's 138th Squadron," Smith began. "The devastation extends over an area of about twenty square miles, 32 square kilometers. The city of Saarbrücken and its railroad complex have been decimated. Water continues to fill the impact crater as we speak. The devastation spread across the border into France. Damage from the blast has been documented as far away as ten miles, 16 kilometers, from the epicenter. You'll note however, no evidence of the massive fires our own scientists predicted in an atomic explosion."

Sarah searched for the Holocaust Train in the footage. She caught sight of a line of boxcars moving away from the blast area, possibly headed south, but there had been so many trains. She couldn't be sure if it was *the* train.

Churchill said, "Casualty estimate?"

"Over a hundred thousand dead or injured, maybe more," Smith said. "Mostly civilians." Sarah's heart rose up into her throat, followed by the contents of her stomach. She bolted from the room, searching for a bathroom. A guard stationed outside the door took one look at her and pointed across the hall. She shouldered through the door, hand over her mouth, and headed for the nearest toilet. She thought she'd never stop retching, but eventually her stomach calmed. She went to the sink and splashed her face with water. As she straightened up and caught the reflection of the room in the mirror, she noticed Lord Mountbatten standing in the open door.

Sarah dried her face on the towel. "We estimated a high number of civilian casualties, but not so many from a single attack. What have we done?"

"It needed to be done, my dear. Retaking Europe from the Nazis will be costly work. I fear many more lives will be lost. The Russian armed forces have suffered almost eight million casualties, plus a like number of civilian deaths. If what you told Ike about Hitler's Final Solution is true, another twelve million are scheduled to die in the camps. And that doesn't include the hundreds of thousands of British and French laid to rest so far. Every month we shorten this war will save a million lives. If your nuclear weapons accelerate the conclusion, we'll endure the cost, whatever it might be."

Sarah nodded. She had made similar arguments herself – all of them theoretical. Now, the visual evidence of the bomb's power confronted her. It was real. "I understand. Just give me a few minutes."

Mountbatten nodded, backed out of the doorway, and closed the door.

Sarah sat on the cot in the room. She bent her head, closed her eyes, and prayed. She prayed for the families that had been destroyed by Hiram's nuclear weapon, for the friends she feared she might never see again. When she opened her eyes, they fell on a poster tacked to the back of the bathroom door. It depicted a young mother sitting at the base of a tree with two children. In the distance, plumes of smoke rose up from the city toward the barrage blimps floating above. A ghostly Adolf Hitler whispers in the woman's ear "Take them back!" urging her to return her children to the city. Printed below the picture were the words "DON'T DO IT MOTHER – LEAVE THE CHILDREN WHERE THEY ARE – A Message from the Ministry of Health."

Sarah made up her mind. She stood, straightened her clothes, attempted to fix her hair, and returned to the conference room. They had an invasion to plan.

28

1300 hours, Friday, August 7, 1942, near Lutzelbourg, Moselle department, Occupied France

The heat rising from the decimated landscape around Saarbrücken had provided additional lift, which enabled him to drift all the way to the rendezvous point in Lutzelbourg in four jumps. Each landing sent screaming hot pain from his ankle up through his leg. Once the meadow north of town revealed itself in his night vision goggles during his final jump, he had taken a small chance and deployed his parachute rather than put himself through another hard landing. He settled down to rest the ankle and wait for Danette and Deborah.

Hiram grew frustrated as the day wore on with no sign or signal from the two women. He had taken a few more of the pain killers, but the pain in his left ankle only grew. Repairing the damage took a back seat as his body combatted Hagar's Curse, a result of the hours spent inside the pod waiting for the initial contamination generated by the Mark XII explosion to dissipate.

He'd launched two drones earlier in the day, a surveillance drone to search for Deborah and Danette, and an Icarus drone to establish communication with the rest of the team. Neither had accomplished the assigned task. That the latter wasn't working did not come as a surprise. The Icarus drone's manual stated that upper atmosphere ionization – a side effect of the bomb – temporarily disrupted communications. Hiram expected it to clear up soon.

His inability to locate the two women closest to him troubled him more.

The farmhouse where they had planned to take refuge had been blown away, but they should have been able to survive in the cellar. Now, he couldn't even tell if the place he sent them even had a cellar. *Had they made it to the farmhouse?* He found no sign of the railbike anywhere between Lutzelbourg and Spicheren. *I can't have lost them now, after all it took to get them out of the camp. Ozreini Adonai elohai.* Help me Lord, my God.

29

1630 hours, Friday, August 7, 1942, Lutzelbourg, Vichy France

Hiram climbed down into the pod to grab an HF radio. His ankle screamed in its cast as he climbed back out of the pod.

"Station Nineteen, this is Hawk, over." The Marquis had an agent near Nancy, not far from Hiram's current location. He tried several times before anyone answered his call.

"Hawk, this is Station Nineteen, over." They kept the transmissions short to avoid triangulation of the source from anyone monitoring HF communications.

"Station Nineteen, have my packages been delivered? Over."

"Hawk, affirmative. Primary package delivered along with sky jockey to an Anglo sewer pipe four days ago, over." Sarah had boarded a sub, along with a pilot.

"Station Nineteen, status of the second package? Over."

"Hawk, secondary package lost in transit. No additional information, over."

"Roger, Station Nineteen." *What happened to Maria?* Hiram provided the location where he'd hidden the last eight crates of 40mm grenades, and signed off.

He had a few hours to kill before travelling again, so he headed back into the pod to grab a snack and a few more pain killers. As he reached the bottom of the ladder, pain shot up his leg. It occurred to him that he might be doing more damage to his ankle hobbling down into the pod after each flight than landing in the wingsuit. His body had no time to recover from the injury and each minute he spent inside the pod ensured that any effort to heal his body was negated. At this rate, his ankle would never heal. Parachuting to the ground might provide less impact. He looked up at the ceiling-mounted portal, and then over at the aerial portal. *I wonder…*

Four hours later with his head pounding, Hiram tightened the last bolt, locking the portal that led to his backpack to the frame that held the aerial portal. If it worked, he could jump directly from his backpack to the sky above without having to climb down into the pod. It meant leaving the backpack behind after each jump. The pod allowed him to pick up another, as many as he needed. Remote activation of the self-destruct mechanism with the C2ID2 ensured no trace of the backpack or portal would be left behind.

Now I have to get out of here so I can test it. He'd prepared by retrieving Jacob's backpack. He opened a portal to Jacob's pod from inside his own and climbed down into it. From there, he jumped into the night sky from Jacob's aerial portal. His headache blossomed and his stomach churned from just the few moments he spent in Jacob's pod.

He landed in the meadow once again, then limped to the tent. Once inside, he picked up an uneaten protein bar and tossed it though the portal in his backpack. Without any wind to push the bar away from his location, he expected it to fall the five thousand meters from the open portal in the sky straight to the ground. About a minute later, the bar bounced off the outside of the tent. *It works. Now for something living.* He spied a large beetle on a nearby tree and scooped it into a plastic bag. He blew into the bag, inflating it as much as possible, then sealed it. The beetle earned its airborne wings a moment later. The bag drifted about a hundred meters on the way down, but Hiram easily tracked it with his night vision goggles. The beetle scurried away with no apparent injury when Hiram released it.

Hiram heard the distinct whistle of a nearby train. A bridge on the main railroad line through the Vosges Mountains required crossing trains to slow down to a few kilometers per hour. Hiram jumped once more, this time aiming for the roof of a slow-moving boxcar. On the way down, he used his C2ID2 to close both portals and initiate the self-destruct sequence for the backpack he left behind.

With the clunky cast on his left leg, he lost his balance and sprawled onto the surface of the moving target, grasping for any handhold that would prevent him from rolling off the roof. He caught the protruding upper edge of the boxcar's sliding door mount just before he would have slid off and fallen to the rocky valley below. He crawled to the hatch, lifted the small door, and slipped inside, hoping the train would carry him west, in the direction of Hitler's Atlantic Wall.

* * *

0600 hours, Sunday, August 9, northeast of Loches, Indre River Valley, Vichy France.

Hiram caught three separate trains to get within five kilometers of Team Bravo's campsite. On the first train, the dark provided enough cover for him to slide into a box car filled with personal belongings. Suitcases had been packed on one side of the car in tight rows stacked almost to the ceiling. On the other end of the car lay neat piles of fur garments, organized so that coats remained separate from stoles, muffs, and gloves. Several flattened and beady eyed critters stared back at him as light filtered in from outside. He settled in near the doors, a wall of suitcases to one side of him and a stack of coats on the other. The second train carried Gentile passengers through occupied France, unaware of the horrors taking place around them except for the occasional inconvenience of having to show papers to a policeman strolling down the aisle. Hiram peered through a small window between the cars where he clung to the ladder leading up to the car's roof. During the night, not even the policeman cared to check the outside of the train. It was ill advised to flash around a torch during blackout hours. The third train was on its return trip from dropping off a large group of Jewish prisoners somewhere outside of France. The Star of David had been painted on each of the box cars. Hiram chose a car near the rear of the train. A strong odor of excrement mixed with the scent of decaying meat remained inside the boxcar. The car had been poorly cleaned at some point and the doors left open to let the air do the rest. Despite the boxcar being an easy target, Hiram regretted his decision and found himself vomiting out the open door as the train clacked along the iron rails.

Hiram established communication with Team Bravo's Icarus drone twenty minutes before sunrise. He pushed through the coordinates of his targeted stopping point. An hour later, he jumped from the train as it neared the stop in Loches. Agnes waited for him at the edge of the tree line with her railbike.

"Agnes, I left an Icarus drone and a surveillance drone flying over the northern Vosges Mountains." Hiram said. "Can you contact them?"

Agnes said something in French. He held up his hand, asking her to wait. He poked a few icons on his C2ID2, bringing up the Babel Fish. He despised the thing, but with Sarah in England, hopefully, and Deborah out of contact, he'd have to rely on it. When the ready symbol appeared on the device, he spun his hand in a circle, indicating she should repeat what she'd just said.

For a moment, Agnes stared at him. Then she spoke. "We were worried when we didn't hear from you," the translator repeated in halting Hebrew.

"The plan did not go as intended. I left an Icarus drone and a surveillance drone flying over the northern Vosges Mountains. Can you make contact with Deborah and Danette?" The software proved to be a slow tool. "Hurry! You need to find them. If they survived the blast, they're somewhere in those mountains near Lutzelbourg right now."

Agnes nodded and turned her attention to the C2ID2 display, punching in a set of codes she read off Hiram's C2ID2.

He let out a breath of relief. "Sorry. It's been a long two days." He touched Agnes on the shoulder.

She glanced up and offered a smile. Then, she climbed into the sidecar of the railbike and signaled Hiram should drive. Once Agnes contacted the drones, she would search for Deborah and Danette.

Team Bravo's camp rested about thirty-five kilometers southeast of the confluence of the Le Cher, Indre and Loire rivers near Tours – a scant five kilometers south of the demarcation line between Occupied and Vichy France.

With no more than a set of coordinates from Agnes, Hiram drove the railbike toward the group's temporary campsite. Team Bravo's camp had been nestled in a shallow valley in the woods. Upon arrival, Ida stepped out from behind a large tree wielding an M22 and pointed toward a well-hidden path. The rest of Team Bravo – Nathalie and Isadore – gathered around, anxious for more information before Hiram had time to dismount. Even with Deborah and Danette still missing, having the others gathered here lightened the fear and exhaustion that he had been building since the event in Saarbrücken.

Ida slung the M22 behind her and embraced him. "Is everything okay?" She looked down at the cast on his leg.

"Bad landing. It'll heal." He hoped it would heal. "We had trouble getting close enough to the target," Hiram said.

Ida gasped when the disembodied voice floated out of Hiram's C2ID2.

"The border was more heavily guarded than I expected. The winds were all wrong when we arrived in Spicheren." The Babel Fish struggled to keep up. "Deborah detected a Holocaust train approaching, so we had to act fast." He fumbled with his C2ID2, hoping for a message from Danette and Deborah. Once again nothing. "I jumped across the border, the landing nowhere near the intended target. In order to impact the rail crossing, I had to dial-in a much larger yield than initially planned.

"After the detonation, I made it to the rendezvous point, but they never showed. I tried to contact them via C2ID2." He looked over Agnes' shoulder, scanning her display as he talked. "Then I launched an Icarus drone, trying to expand the range. Wouldn't work either, too much interference in the upper atmosphere."

"What about Vera?" someone asked. Hiram waited while the translator interpreted her words.

He looked up at the women. *I forgot; they don't know.* "*Elle est morte.*" She's dead.

Agnes stopped looking at her screen and turned to Hiram. She shook her head, disbelieving as her eyes reddened. He thought he'd need to set someone else on the task of finding the missing members of the Alpha team. "Danette *et* Deborah?" Isadore asked.

"I don't know. Agnes is trying to find them. If they survived, they'd be moving south from Spicheren towards the rendezvous point in the Vosges Mountains." He pointed to a spot on Agnes' map display.

She nodded her understanding and went back to work. He told them how Vera had died and about the small unmarked grave where she now rested. "Deborah and Danette hid on a farm in Spicheren. I'm afraid they may have been too close to the blast."

"There is some good news." Nathalie handed Hiram her C2ID2 display as the Babel Fish chattered along. "We found Rosette while you were away."

"Is she with her family?" Hiram asked.

"No, we're not quite sure what happened. Dumb luck we found her. Nora was flying the drone in circles around her home. She spotted a policeman watching the house and decided to follow him when he left."

"Go on," said Hiram.

"He drove to a farmhouse about a hundred kilometers southeast, in the town of Saint Chamond. She went in for a closer look and saw Rosette. It could be a hiding place."

"Good work. Tell Nora I said so. Any word from Sarah yet?"

"Nothing," Ida said.

"Without Sarah, this whole plan is FUBAR," Isadore said, the translator repeating.

Hiram smiled at the use of the term "FUBAR" It was an English term they'd picked up from him, although he hoped no one knew the literal translation.

"Fucked up beyond all recognition," the Babel Fish said at the conclusion of Isadore's translation, then helpfully added French and Hebrew translations for the benefit of all those present. Hiram blushed. The others did not seem surprised.

"I tried to contact the Spanish Maquis yesterday for an update. Took me all day to reach the contact they provided in Lyon. I heard back from him a few hours later." Four anxious faces stared back at him.

"Sarah boarded a British submarine with a wounded RAF pilot Tuesday night. Maria didn't make it that far. That was all the contact could tell me." The news added to the emotion of the group. Most now teared up. "I'm sorry." Around him, the women began talking. The Babel Fish grabbed a few words from their mixed conversations, spewing gibberish back at him.

After a few long moments, Agnes looked up, puzzled. "Why can't we reach Sarah?"

"I don't know the answer to that question. I think we have to assume that Sarah made it to England, and that our plan is still a go. She's got the rendezvous coordinates. And, the Americans can't have missed what happened to Saarbrücken."

"Are you sure the bomb detonated?" Ida said.

"No question," Hiram said. "The destruction extends for five kilometers in every direction. Sarah will find a way to make contact. Otherwise-"

Nathalie cut him off. "Otherwise, there's Barbara's plan."

30

2045 hours, Sunday, August 9, 1942, over the Indre River Valley, Vichy France

"Hawk, this is Raven, over," Sarah said for the fiftieth time since the navigator told her they flew in orbit over the Indre River Valley. Still no response. She intended to keep trying until the B-17 Flying Fortress turned back to England. Cruising at about seven thousand meters, her insulated and heated flight suit remained her only protection from the frigid air both inside and outside the aircraft.

Sarah looked out through the large, multi-faceted nose window. The dark night sky cloaked everything beyond the nose of the plane. She looked back at her C2ID2.

The aircraft's other passenger, Captain Joseph Trembley of the American OSS, said, "Two P-38 Lightning fighter planes out there. Sneaky bastards, just the way we like 'em."

"Raven to Hawk, come in Hawk," Sarah tried once more. If they didn't make contact on the next orbit, the P-38s flying alongside the B-17 needed to break off and head back to England before they ran out of fuel. She expected a second set of P-38s to take their place. Soon, the B-17 would turn back to RAF Uxbridge as well.

"Hawk, this is Raven, over." The C2ID2 covered a range of only a few kilometers, but Teams Bravo through Golf would be within range, somewhere in the valley beneath them, based on the rendezvous coordinates Hiram had sent to the C2ID2. *Where in the hell are they?*

"Raven, this is Hawk. What's your status, over?" Sarah jumped at the sound of Hiram's voice, the welcome sound bringing her to tears. She wiped her eyes, smiled, and returned her attention to the C2ID2.

"Good to hear your voice, Hawk." Sarah blinked back tears that had turned sour. "My companion didn't make it, break. Your demonstration convinced the high command to proceed with our plan, over."

Captain Trembley huddled with the navigator in search of a convenient drop zone. He held up a signboard with a set of map coordinates written on it while she waited for Hiram's response.

"What's your location, over?" Hiram asked. The navigator took the signboard and wrote on it, then showed it to Sarah.

"Angels twenty at thirty-one Tango Charlie November four six two six." She knew what the words and numbers meant. Hiram had spent hours preaching proper radio procedure during the long walk to Spain. Both Sarah and Maria had been prepped so they knew what to expect. Hiram had also given the women a safe phrase that could easily be weaved into the conversation if the interests of their new allies diverged from their own. The stakes remained high. Hiram's weapons promised destruction. After the Saarbrücken display, Sarah wasn't sure she wanted to see more, but she trusted these men to make the right decision. And, she mused, Hiram would verify the intensions of the Allied players before he allowed anyone to handle such power. "We have a package for you." Sarah read from the signboard again, "Drop coordinates thirty-one Tango Charlie November five four five two six four. Codename Falcon, over."

"Copy that Raven." Hiram mapped the coordinates on the C2ID2 and replied. "We'll be in position to retrieve the package in about forty-five minutes." Sarah imagined Hiram signaling those with him to start moving.

"Raven this is Hawk, over."

"Raven, over," she said.

"Raven, can you launch a communications drone from England when you return, over."

"Negative, Hawk," she replied. "Lost everything except the C2ID2. Will be able to establish communication once you retrieve the package."

"Roger Raven. I'll call when we are in position, over."

"Roger, out." Sarah broke the connection.

* * *

Time passed like molasses. She had gotten back in touch with Hiram and the others and she wanted to be the one to jump, to be reunited with them all.

Forty minutes later Hiram called to say they were in position to cover Captain Trembley's jump.

The aircraft made a turn to the right, then the plane slowed as the bomb bay doors opened behind her, the noise deafening. Trembley rose and gave her a thumbs-up before moving into position in the bay. The navigator held up an open hand and counted down by curling in one finger at a time. When he closed his fist the OSS captain plummeted into the darkness below.

31

2055 hours, Sunday, August 9, 1942, Indre River Valley, Indre-et-Loire Department, Vichy France

Hiram trusted no one with the Mark XII weapons and portal technology. He feared American or British commandos waited in the shadows ready to swoop in and seize the bombs once Falcon confirmed their existence. And, if the weapons fell into enemy hands, they could torture the arming secrets out of him if they tried hard enough. So, he'd resolved to bring the weapons through the portals himself. Only he could arm the devices.

But, the OSS man expected six hyperbaric nuclear weapons.

"Agnes, have Team Foxtrot conduct a patrol around this field where the American OSS officer will land. Tell them to be careful, and make sure there are no surprises waiting for us." Once the translator repeated his words, he listened as Agnes relayed his instructions over her C2ID2 to Team Foxtrot.

"And have Team Golf join us here, please," he said.

Five minutes later Team Golf's railbike pulled up. Justine and Emma straddled the bike. Ellen held Myriam in her lap. Myriam's legs rested over the side of the car, kicking at the wind like a little girl. He smiled at the site of them until the memory of Vera, who had been held in much the same way, crept into the moment. His attention returned to the Mark XII devices.

"Okay ladies, we need to pull six Mark XII's through my portal and disarm them. They're waiting in my pod. Should only take a few minutes to extract them with the pulley system. We have to work quickly." Not just because of the visitor on his way. Hiram wasn't sure how long he could stand to stay inside his pod. The headache had died down, but his ankle felt like the bones had been shattered. If he kept going into the pod, he feared at some point his ankle would shrivel up, his foot along with it. The image of that damned, helpless dog kept swimming through the back of his mind. The mutt had wandered into his camp one night as he crossed the Sinai desert, and hung around after Hiram threw him a few scraps. It was a lonely crossing, and Hiram welcomed the company. A few nights later Hiram absentmindedly tossed an empty pod food wrapper through the portal in his pack. The dog darted after it, his font legs and head breaking the milky white surface of the portal before Hiram realized what was happening. He remembered the way the remainder of dog's body had relaxed an instant before sliding all the way through the opening. By the time he got down into his pod, the dog was a shriveled-up husk on the floor.

Hiram shivered at the thought and waited for the translation to complete. The women nodded.

Hiram climbed down into his pod through the portal in his pack. The weapons waited side by side, nuclear soldiers ready to join the fight. He pushed a tripod and pulley system out through the portal. Ellen and Myriam guided the rig out of the pod.

Hiram poked his head out of the portal and watched while the two women setup the tripod and hooked the pulley system at the apex. No need to do anymore climbing on his bad ankle than necessary. "I'll attach the hook at the end to a harness for the first weapon. When I tug the line, turn the crank to lift the device out of the portal. Once you pull the weapon clear, detach the harness, not the hook, and drop it back through the portal." The Babel Fish repeated.

The women nodded. Justine gave him a thumbs-up.

Confident they understood, Hiram ducked back through the portal with the hook in hand. He hooked the line to the harness already attached to the first weapon and gave a short tug. On cue, the line tightened and the weapon ascended. The portal distorted to accommodate the size of the Mark XII. He waited almost sixty seconds before the hook passed back through the portal. He attached the hook to the harness on the second device and tugged the line. They repeated the process for the remaining devices.

Once six of the Mark XIIs had been pulled from the pod, Hiram climbed out through the portal a final time, using his upper body to pull most of his weight up each rung of the ladder. This trip out of the portal was the hardest yet. His arms quivered with exhaustion and he had a hard time catching his breath.

The short grey metal drums, each sixty centimeters tall and fifty centimeters wide across the top, stood in a row. Ellen, Myriam, and Justine stood behind the row, hesitant to stand too close.

"They can't do any damage like this," Hiram said as he leaned on one of the metal drums. "Justine, hand me the screw driver." He waited for the translator to finish and put a shaky hand out.

The three women stepped a little closer. Hiram attempted to unscrew the top lid. He couldn't manage to set the driver into the head of the screw.

Justine stepped forward, put a hand over his, and eased the screw driver away from him. "You tell us what to do," the Babel Fish said.

Hiram nodded. "Unfasten the lid by removing the screws." He waited for Justine to complete the assignment. "Then remove the top lid." He wanted to sleep, so badly. Every part of him seemed heavy and uncooperative. "Each drum is made up of three sections. This top section holds a set of seven titanium discs. You'll notice the size of the discs decreases as you move toward the bottom."

Justine peered over the edge of the drum and into the Mark XII, still hesitant. "It looks like an upside-down layer cake," she said. "Come see."

Ellen and Myriam approached with caution. Once they peered inside, the device seemed to be less dangerous and more interesting. He wondered if they had expected a demonic creature to emerge.

"Each titanium disc contains a two-centimeter-thick portal, like the one in my pack. The discs keep the portals stable just long enough for the blast wave to pass through after detonation, which happens in less than the blink of an eye. The design allows the user to select the desired yield, the larger the disc, the more energy it transmits."

Ellen, Justine, and Myriam accepted his explanation and nodded.

"You'll need to remove the portals from all of the devices. Take the screw driver and pry open the clips holding each disc in place." His breathing was wrong. "Then, you'll need to unplug the wire that provides power to the portals and connects the arming mechanism. See those ribbed sections, squeeze them together."

Justine took a few seconds to figure out what he meant. She seemed pleased with the result as the plug released with little effort."

"To remove the portal from the disc, you need to grasp this tab and pull away." Was the translator speaking faster than he was?

Ellen pointed to the portal. "Is it safe to touch the portal?"

"The portals are not active without the power source. Be sure to unplug the wire before removing the portal from the disc." he said. He thought again about the shriveled body of that poor dog. The portals needed little power to function and the small electric battery could handle the job. If not disconnected from the power source first, the portals could be activated. "Please take your time."

Justine removed the next portal, careful only to touch the titanium disc and the directed tab. Hiram left her to finish and headed to the next Mark XII. He instructed Myriam as she removed the lid. When all the lids had been removed, Hiram returned to the first device. Justine pulled out the last disc. She moved to the next Mark XII and continued.

Ellen moved to the third device in the line. "I'll take this one." She pulled another screw driver out of her thigh pocket.

"Myriam, I need you to help remove the electronic components." He lifted the lid and struggled to line it back up on the top of the drum. "We'll need to flip the device over." The translator repeated.

Myriam grabbed another screw driver and fastened the lid back in place. Hiram tried to help her lift the device, but almost fell over. Justine guided him out of the way as the work on the second device was completed. Together, Justine and Myriam inverted the heavy Mark XII. "This is the door to the electronics panel. You'll need to remove the screws to open the panel." Myriam got to work with the screw driver.

"Now, pull the box out slowly so you don't damage the wire coverings. The electronics are housed inside. We'll need to remove the boards and store them." As Myriam removed the box, Hiram pulled an electronics baggy from his pocket.

"Open the door. Press against the clip holding the board in place."

Myriam paused, searching for the clip. She put her hand on it and looked to Hiram.

He nodded. "Push with your thumb." With the clip fully depressed, the board ejected itself from the connector.

Myriam jumped as the board lifted itself out, then laughed as she slid the board out of the box the rest of the way with ease and handed it to Hiram. He slid it into the baggy. Myriam moved on to the next one, Justine helping to flip the device over. He sealed the baggy once both boards were inside.

Agnes joined the group, with her C2ID2 display in hand. She held the device up for him. "The drone picked up something on the north side of the pasture. What does this look like to you?" she asked, pointing to a cluster of heat signatures on the image.

Hiram glanced at the display, irritated that she'd bothered them as they raced the clock to dismantle the Mark XIIs. "They're pigs."

"Oh," she said as she stepped back. "I worried they might be men trying to conceal themselves. I did not mean to interrupt your work." She turned and walked away before he could apologize for his gruff tone.

Myriam completed the final device. Now, in front of each of the weapons sat a stack of portals, and two electronics boards in antistatic plastic bags. Satisfied with the work, Hiram said, "Let's pack it all up."

Justine collected the stacks of portals, Myriam the bags of electronics. They handed Hiram the items and he eased them inside his pod via the portal in his backpack, ensuring he had six stacks of portals and six bags of electronics. He closed his pack.

"We need to get moving if we want to reach the drop zone in time." The thought occurred to him that he hadn't bothered to count the portals in the stacks or reviewed the electronics bags. He just wanted to get the job done. He needed to close his eyes, only for a few minutes. Besides, he trusted his team and they couldn't afford the time.

Teams Bravo and Golf stayed behind to watch the neutered weapons. The rest of the women accompanied him to the drop zone. They mimicked his slow, uneven pace as if they feared leaving him to make the walk on his own.

* * *

"Six mois!" Barbara shrieked when Captain Trembley, aka Falcon, explained the Allied plan. The Babel Fish repeated her words with similar inflection. "Six months! Our families could be dead in *six days!*"

"It's the best we can do," Trembley said. "We simply don't have the forces available to mount a cross-channel invasion, even with the help of your atomic bombs. Yes, we could punch a hole in the Atlantic Wall, and yes, we could destroy most of the mobile German divisions, but then what? The Nazi's would drive us back into the sea by sheer weight of numbers within a month, with tremendous losses. And it would take years to launch a second invasion if the first one failed."

"What about the forces for Operation Torch?" Hiram said. He had spoken in English, the Babel Fish providing a French translation. Trembley spoke both languages, but spoke French for the benefit of the women.

Trembley said, "That's only about eight divisions. We'll need ten times the number to take and hold France. American forces pour into England as we speak, but they're not fully trained, and our officers and men have no combat experience. And the Germans can shift armored forces to the west by rail far faster than we can move similar forces across the channel by boat."

"Not if the rail lines don't exist anymore," Barbara said, eyes blazing. "What happened in Saarbrücken can happen to all the major rail hubs along the border."

"They could still move units through Belgium and Luxemburg," Trembley said.

Hiram held up his hand, silencing Barbara before she could say more. They had shown Trembley the six weapons after he arrived. Not functional weapons, but Trembley hadn't known the difference.

"The weapons have to be placed manually, not dropped or launched. We can't reach all the major crossings in time anyway." Hiram tapped an icon on his C2ID2, turning off the translator, then continued in English. "I'm not willing to incinerate half the French population."

"With that leg, you aren't going to be doing much of anything," Trembley said.

"Needs some time to heal. Unfortunately, time's something we don't have." He looked around at his soldiers, all hopeful. "Regardless, there has to be another way."

Barbara clapped her hands together, her face contorted in anger. "Pas de secrets," she said. "Parle Français." No secrets. Speak French. She pointed to the C2ID2.

Hiram sighed, and tapped the translator icon. "There has to be another way."

32

0145 hours, Monday, August 10, 1942, Saint Chamond, Loire Department, Vichy France

The betrayal by her husband stunned Rosette. She considered Garon an ideal husband. He worked hard, brought home enough money to support their family. On Sundays they went to St. Ennemond's Catholic Church. When services concluded, they spent the day with Garon's parents, where he ran around the back field with the little ones, laughing and playing. During the week, he escorted Rosette around the community, helping to deliver meals to a few of their elderly neighbors, even after a long day at the office. When they arrived home, Leverette and Sophia would be enjoying a story with Mabel Roussel, the energetic, young primary school teacher, who had befriended Rosette. Garon would scoop up Sophia and the two would race Leverette up the stairs to the nursery. When all was done, he would wrap an arm around her and kiss the top of her head. *He had loved them, hadn't he?*

For two days, she wept for her children and for herself. When the weeping stopped, she found her heart had turned bitter. *Barbara was right about the French Gentiles!* She needed to save her children, and to do that, she had to get back to the others.

Rosette had paid no attention to the route when Detective Locard had driven her away. She didn't remember the few road signs they passed or the direction they had traveled. Rosette did recall a field and a farmhouse, a small stone bridge, and long stretches of evergreens. She had a vague feeling they'd travelled south, towards Rivesaltes. Still, how was she going to find her way back to Hiram and the others?

She lay on a cot in a root cellar beneath a farmhouse, a blanket pulled up tight under her chin. She had spotted a trowel among the baskets of potatoes and had stored it under the cot, just in case. A pitcher of water sat on a nearby shelf, last night's uneaten meal on a tray beside it. Unable to sleep, she stared at the dark ceiling. The sunlight seeping through the floorboards faded away hours ago, and the sounds of footsteps and muffled conversation had ceased as well. She thought it might be after midnight, in the small hours of the day.

The sound of a car engine shattered the quiet, followed by the crunch of tires on gravel. She grabbed the trowel from beneath the cot and moved as far away from the ladder as possible. With the trowel in her right hand, she waited and wished she still had her M22.

She heard the front door open. Slow, heavy footsteps grew louder as they came close to the cellar door. Something heavy above her slid across the floor, the initial squeal of wood on wood made her clench her teeth. Then, the trapdoor to the cellar opened. A silhouette lingered in the opening.

"Come up now," Locard said, his words gentle and encouraging. He left the door open and disappeared from view.

Rosette slipped the trowel into a pocket of the dress she'd stolen the day she left Hiram and the others. She climbed the ladder out of the dark cellar.

Locard sat at the kitchen table, struggling with a silver lighter. After a couple of tries, flame erupted. He lit the candle on the small table and slipped the lighter back into his pocket. The dim light accentuated his pale skin and the dark bags beneath his eyes. He hadn't shaved and sleep did not appear to be his ally.

"Please, sit." he said, directing her to take the seat opposite him.

She remained standing.

"Please. I have news of your children."

Rosette circled the table and took a seat at the table, praying the wariness of this man was not a sign of the news he had to share. "Are they alive?"

"Yes," Locard said.

"Where are they?" she asked. "I beg of you to tell me!"

"I'll tell you," he said, "in return for information."

"All right. What do you want to know?"

"Who freed you from the convoy in the Pyrénées?" Locard said.

"I can't tell you that," she said.

"And where did he come from?" he continued.

"I can't-"

"*Quid pro quo,* Madame Bertrand. You tell me what I need to know, and I'll tell you what you want to know."

Rosette shifted in her chair, uncomfortable with her options.

"If you answer my questions, I'll do everything in my power to get your children to safety."

"What about the families of the other women who escaped with me?"

"I'll do what I can. Can't promise more than that. Getting two children out is a lot easier than a couple dozen families, especially adult men."

Rosette looked into his eyes, thought she saw sincerity behind the weariness. And something else. *Fear?*

"Who freed you and the other prisoners? I need to know, please."

"Something has happened, hasn't it?" Her bitter heart raced, as if it knew what happened. "What is it?"

For a moment, he looked down at his hands. His eyes grew glassy, as if he held back tears. "A powerful weapon has been used," he said. "Nothing we have ever seen before. On the radio, they are saying hundreds of thousands of people are dead. How can a single explosion wreak so much havoc? Waging war with such weapons is madness. France will be destroyed!"

Rosette couldn't take her eyes off of him. *He worries for his people, just as I worry for my own.*

"I can see it in your face. You know something."

Rosette shook her head, not knowing if he'd understand. "Do you know what Hitler plans for the Jewish people? What is to happen to them when they get shipped out of France?"

"Nazi labor camps in the East."

"No," she said. "We go to *extermination* camps where they plan to gas us like an infestation of rats. The Nazis plan to kill every single Jew in Europe. And the Vichy are helping them. *You* are helping them commit one of the greatest crimes in the history of the world."

"You have proof?" Locard asked.

"Hiram showed us proof."

Locard leaned toward her. "Hiram?"

The information was free, she couldn't take it back. "That's his name, the man who helped us. He comes from another time, another place. He is Danette Halphen's great-great-grandson."

"Impossible," Locard said. "Mrs. Halphen is only in her early thirties."

"Do you have a better explanation for what happened in Saarbrücken?"

"No, but neither do I believe that the man you call Hiram has one of Mr. Wells' time machines. I'm not just a detective, I'm a forensic investigator. I've studied science. Time travel is impossible," he said.

"You've heard of the scientist Albert Einstein?" When Locard nodded she continued. "Well one of our group is a physics teacher, and she says that Professor Einstein has theoretically proven that time travel is allowed. Hiram proved it to us in a much more practical sense."

"But-," his eyes narrowed. "I never mentioned Saarbrücken."

Rosette shrugged. "That was the plan. By bombing the bridges and rail crossing near Saarbrücken, Hiram hoped to stop the Holocaust Trains, at least temporarily, until the Americans and British can invade."

"Holocaust Trains?" he asked.

"The mass murder of Jews in Europe by the Nazis will be known as the Holocaust. The trains that carry the Jews east from France and the Low Countries will be called Holocaust Trains."

"Does this man Hiram have more of these weapons?"

"Yes, many more." She let him think for a moment, then said, "Now you tell me about my children before I tell you anything else."

Locard sighed, his weariness growing. "Your children were sent to separate camps by the police. Leverette to a camp for men and boys near Marseille, called Camp des Milles. Sophia to *Frontstalag* 194 in the town of Vittel, in the Vosges Mountains. Both children are relatively safe for the moment."

"And the rest of the families from Camp Joffre?"

He settled back in his seat, took a heavy breath. "On July 22nd the Jewish detainees from Camp Joffre were sent to the concentration camp at Drancy. This past Friday, most of them boarded a Holocaust Train, as you call them." Rosette's heart caught in her throat as Locard continued.

"The train approached the French-German border when the explosion occurred, so your plan-"

"Hiram's plan," she interrupted. "I thought my children were safe in Saint Chamond."

"I understand," he said. "After the explosion, the train was diverted to the south to Vittel - the nearest available option. The prisoners are being transferred from the train to the Camp in the morning. My contact tells me the guard on patrol is light. I assume it will be supplemented by the guard assigned to the train." Locard paused, and then smiled. "My superior, Captain Petain, is not happy they are still in France."

33

1100 hours, Monday, August 10, 1942, northeast of Loches, Indre River Valley, Indre-et-Loire Department, Vichy France

Hiram and Captain Trembley spent the morning reviewing the intelligence reports Trembley brought from England. Most of France's "Army of the Armistice" and Army Air Force soldiers were stationed in North Africa, along with about half of France's Navy. The remainder of the French Navy was reported in port at Toulon, on the Mediterranean Coast.

"Hiram," Agnes said, hesitant. The Babel Fish translated the rest of her words. "There's something you should see."

Engrossed in one of Trembley's maps, Hiram thanked her. He heard whispering behind him.

"Hiram," Trembley said, "I think it's important."

For a second time, Hiram realized he had shooed Agnes away. He handed the map back to Trembley.

Agnes looked at Trembley and then to Justine for guidance. Justine put a hand on Agnes' back and pushed her forward. She handed Hiram her C2ID2 display unit.

The monitor showed a rambling farmhouse surrounded on three sides by fields of grain. In an open area of dirt and grass between the house and barn, someone had placed a large number of painted white rocks and spelled the phrase *FAMILLES ENVOYÉS VITTELCAMP* and below it *DÉPARTEMENT VOSGES* followed by *DANGER EXTREME*.

"What is that?" Trembley peered at the monitor over Hiram's shoulder.

"Video feed from a drone flying over a farmhouse where one of our people is being held," Hiram answered. He read the words over again, considering the implications of the message.

"Huh," Trembley said.

"Think of it like a film that you can see as it's being made," Agnes said.

"I'll show you," Nathalie said. She took out and activated her own display unit, which showed the view from a drone circling above their position. "Ida, step out into that clearing over there and wave your arms about a bit."

Ida appeared on the display. Trembley looked back and forth between the real Ida out in the field to the one on the monitor. Once satisfied it was not a trick, he walked out into the field with Ida and searched the sky, shielding his eyes from the sun.

"You can't see it," Ida said joining him in his skyward search. "Too small and too far up."

"It flies without a pilot?" Trembley asked.

"We tell them where to go, but they fly on their own," Ida replied. "We have three in the air at the moment. One flying above us like this," she made figure eight motions in the air with her finger, "one over Saint Chamond and one searching for two of our people near Saarbrücken."

Hiram had only been half paying attention to the conversation the Babel Fish repeated in his ear. By the time he checked back in to the discussion, it was too late. He hadn't intended to expose the drone technology to the Americans.

Protecting his team's technological advantages for as long as possible would increase their bargaining power, but he couldn't blame them for the drone lapse he had caused. To their credit, neither Nathalie nor Agnes had mentioned the Icarus drone also flying above them. The Americans and Brits knew about the C2ID2s. As for the portal technology, he wouldn't disclose his *piece de resistance*, unless necessary.

Hiram looked away from the display and out to Trembley and Ida, still peering up into the sky and talking. Agnes stood close to him, focused more on the terrible words on the display than the thing that captured them.

"What do we do, Hiram?" Agnes said, her words soft, desperate. The Babel Fish failed to capture her emotion.

Before he could respond, Barbara pushed past Agnes and stood in front of him. She stabbed a finger at Rosette's message on the display. "We go to Vittel now! We save the families!"

"We'll send a team south as soon as it's dark," Hiram said. "We don't want the railbikes spotted during the day."

Satisfied with Hiram's response, Barbara nodded then walked off with purpose, ready to kick everyone in gear to save their families. He returned Agnes' display unit and said, "Keep an eye on the farm. Search for any signs it might be a trap. Find out how many people are in that house and the area around it."

"We are going to save them," she said. Hiram debated whether she was asking a question or telling him it was going to happen.

"We are going to try."

She nodded and walked away with the C2ID2. Hiram doubted Agnes would look away from the display without more news to report.

Trembley, still searching for the drone above them, sidestepped his way back to Hiram. "What else do have hiding in your bag of tricks Hiram? I'd swear you practice witchcraft if we didn't need what you've got to win this war."

Hiram took out his own display unit and set it to show a map of France on which he'd already superimposed a line of demarcation between Occupied France and Vichy France. Working with Trembley, he added the locations of major German units and headquarters.

"Defensive preparations along the Mediterranean Coast are minimal compared to the Atlantic Wall," Hiram said. "Except for the French fleet at Toulon."

"I agree. I suppose the Germans think they can shift forces to the coast faster than we can mount an invasion from Great Britain, despite the limitations of the terrain. Movement from north to south in southwestern France is constrained by the mountains, dormant volcanoes, and river gorges of the Massif Central and the westernmost Alps. Their spies have probably learned we intend to attack western North Africa before invading Europe. At least we did until a few days ago."

"For the sake of argument, if the fleet at Toulon no longer existed, and these two divisions belonging to 1st Army were also eliminated." Hiram indicated the position of an infantry division near Moulins, across the demarcation line north of Vichy, and a panzer-grenadier division near Libourne, south of Bordeaux. "Then Vichy would have a difficult time repulsing a surprise invasion from the Mediterranean. What's left of the German Army's forces in France remain static divisions along the Atlantic

Coast. They can't move without significant transportation support."

"Don't forget the 2nd Waffen SS Panzer-Grenadier division here," Trembley said as he pointed to Dijon in the Côte-d'Or Department. "They have a high-speed avenue of approach south along the roads paralleling the Rhone River all the way to the coast."

Hiram studied the map, looking for a choke point. "Here, south of Valence," he said. "Minimal casualties if we plug them up here."

"If we put the eight divisions slated for Operation Torch ashore here," Trembley indicated the broad sweep of coast from the French-Spanish border to Marseille. "And seize the passes coming down from the north before any additional German reinforcements arrive."

"And hold them long enough for the rest of the invasion force to arrive," Hiram said.

"But we leave a wide gap between the southern end of the Massif Central and the Pyrenees." Trembley indicated a ten-kilometer-wide by fifty-kilometer-long valley of open farmland between Alzonne and Olonzac in the Aude Department. "That will be difficult to hold."

"It's sparsely populated farmland," Hiram said. "We can use the atomic weapons there without a lot of collateral damage. It's a lot easier to employ them as we retreat than to set them on ground we are trying to take."

"Sounds like we have the beginnings of a plan," Trembley said.

A plan that will speed the end of the war. But not one that will save the families. Hiram excused himself, saying he needed to go talk to his team. He found Agnes near her railbike.

"Can you cover for me for a little while? I need to do a little research. If Trembley shows up, let me know via C2ID2," Hiram said. "Have you ever heard of *Frontstalag* 194?"

Once the translator completed its work, Agnes shook her head.

The camp must have been a minor one compared to Joffre. He found a quiet spot away from the group and sat down on a fallen tree. He searched for the unknown camp on the C2ID2, though he found few references that provided any detail. Initially, the place had been the spa town of Vittel with several well-known, glamorous hotels. Early in the war, a few of the buildings served as a hospital for French soldiers. Over a short period of time, Vittel transitioned into an internment camp for foreign citizens stuck in France during the German invasion. Vittel served as a poster child for the way an internment camp was meant to be run. The staff provided fresh, generous rations supplemented by packages from the Red Cross, running water, and medical care, and facilities for leisure activities. The guests at Camp Vittel had been encouraged to partake in leisure activities. They had even been allowed to receive mail and visitors from outside the camp.

When he returned an hour later, he relayed his findings to Agnes. "Security is most likely lacking compared to an SS-run camp."

Agnes grinned. "Then it should be easier to free the families. Once we get them out of there, where do we go?"

"It might be safer to leave them in Vittel. The Germans won't start shipping prisoners out of the camp until 1944." He refrained from adding that he had changed this version of history.

"Barbara will never go for it," Agnes said.

"So, we send teams Foxtrot and Golf to keep watch from a distance. *Frontstalag* 194 is small and in the middle of the mountains. If they try to move the prisoners, we can set up an ambush."

34

1800 hours, Monday, August 10, 1942, northeast of Loches, Indre River Valley, Indre-et-Loire Department, Vichy France

Captain Trembley coded a message to be sent by HF radio to London, using a one-time cipher. Hiram took the time to relay the plan to invade southern France to his troops. He referred to the plan as Operation Roundup, a homage to the plan the Allies would not develop now that Hiram had meddled with the timeline.

"Team Charlie," Hiram said, "you're going to work your way southwest toward Bordeaux. You'll need to position yourselves near Libourne, where the 7th Panzer Division has set up camp. When you are in place, I'll join you and employ one of the Mark XII's." Hiram didn't relish playing another game of hop-scotch on French trains, but it was the only way to ensure that only he could bring a working Mark XII into the world.

"The rest of us will travel southeast towards Vichy," Hiram said. "Teams Delta, Foxtrot, and Golf will break off before we reach Vichy. Team Delta you're going northeast to Moulins, where the German 15th Infantry Division is stationed. You'll notice your proposed route has been programmed on your C2ID2." The translator repeated his words.

The individuals with the C2ID2s pulled up the maps on their display, while the others in their team looked on.

"Teams Foxtrot and Golf, you'll continue north to Vittel. You'll need to monitor the camp until we can liberate the prisoners and get them to safety. Teams Bravo and Echo, you're with me. We're headed to Saint Chamond to free Rosette. Once we get Rosette out, Team Bravo will proceed south towards the coast. We'll be deploying a Mark XII at Toulon to take out the French fleet. Team Echo, we'll drop you off along the way near Valance." No one seemed to contest the effort to save Rosette, not even Barbara.

Agnes stepped forward. "Should we send the Icarus drone towards London," she pointed upward. "Might take five days or more to get there, but we'd need to shut it down anyway. It's too slow to keep up with us. I expect it'll arrive before the invasion fleet departs, assuming our plan is approved in the first place."

"Good idea. Ida, tell Captain Trembley to include a note in his radio message for Sarah to begin checking her C2ID2 for a signal in four days." Ida nodded and stepped away from the group to relay the message.

"Team Charlie, you'll have to launch an Icarus drone upon arrival at your staging point," Agnes added, the Babel Fish translating for Hiram's benefit. "We won't be in contact with you once you move out of C2ID2 range."

"She's right," Hiram said. "The distance is going to push the limits of the drones. Make sure each team has the necessary equipment before we leave."

After Rosette's unexpected departure and his inability to locate Deborah and Danette after the event in Saarbrucken, Hiram had learned his lesson. He refused to let the modified railbikes out of his sight without a means to find them. He handed Isadore a bag full of radio-frequency identification chips and a tube of superglue.

"Glue one of these on each railbike, somewhere under the driver's seat," he said. "Record the number of each chip on your C2ID2. We'll be able to track the railbikes with the Icarus drones that way."

As the women around him discussed the plan, Hiram thought of Deborah. He had convinced himself Deborah and Danette had survived the blast in Saarbrücken, but the more time that passed the less likely the possibility he would see them again. *Why in the hell had he taken such a risk!* He would not give up on them – on Deborah. "Any sign of Danette and Deborah?"

"Nothing yet." Agnes offered a hopeful smile. "Isadore continues searching the area with the drone."

"We need another railbike, which means I have to go into the pod. And I don't want Trembley to see me do it," he said.

Agnes looked in Trembley's direction, Hiram joined her.

"Do you think Ida could keep him occupied for a while?"

Agnes' left eyebrow went up as she searched for the reason of his request.

"I'm going over to Team Golf's position on the other side of the ridge. I can open the portal there. It will take Justine and Emma at least an hour to assemble another railbike."

"You need a little privacy. Understood." Agnes headed off toward Ida while the Babel Fish continued its translation. Hiram headed up the hill.

Two hours later, Hiram's band of nuclear insurgents stood ready to head off into the darkness. Everyone bid goodbye to Irene, Denise, Camille, and Joanne. As Team Charlie disappeared, Hiram and his remaining troops headed southeast.

Captain Trembley and Charlotte rode in Hiram's sidecar, first in line for another long journey down the tracks. Charlotte scouted ahead via the drone, running figure eights around the tracks, searching for concentrations of troops and ensuring the train stations along the way posed no imminent danger.

The American marveled at the speed of the railbikes and seemed enchanted by the night vision goggles. Hiram had also armed him with an M22 assault rifle. While Justine finished assembling the railbike, Ida convinced him he needed proper training to be able to carry such a powerful weapon. Barbara, eager to destroy as many of the bad guys as possible, jumped at the chance to get one more soldier up to speed.

Hiram ignored the man's delighted observations as they sped down the tracks. His thoughts travelled eastward, toward the area just outside of the devastated city of Saarbrücken. *Deborah, where are you?*

35

1845 hours, Thursday, August 13, 1942, Saint Chamond, Loire Department, Vichy France

Rosette stared out a west-facing window, searching for any sign that her message had been received. The sun had sunk below the horizon, but twilight would linger another couple of hours. In the distance, a hunched shape, Alphonse Benoit, the farm's owner and Emile Locard's uncle, cleared debris from an irrigation ditch. Alphonse's wife Janel milked cows in the barn, leaving Rosette alone in the small kitchen, tasked with peeling potatoes.

"Rosette," a women's voice called from the open doorway behind her. She spun at the sound, adjusting the paring knife to a fighting grip as she did so.

"Ida!" She dropped the knife in the bucket of potato peels and rushed to embrace her. "I can't believe you made it here."

"It wasn't easy with the police checkpoints on the roads near every town."

"What about the others?"

"You don't think they let me come after you alone, do you?"

Rosette peeked outside, searching for signs of the others. Janel returned from the barn with a bucket of fresh milk, Alphonse continued his task along the edge of the field, and a cloud of dust drifted up from the road not too far away. "Where are they hiding? Is Hiram with you?"

"I've got another six with me. Hiram's off making life difficult for the bad guys. He said something about blowing up a bridge or two. He'll meet up with us tomorrow."

"I made it home, Ida. But, Sophia and Leverette – my babies – were gone. I can't believe he did it. They are children." She tried to contain her tears. "My bastard husband turned them over to the police after I was taken. Said they were tainted by my blood. How could he throw away his own sweet children?"

"Oh, Rosette. I am so sorry," Ida hugged her friend. "We need to focus on slipping out of here, then we can get your children back, along with the rest of our families. The policeman is on his way back. Follow me."

As Ida reached for the door handle, they heard the car coming up the dirt drive. Rosette risked a peek out the front window and recognized Locard in the driver's seat. Another man sat beside him.

When the car stopped, Locard stepped out of the car, then the passenger door opened. Rosette looked at Locard and at the other man now climbing out. She refused to let him take her away. "Come on! We have to go." Rosette guided Ida to the open side window, which looked out over the Benoit's field. Alphonse, now distracted by Locard's arrival, headed back toward the house. "Stay close to the house. We can get to the woods around back."

The two crept around the outside of the weathered, stone farmhouse. Once around back, they took off toward the thick border of trees separating the property from the one behind it. Once hidden, they could make their way to the woods less than a kilometer away.

As she cleared the garden, a familiar voice called out. "Mère!"

Rosette stopped.

"What are you doing? Run!" Ida said.

"Mère!" the small voice called again.

"Leverette," Rosette whispered. She turned and ran back to the farmhouse, not caring who might see her now. She cut through the garden and almost demolished a row of Brussel sprout stalks.

When she reached the front of the house, a little boy of about five, stood next to the policeman.

"It is you!" Leverette cried.

Rosette took a few steps toward him and fell to her knees. The child ran to her, moving as fast as he could go. Mother and son reunited in the dirt driveway. Locard and the stranger watched from a respectful distance. "Are you here to take us away?" Rosette said with the boy in her arms.

Before Locard or the other man answered, Ida stepped around from the back of the house with her M22 assault rifle held against her shoulder.

155

"Hands up!" she said. Their hands went up without hesitation. Ida's six companions appeared out of the fields surrounding the farmhouse, weapons aimed toward the policeman and his comrade.

36

0610 hours, Friday, August 14, 1942, Saint Chamond, Loire Department, Vichy France

Hiram, Trembley, and Charlotte joined teams Bravo and Echo in Saint Chamond just before daybreak. It had been a productive, or rather, a destructive night. Hiram had planted satchel charges on each trestle of the two bridges crossing the Loire River, then detonated them as freight trains crossed from the east. The train carrying munitions had provided a spectacular fireworks show. Now, two fewer routes existed for the Holocaust Trains to travel.

They left the railbike with Charlotte's Team Echo compatriots in the woods west of the farmer's fields. Isadore informed Hiram that Team Delta had checked in from Moulins. As they walked up to the farmhouse, he wondered how far Team Charlie had gone on their move south toward Liborne.

Ida greeted them at the door, then led them into the parlor where two men sat in straight-backed chairs, guarded by Charlotte. The taller man wore a rumpled grey suit, his long legs crossed at the ankles well out front of the chair. His thick framed glasses disrupted the style of his hair, which lay at awkward, messy angles around his ears. The other man was older, maybe mid-fifties with greying hair and piercing blue eyes. In contrast, he wore a tailored black suit and expensive, well-shined shoes.

Hiram turned to Ida. "Rosette?"

As Ida spoke, Trembley translated for him. Hiram did not want to expose the secret of the *Babel Fish* to either prisoner.

"Upstairs in one of the bedrooms with her son. These men brought him back from Camp des Milles. The farmer and his wife are in the kitchen." Ida's words sounded grim despite the good news she had just delivered.

"What's wrong?" he asked.

She pointed her gun at Locard. "This one is Inspector Locard, says he's a French policeman. He says our families are being moved again. By train, through Belgium, and then east."

"Kak!" Hiram said. *Shit.*

"Who's this guy?" Hiram directed his words to Locard, and was surprised when the man answered in English before Trembley completed the translation.

"May I present my good friend, Oberst Hans Paul Oster. Deputy Director of counter-espionage, German military intelligence," Locard said.

Without thinking, Hiram took a step backward and leveled his rifle at the German colonel.

"Delighted to meet you." Oster held out a hand to Hiram, the motion quick and confident.

"Yasher koach," Hiram tested whether the man spoke Hebrew. *May God grant you the strength to continue your good deeds.*

Oster said, "Shalom. And that, I'm afraid, is the full extent of my Hebrew," he continued in English. Hiram lowered his gun and Oster rescinded his offer to shake.

The German's name sounded familiar to Hiram. His father had mentioned a General Major Hans Oster several times in connection with his research. Probably the same man, not yet promoted from the German equivalent of full colonel to brigadier general. *Of course, the Oster Conspiracy!* Oster plotted to kill Hitler back in 1939. He would be arrested in 1943 for helping Jews escape Europe, which precluded his personal participation in the Operation Valkyrie plot to supersede Hitler's regime in 1944. His execution in 1945 followed another attempt to terminate Hitler. But Oster's story had changed. Everything had changed.

"Hiram," Charlotte said as she burst into the room. She said a few more words that Hiram didn't understand.

"Sounds urgent," Trembley said.

"Ida, these men are not our prisoners. Let's get them more comfortable accommodations," Hiram said.

Hiram and Trembley followed Charlotte out into the hallway. Charlotte spoke again in French.

"She's found Deborah and Danette," Trembley said.

"Where? Are they safe?" Hiram wanted to leave immediately to get them.

"Vosges Mountains, south of La Bresse. About seventy-five kilometers east of Vittel. They lost the railbike somehow. Not in imminent danger, but travelling on foot. They're following the French-German border south, staying well west of the demarcation zone."

"Show me," Hiram said

Charlotte held up the C2ID2 display. Danette and Deborah walked up a steep mountain path among heavy woods. Both alert and watchful. They each carried their M22 assault rifles at port arms. Hiram noticed their backpacks had changed from the IDF-issued ones to smaller canvas packs, the C2ID2s nowhere in sight. It explained his inability to contact them.

"Can we get the drone down where they can see it, so they know we've found them?" He was eager to see Deborah's face again.

Trembley translated.

Charlotte zoomed the view back out and looked further up the trail the women climbed, then zoomed in closer.

Trembley said, "She can bring the drone down and buzz them when they enter that clearing."

"Do it," Hiram said. Charlotte directed the drone to descend to just above the tree tops where it circled, waiting for its quarry. Deborah and Danette lingered at the edge of the clearing, weapons high. As they stepped out into the open area, Charlotte sent the little pilot-less aircraft into a tight, low orbit around the clearing. Charlotte, Hiram, and Trembley watched Danette lock onto the little plane with her rifle as the drone passed. Two more passes and she jumped up and down, waving and pointing at the drone. Soon Deborah joined her. Charlotte settled the drone into a hovering position and zoomed in on both of them as Hiram fought back tears.

"She has one more thing to tell you," Trembley said.

"What?" he asked, irritated at the need to have Trembley translate in Deborah's place.

"Team Delta reports that the German 15th Infantry Division near Moulins is packing up to move. They don't know where yet," Trembley said, his translation slow as he took in Charlotte's words.

Before Hiram could respond, Trembley said, "That could be good news, or bad news. Can we see the view from their drone?"

Hiram removed his C2ID2 display from the pouch on his body armor and handed it to Trembley. "Tell Charlotte what you want to see. Since Inspector Locard and Colonel Oster speak English, I won't need you to translate. See if you can figure out where that division is going."

"Charlotte, the minute you hear from Foxtrot or Golf, give them Deborah and Danette's coordinates." Hiram paused, to clear his throat. "Tell them I would be most appreciative if they would send a team to fetch them."

37

0930 hours, Friday, August 14, 1942, Perpignan, Pyrénées-Orientales Department, Vichy France

Captain Petain replaced the Ericsson Bakelite telephone handset in its cradle and made a note in the case file spread out before him on his large desk. *Yet another delay.* He thought he'd succeeded in scheduling a train to take the troublesome Jews out of *Frontstalag* 194 in Vittel and off to wherever the Germans deported them in the East, not an easy task. Rail transit across the German-French border remained restricted by the *event* in Saarbrücken and the subsequent response by the German and Vichy governments. But he'd found a French National Railway Company dispatcher willing to route the train northward through Belgium.

Now the dispatcher had called to report a delay. Two bridges over the Loire were gone, blown up by partisans, and the train had to be rescheduled. On top of that headache, ration deliveries to the German soldiers took precedence over his requests. Sometime tomorrow the train *would* leave, along with the last remaining ties to the missing prisoners and the evidence that his men had failed in their duties. Petain had called in numerous favors to get the women's families on the first outbound train from Drancy after their arrival. Had the event in Saarbrücken taken place an hour later, the train would have reached Germany and been out of France for good. A half an hour later and the explosion might have destroyed the train. He would have enjoyed watching that fireworks display. Instead, his prisoners had been sent to a fucking resort in the Vosges Mountains.

The idea that the mysterious man, who had created such a headache, had caused the *event* in Saarbrücken crossed his mind. He had used advanced weaponry to take out Petain's men, but he found it hard to believe one man could have taken an entire city down to the ground. *Surely an industrial nation-state developed the thing that destroyed Saarbrücken. Most likely the Americans.*

"Sir, you have a call from Lieutenant Lebeau," Rubi called from her desk outside his office.

He snatched the phone. "Lebeau, what have you found?"

"One of the missing maids, sir. Inspector Locard picked up the Bertrand woman's son from Camp des Milles. Then, he drove to Lyon where he picked up a man at the train station-."

"Who?" Petain interrupted.

"We haven't established that," Lebeau said. "He's German. Came all the way from Berlin according to another passenger I interviewed."

Petain guessed this new player must be important to have secured passage by train, given the current state of the rail system. "Where did they go?"

"We followed them to a farm outside Saint Chamond, in Loire Department. We did a quick drive past the farm. Don't think we were detected. We saw two heavily armed women emerge from the fields around the farmhouse. They took Locard and the other man inside. One of the women took the boy into her arms. She had to be Rosette Bertrand. I assume the other women are some of the remaining prisoners from the convoy attack we've been seeking."

"Keep an eye on them," Petain said.

"Officer Thibult is watching from the bell tower of a church in Saint Chamond. I'm at the local police station a few blocks away. We'll monitor the situation."

"Thibult's an imbecile. Tell me you have another officer with you!"

"Just Thibult and myself, sir."

"Notify me immediately if the situation changes. I'm on my way." Petain hung up the phone. *Time to go hunting.*

* * *

Petain compared the two maps spread out on the table in his outer office. On the left, was a roadmap of France, marked with existing checkpoints. He expected the four-hundred-kilometer road trip from Perpignan to Saint Chamond to take at least six hours, longer if he avoided the checkpoints. He wanted no official notice of this expedition to reach Vichy, given the risk that someone might connect the dots between the missing female prisoners, the attack on the cargo vessel *M.V. Calais* at Port Leucate, and the *event* in Saarbrücken.

On his right, was a map of the French railway system with the route from Camp Vittel to the Belgian border crossing marked in red. The circuitous train route passed within one hundred kilometers of the farmhouse Lebeau and Thibult watched.

He considered how long it would take to move his men to Saint Chamond. A better option appeared before him as he looked at the rail map.

"Rubi," Petain called. "Did Inspector Locard have access to the schedule and route of the train from *Frontstalag* 194?"

The assistant hurried into his office. "Yes sir. I saw him checking it before he left Thursday morning. But," she paused, "he wouldn't know about the latest delay. Should I try to reach him?"

"No thank you, my dear." *If Locard knows, so must his co-conspirators. And if my evaluation of this mysterious soldier is correct, he can't resist rescuing a train full of Jewish prisoners. I can use the train as bait!*

He would load some of the railcars with armed policemen disguised as prisoners, enough to overwhelm the soldier and his Jew whores. If the soldier didn't bite, Petain's men could disembark in Mâcon and proceed to Saint Chamond by truck.

Petain rolled up the maps and headed out into the open police station. Twelve of his men rose as he entered the room, waiting for the afternoon's assignments. A few more and he'd have enough to mount his attack.

"Rubi, get second shift in here. Tell them we've got a situation."

"Sir?"

"And tell them to forget the uniforms."

"Um, yes sir." The assistant picked up her phone and began dialing.

38

1159 hours, Friday, August 14, 1942, Saint Chamond, Loire Department, Vichy France

Although Hiram was relieved to learn Deborah and Danette remained unharmed, he still faced the problem of rescuing the families, along with the other prisoners. The route for the Holocaust Train Inspector Locard provided passed within a hundred kilometers of their current position. Even if stopping the train and freeing hundreds of prisoners went as expected, moving that many people through occupied France would be impossible.

"Oster has proven smuggling routes to Switzerland," Locard said. "I've been helping him to get Jews out of Germany for years. The job has become difficult now that the French police have enthusiastically joined in Hitler's cause. Captain Petain and many others like him are going well beyond what's required by rounding up minors and mothers with small children. I asked for Oster's help getting Rosette and the children out of France."

"What was the plan?"

"First, we were going to Vittel to secure Sophia's release from *Frontstalag* 194, then we planned to take them to a mineral processing plant in the Jura Mountains. After that, I don't know. For Rosette's safety, the less we know, the better. Talk to Oster. See what he can offer."

"You trust him?"

"Rosette wouldn't have been the first Jewish woman I've gotten out of France." Locard reached into his pocket and pulled out his watch. He opened the watch and pried open a well-camouflaged door on the lid. He offered the watch to Hiram, not taking his eyes off the image of the woman inside.

"Who is she?" Hiram asked.

"She was supposed to be my wife," he said. He pulled back the watch but didn't cover up her picture. "I think our parents had written off the idea of either of us getting married. We were planning to tell them. Of course, at our age neither of us planned to have children." He rubbed the bottom edge of the gold frame, then closed the lid and returned the watch to his pocket. "I trust him." Locard stepped out of the room. No one stopped him.

Oster sipped a cup of tea in the parlor. Agnes stood in the doorway, leaning on the frame with her M22 held ready. She watched the German as if she expected him to turn into a horned beast at any moment.

Hiram touched her on the shoulder and she seemed to relax a little. He signaled for her to step out of the room. She looked from Hiram to Oster and nodded before leaving.

"Locard thinks you can help us get the prisoners out of France, maybe get them across the Swiss border," Hiram said.

"I'd hardly call the women you have here prisoners," Oster said, setting the teacup down on the table beside his chair.

"Not them. There's a train headed this way from Drancy. We anticipate two to three hundred Jewish prisoners on board. Do you think you can move them through the mineral processing plant, the way you planned to take Rosette?"

"Three hundred you say." He looked up at the ceiling, tapped his fingers on his knee as if trying to count them up in his head. "If we factor in the number of children, elderly, and possibly sick, you are looking at a high mortality rate just to move them the first hundred or so kilometers."

"The mortality rate is a hell of a lot higher in one of the concentration camps," Hiram said.

Oster nodded. "I can't make any arrangements without a conversation with my contacts. From what I've seen here, especially the exquisite weapons your soldiers are carrying, we may have another option."

A short time later, Hiram, Locard, and Oster sat around the table in the kitchen. Agnes stood watch in the doorway, listening for any indication of trouble outside the room. They asked the Benoit's to stay in their bedroom upstairs. Rosette played with her son in the front yard. Hiram's remaining soldiers kept watch on the house, both inside and out. A few had taken up positions just beyond the tree line at the edge of the farmer's property.

"We can end this war before the train reaches its destination," the German said.

"How?" Hiram asked.

"We eliminate Hitler and his command staff, then seize power in Berlin and other major centers using the *Ersatzheer.* You might know it as the Replacement Army. Highly placed comrades are in position throughout the German Army, ready to command the *Ersatzheer.* Many German officers believe America's entry into the war makes our eventual defeat inevitable. The recent destruction of Saarbrücken should bring more of them over to that belief."

Hiram recalled the general outlines of Operation Valkyrie and it hadn't turned out well. Hitler had been lucky to survive Von Stauffenberg's bomb at the Wolf's Lair. In retaliation, all the conspirators had been snuffed out. *But I have much bigger bombs.*

"Hitler is closely guarded, which has been a problem all along," Oster continued. "I'd guess the destruction of Saarbrücken will only increase the number of guards on watch."

"Can you get your hands on his schedule?"

"I have contacts on Field Marshal von Rundstedt's staff that can," Oster said.

"What do we need to do?"

"Get me to OB West headquarters outside Paris."

39

0700 hours, Saturday, August 15, 1942, Vittel, Vosges Department, Occupied France

Louis Petain rarely used his granduncle's patronage to secure cooperation from such a valuable asset as the Gendarmerie, the French military police. But, the current fiasco's high stakes deemed the use of his family's influence to secure passage for himself and thirty-nine of his best men aboard a French Air Force Farman F.224 transport. The plane landed at an airfield south of Nancy, where Petain and his men boarded a train to Pont-Saint-Vincent, the northern end of the rail line serving Camp Vittel, at least since the allied bombers had destroyed the bridge across the Moselle River north of the town. The same train his men rode in now would be used to pick up the prisoners at the camp.

When they arrived at *Frontstalag* 194, his men took their places among the prisoners, along with the families of the troublesome escaped maids, and began to board the train. Over two hundred Jewish girls had been added to the roster of those headed east. At the front of the train, a French National Railway locomotive, operated by the engineer and his young assistant, pulled a coal tender and a passenger coach with ten officers from the camp's guard force. Two French railway men occupied the caboose. They monitored the train's status from the rear and were prepared to assist if the train needed to be backed down the rail line.

As soon as the single door to the boxcar was closed, Petain directed his men to chain ten of the adult male prisoners in place across the door opening, forming a human barrier for his men to hide behind when the door was opened. Ten Jewish adults and teenagers, plus thirty younger children, mostly girls, huddled at either end of the boxcar, as far from the policemen as possible. The nine trailing cattle cars held a similar complement of passengers.

* * *

0815 hours, Saturday, August 15, 1942, Suriauville, Vosges Department, Occupied France

The train braked hard, steel wheels squealing on the iron rails. Captain Petain reached out to steady himself. Without a good handhold, he lost his footing and went down to his knees. He wasn't the only one to fall. *So soon? We can't be more than ten or fifteen kilometers from the station. How did they get so far north so quickly?*

He picked himself up off the floor, shouting, "Get ready," to his men.

His men regained their footing and took up positions behind the ten adult prisoners blocking the sliding door opening on the left side of the cattle car. The train jerked twice more and rolled to a stop. A few pops of gunfire came from near the engine. "Fire as soon as you have a target," Petain said, speaking to both the men in the car and into the radio mouthpiece wired to the young operator's backpack. The radio operator darted to the rear corner of the car as the door slid open.

Bright morning sunshine filled the car. Petain blinked a few times until he made out the form of a soldier in a camouflage uniform standing outside the door. *A female soldier. One of the escaped prisoners from Rivesaltes?* She stared up at the chained prisoners, bewilderment plastered on her face. One of his men shot her in the face.

Gunfire erupted up and down the line as the men in the trailing cattle cars slid open their doors and joined the fight. The attackers tried not to hit the prisoners, returning sporadic fire from weapons that made no sound. From inside the box car, Petain made out at least four soldiers gunned down in the ditch between the tracks and the wood line. He jumped backward when a bullet cracked into the side of the car sending a quick spray of splinters centimeters from his right ear.

Gunfire tapered, then ceased. Unwilling to risk hitting prisoners, the women backed out of view, leaving Petain's men without suitable targets.

"Surrender," Petain shouted from behind his human shield. "You have one minute." He grabbed a young girl with dark, matted curls and pushed her between two of the adults, their chains rubbing as they adjusted. She clung to the man on the left. Petain positioned himself behind the other man and pressed his pistol to the back of the girl's head. "Or we'll kill your children." Turning his head and speaking in a lower voice, he said to those in the car, "and if any of you try to interfere, I'll kill them all anyway."

A minute later he repeated the threat, irritated the soldier and his dogs didn't bite. He waited another minute, then pulled the trigger. A spatter of blood fell upon his bare hand. The high-pitched screams of the children behind him made more noise than the fusillade of bullets that poured through the cattle car door. He backed away from the opening. Two Jews sagged in their chains, but the shield did not fall. Petain replaced the dead little girl with another one and waited. This time a scream came from outside the boxcar, beyond the tree line.

"D'accord! Nous nous rendons!" *All right! We surrender!* An unarmed man walked out of the woods, hands held high. "Nous nous rendons." He stopped about ten meters from the tracks. Six female soldiers followed him out of the woods, one wounded and supported by two others.

"I count seven out there. Four more over here. Where are the rest of my prisoners?" Petain shouted.

"Not here," the man replied. A flicker of movement in the woods caught Petain's eye.

"Tell your accomplice skulking in the shadows that I'm a hell of shot."

"He's not one of ours," the man said.

Petain fired off three quick rounds in that direction, though he doubted he hit the target. He waited a few seconds, not taking his eyes off the woods. Nothing moved except the mysterious man, six Jewish escapees, and the trembling little girl still clutched in his hand.

He pulled the girl back into the car and pushed her over to the others. "Seize them," he said. "Search the area for any others. Send a few out that way." His men wriggled though the human chain and jumped down from the boxcars.

A group of his men met the prisoners, searching each one for weapons. The others fanned out. Some headed toward the brush at the edge of the forest. A few walked the length of the train. Petain waited in the cattle car.

"All clear, sir," his second in command, Sergeant Dubois, shouted. "Three burned up sidecar motorcycles over there in the brush, but no one else."

More soldiers hid out there, he was sure. For now, he had what he wanted. *Best to move on.* "What about the rest of the train?" Petain slipped between the chained prisoners and jumped to the ground. He headed toward the locomotive. Black smoke billowed from something burning on the tracks in front of the train.

Dubois chose to explore the passenger car. Before Petain caught up, his second jumped out of the car. "Riddled with bullets, sir. All dead inside."

Petain moved forward and found the engineer slouched in the space between the locomotive and the coal tender, the front of his uniform dark and wet. His assistant's arm hung limp from the window. Two unfortunate losses. "Find me someone who can operate this train," Petain told Dubois.

Dubois nodded and trotted off toward the men grouped near the second boxcar.

Petain walked farther up the tracks. A truck burned astride them. Lazy, black smoke drifted up from the blackened engine. In between the truck and train, a missing section of rails and ties left recesses in the ballast where the tracks began to curve.

He was disappointed with the troublesome soldier. Had he taken the truck out of his equation, the train would have derailed.

He considered sending his men to search for the rails. Even if they found them, no one on his team had been trained to place them. They would all have to go northeast, back the way they had come, to wait for the completion of the repair.

"Move all the surviving prisoners to the second cattle car. Throw anything dead or close to it in the first cattle car, along with the motorcycles. Strip the women of their equipment and put them in the cattle car with the other prisoners where they belong," Petain said.

Dubois nodded and directed his men.

"What about this one?" Barre asked with his sidearm pointed at the kneeling soldier's head.

Petain approached the man. "Quite a headache you and your dogs have caused."

The man offered no response, his eyes sweeping the scene.

He doesn't look at his women, does not pay any mind to the squeals of the children as they are pushed along toward their new cage. For a moment, Petain thought he looked like a man playing chess. Evaluating, calculating, preparing for the move to make next. Perhaps preparing for the tenth one down the line.

"He'll be riding in the passenger coach with me." Petain said. *No need to risk any unforeseen situations that might arise if left in anyone else's care.* "The weapons too. And bring me anything interesting you find on the women."

Within a few minutes, the men had relocated all the prisoners, both dead and alive. The troublesome man, now bound inside the passenger car, waited for interrogation. Petain climbed into the car, where Dubois and one of his men sat inside, weapons trained on the prisoner seated toward the middle of the car. A mix of blood and brain matter speckled the wall behind their captive. Petain took a seat across from him.

"Why don't you tell me what you've done with the escaped prisoners?"

The man said nothing, but at least now he met Petain's eyes.

"Fine. How about your name?"

Still the man kept quiet.

Before he could ask again, the door at the back of the car opened. "Sorry to interrupt sir. Radio call," the radio operator said. Blood spatter covered the young man's face, dotted his civilian clothing. "It's headquarters relaying a call from Lieutenant Lebeau."

Petain took the microphone and stepped to the rear of the car still focused on the soldier. "Who is this?" he asked, signaling Dubois to continue the interrogation.

Dubois' fist connected with the soldier's stomach. Petain smiled.

"Miss Brodeur, sir. There's no one else here. Lieutenant Lebeau said he needs to speak with you."

"Out with it," Petain said, his patience faltering. He was anxious to break this prisoner who had caused so much turbulence in his department. He needed it.

"He says Inspector Locard, the German officer, and another man got into Locard's car and left Saint Chamond heading north about an hour ago," Rubi Brodeur said, her voice tinny. "They pulled off the road outside Roanne. They seem to be arguing. Says this is the first chance he's had to call in."

"A German officer?" Petain said, surprised.

"Yes, sir. Lebeau said it's the same unknown German that was at the house with Locard this morning. Colonel's insignia on the uniform."

What the hell is that all about? Is Locard working for the Germans? "Let him know we're serious," Petain spat across the passenger car.

"Sorry, sir. I missed that," Rubi said.

Dubois's hit the soldier several times across the face. One serious shot to the jaw sent his body backwards and he fell onto the bloody seat.

"Nothing. Tell the Lieutenant to keep following them. I want an update within the hour if he can manage it. He must keep me informed." Petain handed the microphone back to the radio operator who headed back the way he had come.

Petain sat down and picked up the mysterious soldier's exotic weapon. "Let's have a look at this rifle of yours. I'm sure the Grand Marshall would appreciate a weapon like this for his collection."

The soldier shifted on the seat. Still, he said nothing.

40

0900 hours, Saturday, August 15, 1942, Suriauville, Vosges Department, Vichy France

Charlotte held Maxime close to her in the side car of the railbike. The death of a child always hit the mother hard. But even Charlotte, who had lost an infant a couple of years before the roundup began, could not imagine the pain of seeing your child die arms-length from a madman with a pistol.

"Solange," Maxime said. She repeated the name, her words slurred by grief. Mucus dribbled from her nose and lips as she sobbed. *Poor, innocent Solange.*

Maxime's tears soaked through Charlotte's uniform. Her body heaved with each intake of breath. The policeman would pay for his cruelty.

Barbara drove southeast, deeper into the Vosges Mountains. The M22 assault rifles, portal containing backpacks, and C2ID2's of those who had surrendered filled the extra space in the side car. A rifle barrel dug into Charlotte's side each time the bike hit a rough patch of road. She refused to readjust to avoid disturbing Maxime's mourning.

When the trio fled, they left behind the bodies of Justine, Ester, Stephanie, and Anna, along with all of their gear. The others taken prisoner aboard the train compounded the loss. But the image of little Solange clinging to the chained man beside her, dark eyes searching for salvation, dug claws into her mind. Charlotte's vision clouded with quiet tears. *Poor, innocent, Solange.* She wiped away the moisture, hoping Maxime would not notice.

Maxime's sobs faded after an hour, leaving a shell of the former woman behind. Her eyes targeted a point somewhere beyond what Charlotte could see. Trees and service poles passed between her and the target, yet her eyes remained fixed.

Another hour passed before Charlotte activated her C2ID2 to message the other teams. Every second that passed seemed longer than the last. She prepared to send through a second message. "Give them time," Barbara said as she reached over and put a hand on Charlotte's shoulder.

Charlotte nodded. The world moved too slow around her. She started counting to herself. *To one hundred then I'll try again.*

At fifty-seven, Hiram sent a return message: "Pick up Deborah and Danette, then go to Mamirolle. Await further instructions."

"What? That's it." Charlotte needed more information. Mamirolle was the rendezvous point in the Jura Mountains, where they'd hoped to hide out until the Allies invaded, or follow Oster's route into Switzerland. She looked at Barbara. "What do we do now?"

"Can you track the train?" Barbara said. "Find out where it's headed?"

"I expect it'll go back to the camp," Charlotte said.

"Nothing to go back to," Barbara said. "Assuming the incendiary rockets did their job." Minutes after the train left Camp Vittel, Stephanie and Anna launched a fusillade of rocket-propelled firebombs into the two hotels that held all the Jews in the camp, before racing to catch-up with the rest of the teams attacking the train. Neither had survived that attack.

"They'll have to figure out how to jam their captives back into the remaining hotels," said Charlotte.

"We have to do something." Barbara said. "We can't just go to Mamirolle!"

"I don't know. Colonel Oster's plan might work before the train heads north again."

"And if it doesn't? You saw what they did to Maxime's little girl."

Charlotte stared at the red dot traveling along the tracks on the display, the path edged by forest. The view offered her no ideas. *It's just a dot.* "I don't know what to do." The train slowed as it passed through Vittel, then kept going north. "They didn't stop. I bet they go all the way back to the railyard in Pont-Saint-Vincent."

Charlotte zoomed the view out to see the train's path as it moved north toward Pont-Saint-Vincent.

"What's that?" Barbara asked, pointing to a cluster of large buildings north of Xeuilley.

Charlotte tried to remember. She hadn't ever been to Xeuilley. "Looks like an industrial complex of some sort." She maneuvered the drone to get a better look at the facility. Large cylindrical towers sat on either side of the railroad tracks, connected by enclosed bridges that she assumed contained conveyor belts. "Cement factory, maybe?"

"We could drop those on the tracks," Barbara said. "The allies destroyed the bridge in Pont-Saint-Vincent, blocking the northern route. If we block the tracks there, we trap the train between Pont-Saint-Vincent and Xeuilley."

Charlotte looked at Maxime, her expression vacant. She thought about Trembley and the other prisoners on the train. "You're right Barbara. We have to do something."

Barbara turned to Charlotte for a moment, as if she needed to validate the plan. Charlotte nodded. Barbara smiled and then started the bike up again. At the next junction in the rail line, the bike turned to the left and headed northeast.

41

1020 hours, Saturday, August 15, 1942, Lapalisse, Allier Department, Vichy France

"Team Delta, this is Hawk, over." Hiram spoke into his C2ID2 from the backseat of Locard's car. Oster sat next to him. The Colonel donned an impeccable German uniform, while Hiram wore an ill-fitting suit borrowed from Alphonse Benoit, a much larger man.

He tried to contact Delta Team again. Still no answer. After the third attempt, Hiram tried to remain calm. *Anything could have happened to them. Splitting up was a bad idea.*

"Hawk, this is Team Delta, over." Hiram jumped at the sound of Nora's voice. "I think we've got a problem. A new unit is moving through Moulins. Doesn't look like they're stopping, over."

"Team Delta, can you tell what the unit designation is, over."

"Hawk, looks like Waffen SS. We're not close enough to see unit markings, over."

"2nd Waffen SS Panzer-Grenadier Division would be my guess," Oster said. "If they're heading south from Moulins, Vichy, maybe Lyon, seems like the next logical stop. Hitler is reacting to the event in Saarbrücken. I'll wager he's planning to occupy all of France. It wouldn't surprise me if the little Austrian corporal went to Vichy himself to personally deliver the coup-de-grace to Marshall Petain."

"Then we can assume the 15th Infantry Division is headed south, towards the Mediterranean Coast." Hiram scratched his head. *There goes our invasion plan. Which leaves Oster's plan as our best shot.*

"Team Delta, track the Waffen SS unit from a safe distance with your drone. Report back when they reach Vichy. Or, if they stop before then. Hawk out." *I sure as hell hope they stop.*

Turning to Locard, he said, "Find a safe place to park off the road. I need to make another radio call. I can't do it from the car."

"Don't trust us yet?" Oster said, peering over the back of the seat.

Hiram looked at Oster, not answering. Trust was a hard thing to sell. Locard defied the French police, Oster the German army. He wanted to trust them, but he'd read too many documents about spies and double agents to assume men who turned on their own wouldn't turn on him.

Oster put his hands up and sat back in his seat. "I understand. I suppose I wouldn't trust me either."

Locard turned left off the main road onto a hard-packed gravel path. At a break in the tree line, he turned left again and followed a narrow dirt track into the woods. He stopped just past a bend in the track, shut off the engine, and Hiram climbed out. He walked far enough into the woods to conceal his call from the two men in the car. He moved slowly and held on to some of the trees along the way to keep his balance on the uneven ground. The moldable cast stabilizing his ankle grew more annoying with each passing day, but it helped with the pain and stopped him from injuring himself further.

The Icarus communications drone Agnes had launched towards London reported its arrival the previous evening. He had instructed Nora, who took over responsibility for the drone when Team Delta broke off from the group, to keep the drone above the city to ensure the ability to communicate with Sarah. But Sarah's delicate position in the hands of the OSS could not be guaranteed. Trust wasn't easily bought either.

"Raven, this is Hawk, over." Hiram waited five minutes and repeated the call.

"Hawk, this is Raven, over. Good to hear your voice Hawk, over." Sarah's words muted his worry.

"How are your hosts treating you? Over."

"We're getting along fine. The mood here is tense. Everyone is waiting for news, whether good or bad. So, fill me in, over."

Hiram laid out the events of the past three days, including Rosette's and Leverette's rescue and Team Foxtrot's rendezvous with Deborah and Danette. The formality of their radio call faded, turning more conversational, each pausing between statements to ensure one didn't talk over the other.

He faltered when he started to tell her about the morning's train mishap. He had been holed up with Locard and Oster while his soldiers took a stand. Trembley had accompanied teams Echo, Foxtrot and Golf. Trembley had witnessed Justine, Ester, Stephanie and Anna dying while fighting for the lives of their families. Hiram understood why Trembley had to go in his place. Still, he carried the guilt of leaving them with the OSS man. And brave Trembley, now a prisoner of the French police, would die along with all the others on the train.

"Hawk? Are you with me?"

"Today was rough," he said. "We lost four."

"Who?"

"I don't think you should worry about that now."

"Who?" she said.

"Justine, Ester, Stephanie, and Anna."

The radio silence continued. He worried she'd disconnected, but he didn't want to say anything more.

"Did we take out at least that many?" Her voice quivered.

"And many more," he said.

"Good. Tell me the rest."

"They couldn't keep fighting," he said. "The man on the train – Locard says he is known as Captain Petain – he threatened to kill the children. They tried to call his bluff."

"Hawk?"

"Maxime's daughter was killed."

Again, the silence remained too long. "Her suffering is over." Whether she spoke of Maxime or the girl, Hiram agreed with Sarah.

"Ellen, Emma, Myriam, Isabelle, and Diane were captured. They're on the train." He considered telling her about the loss of several M22 assault rifles, four C2ID2 units, and four portals. He assumed that someone from the Allied High Command listened to their conversation, raising the possibility of a leak. Hitler had survived many a plot, some due to informants, some due to blind luck.

Hiram waited for her response, not sure if she understood the impact of what had happened. For a few seconds, he heard the crackle of the call trying to come through and thought he must have lost her.

Her words boomed out of the speaker, voice strong and willful as ever. "What's the plan? Over."

Hiram took a breath, the first that seemed full after the day's rough start. Her eagerness to move forward propelled him to focus on the next thing to be done. "Raven, inform General Eisenhower that Operation Roundup is in jeopardy. We think the German 15th Infantry Division is headed toward Toulouse and the coast, and the 2nd Waffen SS Panzer Grenadier Division is going to occupy Vichy, and maybe Lyon, the regional capital. Will advise when we have more information, over."

"Wilco, Hawk," Sarah replied. After a brief pause, she added, "Hawk, request status on Team Bravo, over."

Hiram assumed the question had come from one of Eisenhower's men. Team Bravo's mission put them in position to destroy the French fleet at Toulon. If the Allies abandoned Operation Roundup in favor of Operation Torch, initiating the invasion of North Africa, then the elimination of the fleet at Toulon would be high on Eisenhower's wish list. When Eisenhower made the call, Team Bravo would take the job, if he could reach them. "Raven, Bravo left radio range last night. Will advise when we make contact, over."

"Copy, Hawk. Anything further, over?"

"Negative Raven. Hawk, out." Hiram punched a new code into his C2ID2 and tried to raise Team Bravo for the third time that day.

Hiram returned to the car after one last attempt to communicate with the missing team. Locard and Oster leaned against the front end, a picnic basket perched on the hood between them. The French detective took a sip out of a small metal cup, then passed it to the German officer.

Locard spoke as he approached. "Glad you found your way back. Thought maybe we should send out a search party."

Oster pulled a heel of bread out of the basket. "You must try this bread. Locard's aunt makes wonderful bread."

"And cheese," said Locard as he held out an open tea towel. "Not like the rations we've been getting in town."

Hiram looked at the chunk of bread and the rough block of cheese. He had packed a few meal bars for himself and his newest accomplices just in case. After a brief pause, Hiram accepted their offer. He joined the two men leaning on the front of the car and enjoyed the unexpected meal.

After lunch, Locard drove back toward the main road. Oster sat in the front, Hiram in the back. When they reached the main road, the third brigade of the 2nd Waffen SS Panzer Grenadier Division rolled down both lanes of the highway. They looked at each other for a moment, surprised. The ground shook as Tiger tanks passed.

Oster, still in his uniform, left the car and walked to the edge of the road. Vehicle commanders saluted him as they passed, holding their stance until it looked both awkward and uncomfortable. The vehicles maintained speed. After a few minutes, Oster waved down a six-wheeled Mercedes command car. Hiram and Locard watched from the car as Oster presented his papers. He conversed with one of the officers seated in the backseat of the Mercedes.

Without warning, the officer stood up and waved a passing half-track to a halt. He pointed at Locard's car shouting something in German. The soldier on top of the huge armored vehicle swung his machine gun around to face them. Locard ducked behind the dashboard. Hiram dove to the floor. Gunfire erupted around them.

42

1200 hours, Saturday, August 15, 1942, Pont-Saint-Vincent, Meurthe-et-Moselle Department, Vichy France

"Enough," Petain said. He regarded the bloodied American, his face a swollen mess. "When we stop, fetch one of his dogs. We'll see if he's willing to talk then." The train rolled into the railyard at Pont-Saint-Vincent, seventy-kilometers north of the ambush point. It had taken several hours to complete the move. The damage to the boiler controls during the attack, the need to travel down the tracks in reverse, and the limited skills of the two surviving railway men had contributed to the long ride. He expected a repair team and replacement engine crew to arrive within the hour. A team of railway workers, dispatched from a nearby office, headed back toward Suriauville with a heavy guard, to fix the tracks.

"Sir, I have Miss Brodeur on the radio with an update from Lieutenant Lebeau."

Petain snatched the microphone from his radio operator and said, "Rubi, give me something useful."

"Sir, the Lieutenant says they followed Locard and the others to Lapalisse in the Allier Department. They pulled off onto a side road. By the time they came back out, a Waffen SS column blocked the main road. He says the German officer got out and talked to-."

"What is a Waffen SS column doing in Lapalisse?"

"Sorry, sir. I assumed you'd heard."

"Heard what?" he demanded.

"The Germans have moved into Vichy. Marshall Petain has been detained. I received a call an hour ago from his assistant. She must not have been in the office when they showed up for the Marshall. Says she heard some of the soldiers outside talking about a column in Lapalisse heading towards Lyon." She hesitated, "And sir, another Infantry Division is en route to Toulouse." Petain could almost hear the tears running down Rubi's cheeks. Southern France had so far avoided the depravation and most of the horrors of the Nazi occupation. It seemed their respite would end. "When do you think they'll be coming here?"

Why have the Germans suddenly decided to occupy southern France? If they've arrested my uncle, what does that mean for his relatives, especially me and my family?

"Listen to me. We need more information," he said. "Call the station chiefs in Lyon, Toulouse, and Avignon. Find out what they know. Keep it brief." Petain paused to let her write that down.

"Yes, sir," she said. "Should I warn them?"

"No reason to incite panic without the facts. Now, tell me the rest of Lebeau's report."

"He said the German officer travelling with Locard got out and spoke to an SS officer in the column. The Germans fired a heavy machine gun at Locard's car, which exploded. Lebeau believes Locard, the German officer, and the other man in Locard's car to be dead. Sounds like three casualties in the German command car as well. He's requesting further instructions."

"Send him to Brugheas to pick up the Bertrand woman's husband. I'll meet him in Lapalisse. I want to see the site myself."

He waited for Rubi to pass along Lebeau's acknowledgement of his orders and broke the connection.

He turned to Dubois. "Sergeant, once we stop, send someone out to find a truck."

"Sir, I don't think we have any resources in the area."

Petain stared at Dubois for a moment, not willing to state the obvious. "Once you've secured transportation, load up the equipment we confiscated from the prisoners. I'm taking a team to Vichy. I need you to stay here with the rest of the men and guard the prisoners until the train is ready to move."

The Sergeant acknowledged the order and Petain dismissed him. *Maybe I can make some new friends. I'm going to need them.*

The American sat leaning against the wall of the boxcar. Petain sat down near him on the blood-spattered bench. "How did you do it?"

He said nothing, but the corners of his swollen mouth turned up a little. For a moment, Petain considered peeling the man's skin away from his bones with a dull knife, anything to make him scream.

Petain leaned over toward him. "Your women are all going to die. If I need to break every last one of them with these two hands, I will. And, you won't be able to stop me."

The prisoner smiled, teeth bloody.

"Sir," Dubois pushed one of the Yank's dogs into the car. "What should I do with her?"

Petain had forgotten about his earlier request. But, he mused, she might do more talking than the Yank. "You can start by getting her out of that uniform. She looks like a man." Petain put his pistol back in its holster.

"Sir?" Dubois asked.

"Dogs don't wear clothes," he said. "After that, she's yours. Do what you want with her. Maybe you can get some information out of her."

Dubois pulled out a field knife, but the blonde woman put her hands up. "I'll do it," she said. Although speckled with mud and dirt, the woman reminded Petain of a much younger version of his wife. Pale skin, deep blue eyes that begged for his attention. She opened the neckline of her uniform, the swell of her breasts peeking out in the dim cabin.

"What's your name?" Petain asked her.

"Emma." She pushed the fabric off her shoulder. "Emma Rosecrans."

On other occasions, he might have enjoyed this one. "Don't let her out of your sight," Petain told his second.

Dubois nodded and shifted his attention back to the woman.

Petain peered out the window, expecting to see a replacement engineer and engine repair crew. A single man, dressed more like a dispatcher than a mechanic, awaited them.

"Not another problem," said Petain. "Dubois, get whatever you can out of this dog and then dispose of her. Make sure he see's everything. Oh, and one more thing, make sure she screams loud enough for the others to hear." Petain glanced coldly at his nemesis laying battered on the seat. "I'm glad I didn't kill you earlier; I wouldn't want you to miss this." He turned and walked out, smiling as he heard the first blow hit the nearly naked woman.

"Where are my mechanics and engineers?" Petain yelled at the railway man as he disembarked.

"I'm very sorry sir," the railroad man said, taking his hat off. "The partisans have blown up the cement plant in Xeuilley. The rail line is blocked in both directions until we remove the debris."

Petain closed his eyes, tired from the day's unfortunate turn. From inside the passenger car he heard the first of the screams. When he opened his eyes, the dispatcher remained. "Get on with it, then."

"Sir." The railroad man put his hat back on as he left.

43

A temporal artifact of May 6, 2050

Hiram wriggled through the portal in his pack as a barrage of machine gun rounds pierced Locard's car. He landed hands-first on the floor of the pod and rolled, a maneuver he'd practiced hundreds of times. Somehow his left foot hit the floor as hard as the rest of him, reawakening the pain of his ankle injury.

"Fucking bastard!" Hiram punched the door to one of the storage cabinets. *I never should have trusted Oster.* He hit the door again, leaving a dent this time. His knuckles burned from the impact. *Probably thought having my M22 would swing the war in Germany's favor. Or maybe the SS bastard suspected something and ordered the attack on his own. Doesn't matter now.*

And Locard? If the German MG 34 machine gun rounds that ripped through the hull of the oversized car hadn't cut through the detective, the satchel charge Hiram pulled from the wall of the pod and pitched through the active portal finished the job. The outward blast of the ten kilo C4 charge would have obliterated both Locard and Oster, along with the M22 and backpack. *Now what?*

He punched the compartment door again. This time it swung open. The edge of the wooden box his father had given him all those years ago sat inside. Memories of his family – past, present, and now future – sat inside. Their imagined doubt and judgment gnawed at him, magnifying his dark mood.

Every scenario for saving the families of the women he had rescued seemed impossible now. He could take Rosette, little Leverette, Deborah, and Danette, and as many as of the other women willing to leave their loved ones behind and make a break for the Swiss border. Sarah's contacts provided a means for passage to London. Operations Torch and Overlord could certainly benefit from Hiram's nukes, but it would still be months before the Allies managed to mount a European invasion. *Too late to save the families.*

Besides, Barbara would never agree to leave. And, she would round up anyone else willing to stay behind and continue fighting. He suspected they would all stay and fight. Deborah would be at the front of the line – right beside Barbara – encouraging the others to put up a fight regardless of the consequences, her refusal to accept defeat acting as a torch for the others to follow. He smiled. Even he would follow her.

Five hours later, his C2ID2 chimed. A dull, consistent ache had settled into his head. The throbbing in his injured ankle had once again intensified. His knuckles had transitioned into a tender, purple black, from where they had come in contact with the compartment door. He wondered if his body would ever be the same again after this continued and repeated torture inside the pod. His cells were dying, and he was not familiar enough with the equations to determine how long he'd need to avoid the pod to get back to normal. Whether or not he had a plan, the pod no longer provided a safe haven. He brushed past the open storage door and prepared for a daylight jump through the aerial portal. *Hopefully the Germans have left the area.*

Hiram dropped a surveillance drone through the aerial portal. It took the little aircraft a moment to stabilize. Then, as instructed, the drone began a slow downward spiral centered on the burned-out wreckage of Locard's car. The military convoy was gone. The command vehicle lay off to the northern side of the road, as charred and mangled as the dead inspector's car. Further east, a grey Citroën Traction Avant sat in the shade of several pine trees that bordered the road. He sent the drone in for a closer look.

One man leaned against the car's right front fender, a cigarette between his lips. Inside the car, one man sat behind the wheel and a second in the back seat. The smoker opened the back door of the sedan and the rear seat passenger made an awkward advance toward the outside in dark slacks and an untucked, white undershirt. As the smoker assisted him, Hiram noticed the man's hands cuffed behind his back. He was led into the trees. *Either they're going to let him take a piss or they plan to shoot him.*

After a few minutes, both men emerged from the woods. The smoker forced the prisoner to take a seat on the ground near the car. Hiram zoomed in on his face. *Well, that can't be a coincidence!*

Hiram recognized the prisoner as Garon Bertrand, Rosette's husband. Rosette had once shown him a picture of the family in happier times, back before the man had turned his own family over to the French police. His current wary appearance seemed crafted out of annoyance more than fear. He could only speculate on the policemen's interest in Garon. *Had he and Locard been followed?* He hadn't noticed a tail, but he hadn't been really looking for one. Without mirrors to see behind the vehicle, it would have been difficult to spot a tail from the backseat. Perhaps the sniveling dog of a man had made a deal with the police. That didn't explain the handcuffs, however.

Another chime from the C2ID2 reminded him that he needed to get out of the pod and back to the real world.

* * *

1610 hours, Saturday, August 15, 1942, Lapalisse, Allier Department, Vichy France

Hiram dropped through the aerial portal into France five thousand meters above Garon Bertrand and his captors. He angled the wingsuit to land in a clearing near where he'd eaten fresh bread and homemade cheese with Oster and Locard. He managed a rather gentle landing though his ankle felt as though it folded beneath him despite the support of the cast. The sudden, intense pain made his eyes water and he clenched his teeth to avoid screaming. He could not afford to announce his position. He shed the wingsuit and stuffed the fabric into a thick patch of brush out of sight. He contacted Teams Charlie and Delta on the C2ID2. "Meet me in Mamirolle, over."

Once each team responded, he headed towards the men in the Citroën. Dry branches and leaves crackled beneath his feet as he crept through the woods. He sent the little recon robot in close enough to pick up the conversation between the three men in the car.

"How much longer?" the driver asked. "We've been here for hours."

The smoker said, "I don't know. With the German column hogging the road, delays are inevitable." He blew a stream of smoke upward into the air, not seeming to mind the afternoon break.

"Why am I here?" Bertrand demanded. "I've done nothing wrong! Turned in my wife just as soon as she showed up. I even turned in her Jew whelps."

"Following Captain Petain's orders. He said to pick you up, and that's what we did," the smoker said. "He'll be here soon enough. You can ask him directly. For now, shut up and sit still."

The name went off like a firecracker in Hiram's head. He clenched his fists, sending his fingernails biting into his palm. Captain Petain had shot little Solange. Charlotte's report about the girl's death during the assault on the death train had been quite clear. And according to the late Inspector Locard, Captain Petain had initiated the search for Hiram and his team of escaped prisoners. Petain needed to pay. This time, Hiram would be prepared. He deployed four combat robots.

44

2200 hours, Saturday, August 15, 1942, Lapalisse, Allier Department, Vichy France

Louis Petain cursed the darkness. With only the blackout lights to lead the way, the truck made slow progress across the Allier Department. He understood the restriction and wanted to avoid drawing an Allied night fighter or dive bomber down on them, but every moment of delay allowed the situation in Vichy to spiral further out of control.

"There sir." Corporal Chabot pointed to a sedan parked just off the road up ahead, a few meters from a blackened pile of twisted metal.

"Pull over." Petain looked forward to riding the rest of the way in Lieutenant Lebeau's Citroën. His body complained about the long, bumpy ride in the truck. As Chabot brought the vehicle to a halt, Petain opened his door. He climbed out, ran his hands over his wind tousled hair, and considered stretching to work out the irritating stiffness in his back. He could not afford any more delay and instead approached Lebeau.

"What do you have to report?" he said, without waiting for the man's salute.

"Sir," the lieutenant said, snapping to attention. "Inspector Locard and his companions encountered the military convoy at this intersection. I'm not exactly sure what happened. The German officer travelling with the Inspector got out of the car and waved down a command car. A few minutes later the Colonel – I think he was a Colonel, hard to tell from where we were watching-," Lebeau said.

"I don't have time for this," Petain growled.

"Sorry sir," Lebeau continued. "The Colonel said something to the commander of a passing halftrack. The halftrack opened fire on Locard's car." He nodded toward the nearby debris. "Sprayed bullets all over the damn thing. A few seconds later the car blew up. Hell of an explosion, sir. Destroyed the Inspector's car. Killed the Germans in and around the SS command car. What do you think they were carrying?"

"You don't know who was with Locard? And you don't know why the SS opened fire on them?"

"Correct, sir."

"What do you know Lebeau?"

"Sir, there is one thing." Lebeau took his hat off. "They pulled a body from the wreckage of the Inspector's car. I'm pretty sure it was Locard."

"And the other man in the car?"

Lebeau shrugged.

"We can hope he was blown to bits," Petain said.

"Well sir." Lebeau worked the brim of his hat through his hands. "I've seen a lot of explosions since the war began. German. Allied. Partisans. We always find some fragment of the deceased. An arm or a leg. Always something. I don't know how it's possible, but I think the third man escaped somehow."

"You should probably leave the thinking-." Petain cut himself off, realizing that Lebeau's assessment was accurate. *If the third man escaped, where did he go?*

"Did you search the area?" Petain asked.

Lebeau nodded. "The SS did a pretty thorough search themselves. They questioned us, demanded to see our papers. I told them we were following up on information regarding Jews hiding in the area, showed them that list of names we've been carrying around, told him we arrested Bertrand on suspicion of harboring Jews. When they left, we searched again, didn't find any evidence of him."

Should I have my team search the area again? The men had climbed down out of the truck. They milled around the scene. He noticed a few men taking the time to stretch. Their lackadaisical movements irritated him and he considered throwing orders at them. He looked up at the sliver of a moon. It shed little light on the landscape. It would be a waste of time to send his men out into the woods in the dark.

He looked at the man seated on the ground. "Is this Ber-." Lebeau suddenly pitched forward into Petain's arms. He felt wetness on his face, tasted blood. Whirring filled the air around him, like nothing he had heard before. "Take cover!"

He watched as his men danced, arms flailing and bodies contorting. Ten seconds later, the sound ceased and his men lay still on the ground, twisted into odd poses. Wet blotches spread out over their clothing.

Something moved in the darkness behind him. He spun at the sound, drawing his sidearm as he turned. He emptied the pistol into the shadows, but the thing kept coming. Whatever it was, it wasn't human. Louis Petain turned away from the thing, fled into the darkness.

A man appeared in front of him holding out a strange device.

"Get out of my way," Petain growled as he kept running. *Nothing is going to stop me from getting out of here.*

The device lit up and a strange, yet painful burning sensation exploded in his chest. Every muscle throughout his body tightened. Then, he was falling. He tried to adjust his uncooperative feet, tried to throw his arms out to help with balance. He kept falling. Petain's head collided with something solid on the ground and all at once the seizing stopped.

* * *

Once Petain was securely shackled, Hiram dragged him into the back seat of the Citroën. His training dictated that he do a thorough inspection and sanitization of the site, but his pounding head said otherwise. After dumping the bodies of the dead policemen into a pod, he slipped into the driver's seat and put the car in gear.

* * *

Petain regained consciousness sometime later. The back of his head ached. Soreness radiated from his chest as if the entire front of his torso had survived a severe muscle cramp. He was in the backseat of a car that bumped along much too fast for his complaining head or the blackout conditions. He reached up to touch the aching place on his head. His hands moved no higher than his chest. He was shackled, hand and foot. After a moment, he noticed the man sitting next to him. He rustled the chains, testing their hold. The other man turned to him, eyes wide, terrified.

The driver glanced back over the seat. Petain jumped at the sight of the man's monstrous face before he realized it was just a man in a mask and a pair of goggles.

"Who are you?" Petain asked.

The man in the goggles placed his right arm on the back of the front seat, a dull glow radiated from the man's oversized watch. He spoke in what Petain guessed to be Hebrew. He had heard a rabbi speak in a similar tongue during the roundup as unheard prayers (or whatever the Jews called them) for the safety of his people poured out of him. Petain did not understand. He might as well have been talking in gibberish.

As the man's words ended, a second voice – female – answered in French. "Hiram Halphen. I hear you've been searching for me these past few weeks. Now you've found me, Captain Petain." The voice seemed to emanate from the mechanism on the man's wrist.

"How are you doing that?" Petain's curiosity outweighed his fear.

The man spoke in the Jewish tongue again.

"Magic," the female voice said.

Petain figured it might not be healthy to push for further explanation. "Where are you taking me?"

"To the Jura Mountains. Prepare for a heartfelt reunion between Monsieur Bertrand and his loving wife," Halphen said.

Bertrand whimpered.

"And to allow you to make the acquaintance of Maxime Bisset. You killed her little girl Solange yesterday. I'm sure they'll be thrilled to see you both. I suspect you know both Rosette and Maxime have become quite handy with a multitude of weapons."

If the man driving the car so recklessly was the mystery man Petain had been pursuing, then who did he have imprisoned on board the train? Was it his subordinate, or his superior? More information was needed. "I was following orders," Petain said. "The Germans are running things in France these days."

"Save it. I've seen Reichsführer Himmler's order. The French police were only to arrest Jewish adults. Not children or mothers with young children. You killed a four-year-old girl because you're a monster. Don't blame your cruelty on orders."

"A casualty of war. Look, I can help you, all of you," Petain said.

"How can you possibly help me?" Halphen asked.

"The families on the train, my men hold their documents. I can get them released." Halphen turned and looked at him for a moment, then returned his eyes to the road. "I'm Chief of Police for the Pyrénées-Orientales

192

Department. Camp Joffre resides within my jurisdiction. I can have them returned to the camp, then released."

The man appeared as though he considered the offer.

"Perhaps you could steal another ship," Petain said.

45

0610 hours, Sunday, August 16, 1942, Corgoloin, Côte-d'Or Department, Vichy France

Hiram approached the railway station near the center of town in Corgoloin. The station agent inside had access to a telephone. Hiram, dressed in Alphonse Benoit's oversized suit, followed Petain into the two-story plasterwork building that served as both ticket booth and newsstand.

The pain in Hiram's ankle had crawled up to his knee and settled with such intensity that Hiram doubted he'd have been able to catch the captain if he decided to run. He had managed to sneak a few painkillers in on the trip to the train station. As he fought to keep his composure, he'd have sworn the little white pills were nothing more than candy.

A single wooden bench sat against the building beneath a weathered awning. Hiram and Petain were the only visitors to the station this early on a Sunday morning. Garon Bertrand waited, gagged and shackled, in the trunk of Lebeau's Citroën. Hiram's right hand remained in his pocket holding a nine-millimeter pistol aimed at Petain's back.

"I need to use your phone." Petain flashed his badge at the station agent. The agent picked up the ancient device. He guided the cord and placed the contraption on the counter. He stood, watching Petain, waiting for him to make his call.

"Police business. Go have a smoke," Petain said. The agent hesitated, looked at Hiram, then stepped out the back door of the station. Hiram listened as Petain made contact with the first two operators before connecting with his office in Perpignan. Hiram held the Babel Fish receiver near Petain's right ear and set it to text mode. The C2ID2 translated the conversation, providing an onscreen view in Hebrew text. Hiram pressed the pistol into Petain's ribs, a not-too-subtle reminder of his promise to end Petain's life if he drifted from the script they had rehearsed in the car on the way to Corgoloin.

"Perpignan Station, Miss Brodeur speaking."

"Rubi, you're in early," Petain said.

"Yes, sir. I thought with everything going on, it was best to get an early start."

"Listen Rubi. The railway system is all messed up. I want you to issue orders to the Commandant at Camp Joffre in my name. He is to send thirty trucks to the railyard at Pont-Saint-Vincent to pick up the prisoners on the train. I'll meet the convoy with my men. I've got plenty of men to provide sufficient coverage. We just need the trucks. Got that?"

"Yes, sir. Should I contact Sergeant DuBois and let him know what's happening?"

Petain looked at Hiram.

Hiram shook his head. Sweat slipped into his eyes.

"No. I'll take care of that myself. And Rubi, let's try to keep this as quiet as possible, understand?"

"Yes, sir. Anything else?"

"No, that's all. I'll call you back later this afternoon. I'll need an estimated time of arrival for the trucks." Petain hung up without saying goodbye, then looked at Hiram.

"Let's go." Hiram followed Petain out the door. The station agent rushed back to his post as Hiram and Petain passed on the way back to the parking lot. A few minutes later, the Citroën pulled out of the lot, Petain behind the wheel. He'd find a secluded spot to shackle him up later. First, they needed to stop for petrol.

* * *

1100 hours, Sunday, August 16, Mamirolle, Doubs Department, Vichy France

The grey Citroën turned right off the main road south of Mamirolle and onto a dirt road headed into the hills, Hiram at the wheel. Bertrand had been allowed out of the trunk as the temperature climbed to 30°C and now sat beside Petain in the back seat, both hooded. The road sloped upward through a pine forest and ended at the front door of an abandoned farmhouse. Fields overgrown with weeds surrounded the house. The French civilians that once lived here had fled during the initial German invasion. Many homes in the so-called Zone of German Settlement had been left behind. The Nazis prevented their return, intending to open the area up to settlement by ethnic Germans, but few Aryans opted to move west.

The C2ID2 message he sent to the women waiting in the abandoned farmhouse had been short with no more than a description of the car and his approximate arrival time. As he turned off the engine, Rosette stepped out of the farmhouse door with Leverette at her side.

Barbara and Charlotte emerged from the shadows at opposite corners of the barn, M22's in hand. Maxime was nowhere in sight, and Teams Charlie and Delta had not yet arrived. Hiram opened the door of the car and began to climb out. As he stood, Deborah threw her arms around him and almost pushed him back into the driver's seat. He clenched his teeth as he tried to steady himself on his good leg. She pulled away for a moment, but Hiram drew her back to him. He kissed her and pulled her in tight against him once more. Relief filled the gaping void that had been left in his chest since the mess in Saarbrücken.

When Hiram opened his eyes again, Danette had joined them, standing behind Deborah. Her smile – Rachel's smile – was almost too much to bear. Deborah released him and he turned to hug his great-great-grandmother.

"I never thought I'd see you two again," he said.

"After the bomb went off, we thought we'd lost you," Deborah said.

"Until we saw the drone in the mountains," Danette added, Deborah translating.

Hiram held his right index finger up to his lips, pointed to the two men inside the car. Both Bertrand and Petain now sat in the back seat, each sporting a black hood he had pulled from Jacob's Mossad-equipped pod. Barbara, Danette, and Deborah moved to surround the car.

"Who's this?" Barbara nodded toward the two prisoners. Deborah translated.

"I've got a plan," Hiram said. "Where's Maxime?"

"Asleep in an upstairs bedroom." Charlotte used her M22 to point to the leftmost window on the second floor of the farmhouse. "I gave her a pretty heavy dose of the sedative in the medkit. Valium, I think." Deborah repeated her words in Hebrew. "She'll be out for a while."

Hiram opened the right rear door of the sedan and dragged the thinner of his two captives out of the car. He forced Bertrand to his knees facing the house. He wanted to get Bertrand back to Rosette alive. He'd leave it up to her to address his punishment.

"Papa!" Leverette yelled when Hiram pulled the hood off. Too young to understand his father's betrayal, he broke loose from his mother's grip and ran toward his father. Rosette retreated into the house.

Garon lifted his cuffed hands above the boy to let him in closer. He looked down at the boy and then back at Hiram.

"Papa, papa." The boy said a few more words and Garon responded before kissing him on the forehead. Garon acted happy to see his boy.

Rosette emerged from the house. She addressed Charlotte.

Charlotte said something to the little boy about a biscuit and he took her hand. They walked away from the house together, the boy jumping over sticks along the way.

Rosette held a knife. "Down to the root cellar, please." As she moved closer to the man on the ground, Hiram recognized the military issued can of clotting foam in her other hand.

Garon caught sight of his wife, began to plead with her.

Rosette spoke to Garon in a calm, almost motherly tone. Hiram did not understand her words. She was not a murderer, but he supposed for Garon she might make an exception.

Garon's pleading had no impact. He looked to the other women, eyes wide and begging for reprieve. When no one stepped up to assist, he tried to calm himself.

"Shhh," Rosette put a finger to her lips. "No more worries, my husband. We're just going to make sure you don't ever have any more children you're not prepared to give your life for."

Barbara helped the man to his feet. She pointed her M22 toward him.

Garon's eyes watered. His lips quivered. Rosette, on the other end of the spectrum, seemed serene.

Barbara and Rosette disappeared behind the house with Garon between them. A few seconds later Hiram heard the cellar door slam shut.

Hiram looked away. The man in the cellar screamed. He hoped his other prisoner listened.

After a few minutes, Danette walked up beside him, said something in French. "What about the other one?" Deborah translated

"We need him alive for a while longer for my plan to work."

"What plan?"

"The plan to save the families on that train."

"Who is he?" she demanded.

"Pull him out of the car." He limped after her as she rounded the sedan and opened the left rear door, drew his Taser in case Petain tried to make a run for it.

Petain climbed out of the car, he stood without moving. Hiram reached out with his free hand and pulled the hood off the man's head.

"Capitaine Petain?" Danette said.

Deborah crossed her arms and leaned back against the car. "How in hell did you capture him?"

A muffled scream escaped the root cellar. They turned toward the noise. Petain looked from Hiram and around at the other women, worried.

Hiram slid the hood back on their captive and shoved him into the car. They needed him for a bit longer. Hiram hoped Maxime would get her chance for revenge.

* * *

1300 hours, Sunday, August 16, Mamirolle, Doubs Department, Vichy France

Teams Charlie and Delta arrived and stood guard around the farm. Hiram gathered his surviving team leaders, Barbara, Charlotte, Nora and Irene, in the barn. Deborah and Danette stood with Hiram. Maxime continued to sleep in the upstairs bedroom. He planned to go check on her after the briefing. Denise watched over Petain, ensuring he remained in place in the back seat of Lebeau's sedan and protected from other members of their party who wished him harm.

Charlotte walked beside Leverette as he picked wild flowers at the edge of the overgrown field, his occasional laughter a ray of light in the shadow that loomed over the farm. The boy remained oblivious to the well-deserved horrors his father suffered at the hands of his mother. Hiram wondered what Rosette would tell her son when he asked about his father. For now, Garon Bertrand was in the root cellar with his wife, his current status unknown.

Hiram briefed the team leaders on the events in Lapalisse and the German decision to occupy southern France. The acceleration of the operation put them all in more danger.

Barbara stared out the open door at the Citroën. Hiram expected her to make quick work of destroying the Police Captain if she wasn't kept under watch.

"Listen, we need to focus on getting the families to safety," he said. Deborah translated. "You can do whatever the hell you want to Petain afterward. We need him alive and cooperating for the next couple of days."

"Hiram's right," Charlotte said to Barbara.

"If he can help us save our families, he can draw a few more breaths," Barbara said. "When it's done, I plan to gut him like a fish."

Deborah translated for Hiram. Part of him wished he didn't always know what his soldiers said.

Charlotte turned to Hiram. "What's your plan?"

"Thirty trucks have been dispatched from Rivesaltes to Pont-Saint-Vincent to pick up the prisoners and return them to Camp Joffre," he said. "I don't think Petain's communication with his assistant raised any warning. We should expect the trucks to arrive with drivers, but no additional guards."

Deborah continued to translate before adding, "How can you be sure?"

"I can't, so we'll take no chances. Teams Charlie and Delta will set up in the hills west of the railyard to provide cover fire if it's needed." He called up the overhead drone view of the railyard on his C2ID2 display and pointed out the steep hillside he meant. Several houses rested on the hillside, and along the west side of the railyard, but like almost every other town in the Zone, he assumed they had been abandoned. "It'll be dark, so be sure to have your NVGs. Petain can get the five of us past the railyard perimeter guard." He pointed out the guard stations on the display. "We'll drive to the spur where the train parked. Once we get in position, Petain will gather his men together. We disarm them and herd them into one of the boxcars. Take out anyone who refuses to cooperate."

"Do you think he'll betray his men so easily?" Irene said as she nodded in Petain's direction.

"Petain is looking for the best outcome for Petain. If he thinks it'll save his own hide, he'll sacrifice theirs."

"What happens next?" Irene said.

"When the trucks arrive, we take the drivers hostage. Take them out if you need to. Then, we load every one of the prisoners up and drive out of there," said Hiram.

"Where do we go?" Nora asked.

"Head back this way. We keep going all the way to the Swiss border.

Petain's credentials should get us as far as Besançon without raising too many questions." Hiram pointed out the city ten kilometers north of Mamirolle, at the edge of the mountains. "The border is heavily defended, but if we attack at night, using our night vision scopes, we have a chance. We can arm some of the prisoners on the train as well. And I can jam the guard's radio transmissions so they can't call for help."

He waited for Deborah to finish translating for the group.

"Can I make a suggestion?" Charlotte said.

"Of course."

"I noticed an old style-, current style I mean, HF radio in the Citroën. I assume it's Petain's?"

Hiram watched Deborah as she repeated Charlotte's words. He nodded.

"Can Petain send his men off on some wild goose chase?" Charlotte said.

"They think he's in Vichy, right?" Danette said.

Deborah interpreted and Hiram nodded again.

"Petain can order them to join him in Vichy. Tell them they're getting some type of reward for turning our equipment over to the government."

"It might work," Hiram said.

"What time do we expect the trucks to arrive?" Deborah asked. "How much time do we have to prepare?"

Hiram shrugged. "I'm not certain. Petain told his assistant he would call her back this afternoon, once the Commandant at Camp Joffre had time to organize the convoy."

"Well, I guess it's a good thing we didn't kill him yet," Barbara said.

With no further input from his soldiers, Hiram sent them off to prepare for the mission. Deborah lingered behind.

"We need to cover two hundred kilometers, but the convoy has a lot further to go," he said. What if we-." His C2ID2 squawked.

"Hawk, this is Raven, over." Three seconds later Sarah's voice came over the comm.

"Raven, this is Hawk, over."

"Hawk, we've been contacted by Falcon." Falcon was Trembley's codename and, the last he heard, Trembley was on the train with the rest of the prisoners. "He reports that the train with the prisoners is still in the railyard in Pont-Saint-Vincent with a guard of approximately thirty men, over."

"Raven, Falcon was captured. I think you're being set up, over."

"Hawk, the two OSS officers standing here with me say he used all the proper code words. No reason to think he's under duress. He seems to have made some new friends, over."

"Raven, did you say friends? Over."

"Local resistance fighters. He's been in contact using one of their HF radios. Looks legitimate from here, over."

"Roger, Raven. Send me Falcon's operating frequency, over." Once he had the frequency, Hiram ended the transmission.

Deborah unbuttoned the top two buttons of her uniform. "You were saying?" He caught a glimpse of the inside edge of her breast.

"Not here," Hiram said. Not with the bustle of the camp preparing for battle. "Bit of a buzz kill."

"The woods then," she said. She undid another button, opened her uniform more, before heading toward the woods.

Hiram started to limp out of the barn after her. She was less than two meters from him, yet he held on to the frame of the barn door afraid he'd collapse if he took another step. He wanted to be with her, to feel her in his arms, to sense the warmth of her skin against his even in the summer heat. His body would not comply. "I can't. I-"

"Hiram? What's wrong?" She turned and walked back to him. "You don't look so good." She put an arm around him and guided him to a bench inside the barn.

"Yesterday, things didn't go as planned. The pod was the only place I could go. I think I spent too long inside. I need a place to rest, just for a few hours."

She nodded. "I know just the place."

46

0300 hours, Monday, August 17, 1942, Pont Saint Vincent, Meurthe-et-Moselle Department, Vichy France

Hiram, Deborah, and Teams Charlie and Delta arrived in the hills above the railyard with time to spare. Hiram left Danette, Rosette, and Leverette at the abandoned farm in the Jura Mountains, though Danette put up a fuss about being left behind. Hiram insisted he didn't want the others involved if a firefight developed. "Someone needs to watch over them," he had told her. He would have left Deborah behind with them as well, but he preferred her translations to the Babel Fish's and she was the only one he trusted in his current state.

Deborah, awaiting his return, had found one of Hiram's blackout tents. She had set the small dome up in the woods behind the house with every intention of providing Hiram a homecoming gift, though she had been the one to come back to him after so long away. Instead, she lay beside him as he drifted off into a near coma. When he had finally woken, nearly seven hours later, she was still there and Hiram told her about Hagar's Curse.

Charlotte and Denise moved toward the edge of a stand of trees that stopped atop the crest of the hill. They could observe most of the railyard with their night vision scopes. Nora and Irene launched surveillance drones. Nora's flew west in search of any approaching threats. Irene sent hers southward along the road toward Dijon and spotted the convoy of trucks from Camp Joffre. Under blackout conditions, the trucks still had more than two hours travel to reach the railyard. Irene brought the drone in as low as she dared, counting heat signatures with the thermal camera. Except for the lead truck, which carried two men, she detected a single occupant in the remaining vehicles. The Commandant had followed Petain's instructions. Hiram smiled.

He limped to the edge of the woods, Deborah at his side. They settled in beside Charlotte. He rubbed his sore, swollen ankle. "What do you see?"

"Five men patrol the train at all times." Charlotte paused to let Deborah translate. "None of them wearing police uniforms. We counted ten fixed posts around the railyard, including the two men up there." She pointed to the dispatcher's tower.

Satisfied with her assessment, Hiram activated the HF radio and set it to the frequency Sarah had given him.

"Falcon, this is Hawk, over."

"Hawk, this is Falcon, over."

"Falcon, what is your location? Over."

"Hawk, I'm about two hundred meters up the ridge west of the railyard, over."

"Falcon, I'll join you at your location. Do you need anything? Food? Water? Over." He gave Trembley one last chance to use one of the duress codes, "doughnut" or "burger."

"Negative Hawk. We'll be expecting you. Falcon out."

Hiram led Deborah and Team Delta south toward Trembley's location, leaving Charlotte, Barbara, and Team Charlie in place to keep an eye on the railyard below. The women carried heavy loads of extra weapons and ammo intended for Trembley's partisans. They climbed down the wooded hillside, out of sight of the policemen standing guard, in a travelling overwatch formation, trailing team ready to support those in front if Trembley had been compromised. They crossed a stream flanked by heavy brush and climbed the wooded ridge. Everyone on the team panted as they reached the crest, Deborah more than most, as she assisted Hiram and his worsening ankle.

A familiar, American voice called out "Napoleon." Hiram almost laughed at the sound of it. He had established the challenge and password before the teams set out for the original attack on the train. It seemed like a lifetime ago. Today's challenge, he remembered, was Napoleon.

Hiram responded "Waterloo."

Trembley, accompanied by three French Partisan soldiers, emerged from the woods. Hiram observed his slow, painful steps. As he moved closer, the moonlight illuminated his battered and bruised face.

"Boy am I glad to see you," Trembley said in English. He greeted Deborah and Team Delta in a similar manner.

"What happed to your face?" Hiram asked.

"You should see the other guy," the American said.

"We have his boss, about four hundred yards that way. He's being helpful. Seems to want to save more than just his pretty face."

Trembley shrugged it off. "I'll be fine now that I can see out of both eyes again. Could use a couple aspirin, though."

Hiram fished two ibuprofen tablets out of his first aid kit and handed them to Trembley.

"Take these," Hiram said. "Much more effective than aspirin and they won't fuzz your thinking like something stronger."

"Thanks." Trembley swallowed the pills with a swig of water from a canteen Nora offered.

"How did you escape?" Hiram asked.

"Emma was brought into the passenger car, to be tortured in front of me by DuBois, Petain's number two. He was the one who roughed me up." Trembley smiled, revealing the gap where two teeth were missing on the left side of his jaw. "Petain left to find out what the hold-up was. The second Petain stepped onto the ground, Emma kicked DuBois in the family jewels, then broke his neck. Impressive, truly. She freed my restraints, stomped on the dead man's face and let out a couple god-awful screams. I'm sure Petain thought his henchman was doing his job. We slipped out of the front of the passenger car and into the woods before they sent anyone to check on us. Then we ran into these fine fellows casing the railyard for an attack." Trembley turned and motioned the partisans forward.

"Where is Emma now?" asked Hiram.

"She is monitoring the activity in the rest of the train along with members of the resistance, just in case DuBois's body is discovered. I fear the other men might decide to start hurting the passengers or the others from our Team."

Hiram, Deborah, Nora, Catherine, Pauline, and Simone followed Trembley and the men into the French Partisan encampment. Twelve well-armed men pointed weapons at them until the one Hiram guessed to be the leader approached.

Trembley touched the man's shoulder. "Monsieur Rene Donath I'd like you to meet Hiram Halphen."

Donath nodded, shook Hiram's hand, and the introductions continued. The women who had accompanied Hiram fell into quiet conversation with the French Partisans, whose attention seemed drawn to the advanced weapons they carried.

Donath and Trembley said a few more words before laughter erupted between them. Trembley made friends with ease.

Trembley, Donath, Deborah, and Hiram discussed the guard detail around the railyard. Trembley translated. Charlotte's numbers came in a little shy, but Hiram suspected Donath's men might be the kind who overestimated and prepared for the worst.

"Most of the men guarding the train climbed into a truck and left about two hours ago, heading north," Trembley said. "You have anything to do with that?"

"Captain Petain can be most persuasive when he has a gun pressed to his ribs," Hiram said. "And in case you're thinking of ways to deal with Petain after this is over, we already have plans for him."

"Yes, Captain Trembley told us one of your soldiers is the mother of that poor girl he shot. She deserves her revenge. I presume you have a plan. How can we help?"

"Okay, here's what I want to do." Hiram used a picture of the railyard taken from the overhead drone to illustrate his primary plan. "We enter the camp through the north gate in Petain's sedan. I'll drive. Petain will join me in the front passenger seat, Deborah and Nora in the back seat. Simone, Catherine, and Pauline will follow on one of the railbikes. Everyone will wear civilian men's clothes, including the women. It'll be dark, and Petain's credentials should get us through the gate without much trouble."

Donath and Trembley nodded.

Hiram continued. "Petain will tell his remaining men they are being relieved and gather them together here." Hiram pointed to a spot near the locomotive. "We should be able to get the drop on them."

"And if they put up a fight?" Donath said.

"It won't be a fair one," Trembley said. "Hiram's team has weapons that don't make a sound and goggles that allow them to see in the dark."

"Speaking of which…" Hiram signaled Team Charlie to distribute the silenced nine-millimeter pistols, Milkor grenade launchers, and AT-7 anti-tank missiles they'd hauled up the hillside. "Sorry, I don't have any spare night vision goggles to give you."

"These'll do just fine," Donath said, examining one of the Milkors. "How long to train my men?"

"A half-hour, max," Hiram said. Trembley seemed disappointed that he wasn't getting an M22 with night vison scope, but he said nothing. "And I've got an HF radio for Captain Trembley so we can stay in contact once we deploy the jammer."

"Jammer?" Donath and Trembley said at once.

"As soon as the convoy enters the camp, I'll activate an all-spectrum radio jammer. It can be programmed to allow our signals to go through, but not anyone else's." Hiram had found the tech in Jacob's pod. "Can you have one of your men cut the phone lines leading out of the railyard?"

"No problem," Donath smiled as he admired the sleek pistol. "I'll put Sean on it. He likes to climb."

"Once we've subdued Petain's men, we'll stick them in a cattle car and wait for the convoy from Camp Joffre."

"How long before they arrive?" Trembley said.

Hiram looked at his watch. "An hour, maybe a little less. Once we've loaded everyone on the trucks, we'll leave through the south gate, here." He touched the gate on the map.

"Then we're free to torch the place?" Donath said.

"Right. Tear the place up as best you can," Trembley said. "We'll want as much confusion as possible."

"Looking forward to it." Donath showed his teeth as he traded the pistol for the Milkor.

* * *

Hiram made the excruciating trek back to Team Charlie's location with Deborah and Team Delta. He struggled to stand by the time they arrived and sat on the ground disseminating the plan to his soldiers.

"How far out is the convoy now?" he asked Irene.

"About forty-five minutes," she said.

"Barbara, take Team Charlie and head up to the wood line and assume your positions. Delta, let's get going." Hiram limped off toward the Citroën.

Nora continued to operate her drone from the backseat of the car as they drove around the mountain and down into the town of Peyraud. Hiram slowed the sedan and removed his night vision goggles when the railyard's north gate came into view.

"Nora, better shut it down until we pass the guard post." Hiram directed a quick glance at Petain. "If you want to keep on breathing, don't do anything stupid."

Petain looked at Hiram for a moment while Deborah translated, then nodded.

The sedan stopped at the gate and a guard approached Hiram's side of the car. Petain called out the window, waving the guard over to his side. They exchanged a few words, Petain flashed his credentials, and the guard waved the car and the trailing railbike through.

Twenty meters into the railyard, Nora powered up her C2ID2. She gasped.

"What's wrong?" Hiram said.

"You need to see this," Deborah said.

Hiram stopped the car and Nora handed him the display. She leaned over the seat, reached in, and pointed to a line of red heat signatures moving west on the highway along the Moselle River. Hiram tapped the screen and the view changed from thermal to low-light visual mode. A clear line of thirteen half-tracks, two pulling heavy mortars and led by three tanks, appeared on the screen. He stared at the image. "Well, that changes things." A reinforced mechanized infantry column headed toward Pont Saint Michael.

47

0415 hours, Monday, August 17, 1942, Pont Saint Vincent, Meurthe-et-Moselle Department, Vichy France

Pauline pulled up beside the stopped Citroën, her NVGs reflecting the glow of Deborah's C2ID2. "Pauline thinks they are passing through," Deborah said as she touched Hiram's arm. Simone and Catherine leaned in the left side windows waiting for more.

"With orders to exterminate the families on the way through," Simone said. Deborah translated. "Can we take that chance?"

Pauline looked away from the car.

In the backseat, Nora studied her C2ID2 display while the others talked. She blurted something out in French, interrupting them all. "What if we give them another target?" Deborah said.

"Another target?" Hiram said.

Nora spoke and Deborah continued to translate. "Something on the other side of the river. The company is still well north of the bridge here." Nora pointed to a bridge in Maron, about five kilometers downstream of Pont Stain Vincent. "If we get them across the bridge, we can blow it up behind them. And, be long gone before they could get back across the river."

Hiram looked at the display with Deborah. The La Madon River joined the Moselle in Pont Saint Vincent in a confusion of tide pools, rapids, and tight turns in the two rivers. As a consequence, the French had built the Canal de l'Est to route vessels around the troubled waters. A long narrow island divided the canal from the north-flowing river, stretching from near Flavignysur-Moselle all the way to Maron. The Allies had destroyed any bridges that spanned both the river and canal. A single bridge stood across the canal, about three kilometers north of Pont Saint Michael, which provided access to the island, but didn't extend across the river.

Allied bombing had destroyed the highway bridge connecting Pont Saint Michael with Neuves-Maisons on the north side of the river. The railway bridge over the Moselle River stood fast, though a portion of the bridge that crossed the canal had collapsed.

"What are these?" Deborah pointed to a man-made structure just south of the railroad bridge. Hiram zoomed in.

"Locks on the canal," he said after studying the image for a moment.

Hiram looked at Nora and smiled. "I like it, but let's take care of the guards first."

* * *

Hiram stopped the sedan at the spur where the holocaust train sat idle. His soldier's families waited inside. Pauline and Catherine pulled up beside them on the railbike.

One of Petain's guards approached the incoming vehicles. He readied his weapon, took slow, calculated steps toward them. He called out to the policemen on-site. Two of the men nearby turned toward the incoming vehicle with weapons ready. In the darkness, more watched unseen.

Petain climbed out of the car and said, "I'm Captain Petain."

The man snapped to attention and saluted. "Officer Reynard, sir." He called out to the policemen and Hiram noticed a change in their stance. A man echoed Reynard's words to those waiting deeper in the railyard.

Hiram and Deborah climbed out of the car and joined Petain. The others on the bikes dismounted and congregated behind the police captain.

Petain returned a casual salute and said a few words. He made a familiar motion with his hands as if to invite the men to come in closer.

Standing beside him, Deborah repeated Petain's words in a whisper. "He says there are only five guards on duty. Petain is relieving the men."

Officer Reynard called out again to the men. In minutes, all five of Petain's men stood before him in a line armed with bolt action rifles and pistols. Petain addressed his team, his tone casual.

"He says to prepare for inspection," Deborah said. "Now put your hands up."

The guards looked back and forth at one another and back at Petain.

Reynard said, "Capitaine?"

Petain held his hands up the way he intended his men to comply. One by one, the men became aware of their captain's betrayal and their hands headed skyward.

* * *

0445 hours, Monday, August 17, 1942, North Bank of the Moselle River, Moron, Meurthe-et-Moselle Department, Vichy France

Hiram and Simone touched down in a cornfield one kilometer north of where the river and canal split near Maron. The precision of their landing did not spare his injured ankle. He bit down hard trying not to scream from the pain, catching the side of his tongue. The taste of blood filled his mouth. Hiram leaned on his good leg and took a few deep breaths while Simone fought to gather up the parachute snagged on the tough corn stalks. She had taken a chance jumping through the twin portals, even though he had promised safe passage. They had both made it safely to the ground.

Simone helped Hiram down to the river bank, occasionally bumping helmets on the way down. He opened his pack on the gravel shore, activated the portal inside, and hopped down the ladder into the pod, careful to keep his weight on his good leg. He dragged a quick deploy motorized RHIB and a few drift mines over to the base of the ladder. The small black explosive devices, designed for underwater attacks, contained ten kilos of explosives. He passed the boat up through the portal to Simone, then began the painful climb up the ladder with the mines cradled in his arm. Several agonizing minutes later, they boarded the RHIB and motored out into the Moselle. Hiram scanned the shore with his NVGs.

"Hawk, this is Echo." Charlotte's voice came through his helmet. The Babel Fish translating a few seconds behind. "Reference point Papa Tango, over."

Charlotte had taken over tracking the mechanized infantry company via drone while Nora was busy with Petain's men. Reference point Papa Tango sat at the outer edge of Pierre-la-Treiche, a village six kilometers north of Maron. Under blackout conditions, Hiram expected the column to travel about ten kilometers an hour.

The RHIB approached the bridge. Hiram and Simone maneuvered the small vessel into position adjacent to one of the concrete piles near the center of the span. Hiram picked up a floating mine, powered on the device, and set it into the water. It slipped below the surface, a spaghetti-thin aerial the only visible indicator of its position above the murky water. He secured the explosive to the pile. They maneuvered the RHIB next to another pile, where he repeated the process.

With the mines placed, Hiram activated his C2ID2.

"Echo, this is Hawk, over."

"Hawk, this is Echo, over." Charlotte wore a helmet similar to his. In tandem with the C2ID2's tactical mode, they communicated via the wireless earpieces and microphones built into the helmets.

"Echo, Phase One complete, moving to Phase Two, over."

"Roger, Hawk. Target is midway to reference point Sierra Foxtrot. Hurry, over." The column would make one final turn through the village of Sexey-aux-Forges before reaching the bridge across the Maron. He was running out of time.

"Wilco. Hawk out." They passed under a bridge, the flow of water more disagreeable around the footings. A set of dim lights passed overhead.

Deborah spoke in his ear. "Hawk, this is Alpha, over."

"Alpha, this is Hawk, over."

"Hawk, the convoy arrived. We've captured the drivers. No casualties. We're transferring the prisoners from the train to the trucks as fast as we can. The drivers are cooperating, but it's a slow process, over."

"Roger, Alpha. How much more time do you need, over?"

"Another hour, Hawk. Over."

"Roger, Alpha. Hawk, out."

The railway bridge came into view in their night vision goggles and they headed for the shore.

Gravel crunched underneath the RHIB's bow as it grounded on the eastern shore of the island, one hundred meters north of the northernmost gun emplacement. Simone dragged the boat to shore, while Hiram erected the small tent to mask the glow from the portal. He laid out his pack on the floor of the tent, opened it, and activated the portal inside.

Hiram climbed in and retrieved the parts for four combat robots. Simone pulled the parts out of his hands as he passed them up. He grabbed two more drift mines and headed up the ladder.

By the time Hiram emerged, Simone had assembled the first of the robots. Simone's familiarity with the design and operation of the devices made her the ideal partner on this endeavor. Ten minutes later, the remaining combat robots stood beside the first. Armed with electro-magnetic grenade launchers loaded with a mix of 40mm high explosive and incendiary munitions, Simone sent the mechanical monsters down the riverbank toward the locks.

Hiram tied off the two new drift mines to the boat's main spar. Simone helped him into the RHIB, then pushed him back into the water before returning to her robot controls.

He repeated the process of attaching the floating bombs to the lock gates and motored back to shore. He programmed them to go off in six minutes. If the situation changed, he could detonate by remote control.

"Hawk, this is Echo, over." Charlotte's voice carried more urgency than her last communication.

"Echo, this is Hawk, over."

"Hawk, the enemy column is passing reference point Sierra Foxtrot, over."

"Echo, is Falcon in place, over?"

"Roger, Hawk. Falcon reports all elements are in place. Charlie and Delta are awaiting the signal, over."

"Echo, five minutes to detonation. Hawk, out."

48

0510 hours, Monday, August 17, 1942, Pont Saint Vincent, Meurthe-et-Moselle Department, Vichy France

Charlotte grew more anxious as the enemy column moved closer to the railyard. The line of vehicles snaked down the road past Sexey-aux-Forges. A bright spot blossomed on her screen alongside the canal locks. In front of her, the night sky lit up for a few seconds. The familiar boom followed. A few seconds later, another bomb detonated closer to the shore. Neither bomb inflicted any real damage to the locks. But no one could deny an attack was underway. Water and debris continued to rain down from the twin explosions as the four combat robots opened fire on the lock's control booths, powerhouse, and administration building from positions along the canal's western shore farther downstream. The position of the robots presented the illusion that a more sizable force had dug in along the canal.

The combat robots unloaded high-visibility incendiary grenades and loud explosive grenades. Bright, thundering explosions drove the frightened guards and workers to abandon the locks. A few of the men running from the powerhouse disappeared into the patches of trees that lined the road.

The enemy column slowed to a stop. The assault on the powerhouse continued, although the combat robots slowed their rate of fire.

When the column began to move again, they turned left down a narrow road that followed the shore. Another left and a right led them through the center of a small village and back through La Corvée. The column lumbered toward the only bridge that could get them across the river.

Charlotte touched Barbara's arm, and pointed to the moving column on the display. Barbara nodded and relayed information to Teams Charlie and Delta, Deborah, Hiram and Simone, and Captain Trembley and the partisans.

When Barbara completed her transmission to Trembley, she adjusted her position. She lay down beside Charlotte and aligned her body to form a straight line from her right foot to the muzzle of the M22.

"Targeting the shorter man up top," Barbara said. "Try to keep an eye on his buddy." Barbara spoke of the two guards standing atop the railyard control tower.

"Roger," Charlotte said. The firefight across the river continued to draw the guards' attention and they neglected their watch. She doubted they would notice Captain Trembley and the French partisans moving toward the railyard perimeter, but she kept an eye on the second man anyway, switching between the view on the screen and the tower in front of them.

The weapons fire across the river slackened as the combat robots ran low on ammo. The guards atop the tower kept their eyes on the mayhem.

"A few more minutes," Charlotte said. On her display, the enemy vehicles crossed over the Moselle one by one.

"Merde."

"What's wrong," Barbara asked, not taking her eye off the target in her scope.

"Three Panzers at the end of the column changed direction again," Charlotte said. "They're headed south. I bet the bridge isn't rated for the weight of the tanks."

"Falcon will be waiting for them," Barbara said, "with Monsieur Donath's men and a few anti-tank rocket launchers."

"We should let them know," Charlotte said.

"You're right." Barbara laid the rifle aside and grabbed the HF radio handset. "Falcon, this is Echo, over," she called in French.

"Echo, this is Falcon, over," Trembley replied.

On the display, the Panzers ignored the right angles of the roads as they rolled back through the village, pushing smaller vehicles out of their way.

"Falcon, three Big Boys heading south on the west side of the river. ETA twenty minutes at present speed, over."

Charlotte understood most of what Barbara said, though she struggled with Hiram's military terminology. Barbara, on the other hand, rattled off Hiram's slang with ease.

"Roger Echo. No infantry support, over?" Trembley said.

"Negative Falcon. The Big Boys split off from the infantry before they crossed the river, over."

"Roger Echo. We'll be sure to make them feel welcome. Falcon out."

Barbara put down the headset and took up the M22 again. By Charlotte's calculations, the tower was only about four-hundred-and-fifty meters out, an easy shot for Barbara.

"Ready when you are," Barbara said.

The last halftrack crossed the bridge. Charlotte tapped two icons on her C2ID2. To the North, a bright light flashed. Six seconds later, the faint boom announced the explosion. The ten kilo charges would rupture the two pilings, which would put more pressure on the adjacent pilings. The fast-flowing river would do the rest of the work. The roadway above would collapse as its supports washed away in the torrent.

Charlotte tapped another icon on her C2ID2. "The jammer is on."

Beside her, Barbara pulled the trigger. Charlotte watched as the shorter guard's body tipped toward the center of the control tower and collapsed. Barbara re-sighted her weapon on her next target. The second guard took a shot square in his back. He took two awkward steps forward and tumbled over the railing.

Barbara laid down the rifle and picked up the HF radio handset. "Falcon, this is Echo. Execute. Out." Hiram had changed the plan when the mechanized infantry column appeared. The Partisans, assisted by Team Charlie would execute their attack on the railyard as soon as the German column was trapped on the other side of the river.

Charlotte toggled her view in the C2ID2 to the drone over the railyard. Heat signatures from Donath's men emerged from the woods headed toward the guards patrolling the western perimeter of the railyard. Within minutes, all six guards were down. Not one of them managed to raise an alarm. Donath's partisans, followed by Team Charlie, flowed into the railyard.

Hiram appeared on the other side of Barbara, quiet despite his awkward gait. He settled in beside her, an M22 and his well-worn sniper rifle ready to get to work. Simone crawled up on Charlotte's other side a minute later.

"Is everything on schedule?" Hiram said, voice low, his Babel Fish translating at the same volume.

"Three Panzers headed toward Falcon's team," Barbara said. "He's expecting them."

Hiram nodded, took out a high-powered night vision spotting scope, and surveyed the scene below them.

Charlotte ran through the scenario for Simone. Simone took out her C2ID2 display unit and called up the view of the Panzers on her screen.

"I'll watch the Big Boys. You keep an eye on the railyard. You're much better at flying the drones than I am."

Charlotte smiled at the compliment and nodded. She switched the display back to the video feed from the overhead drone. Teams Charlie and Delta moved into position to assist with the transfer of prisoners from the cattle cars to the trucks.

"Sorry boys, can't have you falling into enemy hands," Hiram said. He tapped an icon on his C2ID2. A second later Charlotte heard four quick booms in succession and assumed Hiram had sacrificed the combat robots.

Hiram tapped Barbara on the shoulder and said something in English about the radio. They got up, Hiram signaling Charlotte and Simone to watch the events playing out below.

"You are our eyes," Barbara said as she put an arm around Hiram. The two hobbled away into the darkness.

On the display, Donath's men eliminated the remaining guard force one by one, with almost mechanical precision. She admired their efficiency.

A sudden ray of light exploded from an open door in the control tower. The silhouette of a man stepped onto the platform surrounding the tower. He looked at the dead guard and surveyed the landscape around the railyard. Then, he turned and scampered back the way he'd come.

Here we go.

A siren wailed, projected from the speakers mounted above the control tower.

A bright white light pierced the darkness once again. Three bright beams bounced across the landscape from the targeting searchlights on the Panzers charging through Pont Saint Vincent.

49

0520 hours, Monday, August 17, 1942, Pont-Saint-Vincent, Meurthe-et-Moselle Department, Vichy France

Hiram waited in silence atop a boxcar in the railyard watching the approaching tanks. A few feet beneath him, Irene tried to convince a group of men, women, and children to board the trucks that would take them to safety, a task complicated by the unaccompanied children who spoke only Spanish or Portuguese. Teams Charlie and Delta worked through the cattle cars down the line, cutting the thick wire that secured the bolts meant to keep the sliding doors in place.

Hiram pointed the barrel of his sniper rifle toward the chest of the silhouetted man protruding from the lead tank's turret. A targeting searchlight mounted on the tank's hull screwed with Hiram's night scope. Hiram shot out the light, then focused on the tank's commander again. The man wore a German uniform and rode atop a German tank. But the patch on his right arm – three vertical stripes of blue, white and red from left to right – and twin lightning bolts on his collar said he wasn't German. *LVF?* His father had told him about the *Légion des Volontaires Français Contre le Bolchévisme*, or the Legion of French Volunteers against Bolshevism, a unit of French Fascists fighting alongside the Nazis.

A burst of machinegun fire drew Hiram's attention to the right. Through the scope, he saw one of Donath's machine gun nests by the railway bridge engaging infantrymen attempting to cross from the island on foot. *They must have crossed over the upstream lock on foot, then climbed onto the railway bridge.* The

LVF men fell one after another. Many dove into the water to avoid joining the slaughtered pile on the bridge. The men in the water struggled against the current. *Drown, you bastards.*

He swung the rifle back to the north. The two lead tanks slew their turrets in the direction of the machine gun nest. The scope flared as an artificial sun passed over him, revealing the lead tank commander in high relief.

Hiram pulled the trigger. The lead tank's gun blossomed flame as its 88mm main gun fired. And, three AT-7 anti-tank rockets leapt out of the night headed for the Panzers. Hiram assumed he hit the LVF officer. Even if the shot missed, an AT-7 struck the tank at the bezel ring, popping the turret off like a champagne cork. The 88mm round from the Panzer landed in the nearest of the two machine gun nests. Dirt, broken weapons, and body parts erupted from the crater.

Hiram turned back to the tanks. Three unmoving, mechanical corpses sat along the road. A legless man pulled himself away from the wreckage. The AT-7s never disappointed. On the railway bridge, the LVF infantrymen made another push to cross the bridge. With one of the machine guns silenced, they had a chance, he supposed. Hiram, armed with his grandfather's trusty M2010, began picking off the LVF men almost seventeen hundred meters away.

"Hawk, this is Echo, over," Charlotte said through his headset.

Hiram took out two more soldiers on the bridge.

"Echo, this is Hawk, over."

"Hawk, the enemy commander on the far shore is gathering up his men and loading them into the halftracks, over."

"Roger Echo. Advise if they begin moving, over."

"Wilco Hawk. Echo out."

The LVF commander would have to find another way across the river somewhere downstream. Their new route awarded Hiram and his teams two more hours to clear out.

Hiram spotted a straggler trying to make his way across the bridge. The man looked down at the water, and then in Hiram's direction. Hiram fired and the man fell across the wooden slats at the center of the bridge. After two minutes, and no further movement on the bridge, he checked on Deborah in the boxcar below.

"Deborah, how is it going down there?"

"We're loading as fast as we can!"

"We need to be gone in an hour, maximum," he said. "Speed it up."

"Almost done the first five cars. The rest should be quicker."

Hiram watched the railway bridge for another five minutes, but no new LVF soldiers appeared.

Simone's voice broke his concentration. "Hawk, enemy column is heading north, over."

The news erased some of his unease. He surveyed the bridge and the area around the train before climbing down to the ground, his left ankle objecting all the way. Nora waited for him at the bottom. She helped him down from the last rung of the ladder.

"Thanks," he said.

She nodded and said, "I've got good news, bad news, and worse news." The translator almost kept up with her.

"Tell me," Hiram said.

"Emma has freed Ellen, Myriam, and Isabelle, with the help of the French Partisans. They're back in uniform and ready to fight. That's the good news." Nora paused. "The bad news - Barbara's family is not here. Her husband and two sons are missing. According to some of the other prisoners, they didn't board the train in Drancy. No one seems to know why."

"Diane?"

"She's going to live, but they roughed her up a bit. Isabelle said they raped her, but Diane wouldn't admit it. She's in bad shape. She's with her family in the first truck."

"And the others?"

She nodded toward the first cattle car in line. "In the next car." She looked down at the ground. "As we thought, all dead. Ester, Anna, Justine, Stephanie, little Solange. The pigs threw them in there like garbage." She wiped her eyes and took a breath. "Fourteen more in there too. Two male prisoners I don't know, two men I think were part of the train's crew, and ten French policemen. Two of them dressed like prisoners. Why do you think they are out of uniform?"

Hiram shrugged. "Don't know for sure. Inspector Locard told me Captain Petain tried to keep the whole matter of your escape quiet."

"Don't suppose he'll be able to keep this quiet."

"Hawk, this is Echo, over." Simone's voice, not Charlotte's. The Babel Fish translated. *Now what?*

"Echo, this is Hawk, over."

"Hawk, pull up the feed from drone one, over?"

"Roger Echo. Checking now, out." Hiram pulled the C2ID2 auxiliary display out of its pouch on his combat vest and powered it on. He tapped a few icons and a thermal image came into focus.

"Echo, this is Hawk. What am I looking at, over?'

"Hawk, I think it's another German column, over."

Hiram tapped an icon to overlay a map on the display. The line of vehicles moved north through the town of Diarville, about twenty-five kilometers south of Pont-Saint-Vincent. The convoy looked similar to the mechanized infantry company they defeated. The vehicles traveled at about twenty-five kilometers per hour, their headlights switched on, heedless of potential Allied air attacks.

"Not German," Hiram said. "LVF. French Nazis working for the SS."

"Bastards," Simone said.

"Can you overlay the route we're taking to Besançon on this map?" Nora said. "If we can reach the town of Pierreville and cross this bridge, we can put the La Madon River between us and them."

"But they could cross further south, here in Ceintrey and cut us off." Hiram pointed to the bridge on the map.

"Not if we blow it up first," Nora said.

Hiram did some time and distance calculations in his head. The LVF column could cross the ten kilometers to Ceintrey in about a half-hour. Port Saint Vincent was about fifteen kilometers from Ceintrey and the railbikes could travel faster than the LVF column, but it would still be a race to the bridge.

It was all academic, if their own convoy of trucks couldn't get across the bridge in Pierreville first.

"Deborah, we leave in fifteen minutes," he said. "Anyone not on the trucks gets left behind."

"Got it," she said, and began shouting orders to Team Charlie.

Hiram turned back to Nora. "I need to get a few more charges out of my pod. Can you keep an eye out for me? We don't need any of Donath's men knowing about it."

"Of course."

Hiram inched closer to the mutilated locomotive, hoping to use the structure for added cover. Nora stood a few feet away looking up and down the train.

Hiram activated the portal in his pack, setting it to the moment he had pulled out the drift mines he'd used on the locks. He reached inside and hauled out the floating mines one-by-one, thanking himself for situating them by the pod entry so he wouldn't have to attempt a climb down another damn ladder. A total of four drift mines sat on the ground beside his pack a minute later. Forty kilos of high explosive, enough to weaken, if not destroy both bridges over the La Madon River.

"Okay, I'll take Barbara with me," Hiram said.

Nora held up her hand. "You need to stay with Petain. I'll take Catherine on the railbike."

He nodded and struggled to get to his feet again. "You're right." He handed her two of the mines. "Take these and go."

Less than two minutes later, Nora and Catherine roared through the railyard's south gate. Catherine waved to the partisans standing guard on the way out.

"May God go with you," Hiram whispered.

50

0615 hours, Monday, August 17, 1942, Ceintrey, Meurthe-et-Moselle Department, Vichy France

"Hurry!" Catherine tucked two pair of night vision goggles back into the pack resting on the floor between her feet. "The bastards have almost reached the bridge." She grasped the sidewall of the speeding railbike's sidecar as Nora guided it down the deserted road toward the crucial bridge in Ceintrey. A dust trail rose behind the LVF vehicles on the other side of the river.

"Arm the mines," Nora said. "It's going to be close."

Catherine picked up each mine and set the timers for thirty seconds but didn't activate them yet.

The railbike careened onto the bridge just as the lead LVF halftrack turned onto the opposite end, a hundred meters away. Catherine struggled to keep her balance as the side car whipped around the turn. She hugged the heavy mines to prevent them from bumping around.

Nora slammed on the brakes and the bike skidded to a halt. The hump at the center of the bridge would protect them from enemy fire for no more than a few seconds. Catherine, arms shaking, dropped the mines out onto the concrete roadbed as Nora turned the bike in a tight circle.

"Go," Catherine yelled as she tapped the activate icon on her C2ID2.

Nora hit the accelerator as the LVF machine gunner in the halftrack let loose an eight-round burst.

A round cut through Nora and she slumped over. The railbike whipped toward the side of the bridge. Searing pain sliced through Catherine's arm as the bike began to tip. The momentum tossed her into the air and back toward the active mines sitting on the bridge. Her shoulder slammed into the hard surface, then her helmet hit.

Catherine tried to pull herself along the road, but her broken body refused to comply. She stopped struggling and decided to watch the show. As the halftrack crested the bridge, she smiled. The mines detonated.

51

1635 hours, Monday, August 17, 1942, North of Besançon, Vosges Department, Occupied France

The late Lieutenant Lebeau's Citroën led the way to Besançon with Hiram at the wheel. Petain sat beside him in the front seat. Trembley and Deborah sat in the rear. Petain had talked his way through a roadblock and two checkpoints with such ease, Hiram wondered how many times the good Captain had wagged his lying tongue in the past.

The 17th century Citadel of Besançon sat high above the city, wrapped by a horseshoe bend of the Doubs River. The German occupiers, recognizing its strategic position on Mount Saint-Etienne, had turned the Citadel into their fortress.

Hiram made a sharp left and stopped the Citroën at a checkpoint manned by French policemen. As a uniformed guard approached his window, Hiram waved him over to Petain's side of the car. Petain greeted the man and showed his credentials.

Hiram scanned the length of the convoy stretched out along the rising road to his left through his side-view mirror.

"*Non. Quatre moto avec side-car,*" Petain said, his tone different than previous stops.

"*Un, duex, trois,*" The guard pointed back up the hill. "*Il n'y a pas quatre.*"

Hiram spoke enough French to understand the man's words. One of the four railbikes had drifted away from the convoy. He looked in the mirror again. *Barbara.* Hiram clenched the steering wheel tighter.

52

2040 hours, Monday, August 17, 1942, Bost, Allier Department, Vichy France

The men Captain Petain had ordered to join him in Vichy made slow progress across France. They inched around every turn and crept through every town. To Corporal Lafayette, it seemed the team could not make it twenty kilometers without running into a military convoy or police roadblock. The entire countryside had morphed into a nightmare over the past few days.

As the car rounded a bend in the road, Lafayette spotted a familiar truck parked off to the side, the front end breaking through a patch of overgrown brush. "Does that look like the Captain's truck to you?"

The driver pulled up beside the abandoned vehicle. "If it belongs to the Captain, he must have found some trouble." He pointed to hole in the door, a wide wet smear of what Lafayette guessed was blood ran down to the sideboard.

"Stay here." Lafayette climbed out and inspected the vehicle. He confirmed that the truck was indeed the one Captain Petain had taken on the trip to Vichy and the smear on the door was someone's blood. The Captain had taken Lebeau and two other men with him. He found no sign of any of them.

"Search the area," Lafayette ordered. No one jumped at the command. They seemed hesitant to climb out of the vehicles. "Now."

One of his men soon turned up a poorly concealed blood pool, but no other signs of the missing men. The armored trunk with the mysterious weapons remained in the back of the abandoned truck. Instead of moving the trunk, he split his men between the two vehicles, and they set off again for Vichy, hoping to find Captain Petain, or at least Lieutenant Lebeau there.

Ten kilometers down the road, the lead car pulled up to a roadblock in the little town of Bost as the sun dipped behind the treetops west of the village. Men in German Army uniforms manned the post.

"I'll do the talking," Lafayette said, fishing his identity papers and police badge from a jacket pocket.

"Guten morgen, mein herr," Lafayette said, his German polluted by the accent of his native tongue. He held out his documents as the German sentry walked up to the truck's window.

"Bonjour, monsieur," the man said in provincial French. "What is your business in Vichy?"

Surprised by the man's response, Lafayette looked over the man's uniform once more, realized he was with the LVF, a unit of French Fascists fighting alongside the Nazis. Now, they helped the Germans take over what remained of the French State. *Traitors, maybe. But who hadn't betrayed the country in this damned war?*

"Your business?" the sentry repeated. He eyed Lafayette over the documents.

"Sergeant Dabney Lafayette of the French National Police," Lafayette said. "I have orders to report to the office of General Secretary Bousquet." René Bousquet had been appointed General Secretary to Police by Marshall Philippe Petain's Prime Minister, Pierre Laval. Lafayette had no idea whether Bousquet, Laval, or his boss were alive, much less still in power. But Captain Petain had ordered them to Vichy, and that's where they were going. "The next truck is with us also."

"Who is your captain?" the sentry asked.

"Captain Louis Petain, Chief of Police for the Pyrénées-Orientales Department."

"Any relation to Marshall Petain?"

"Petain is a common name in Southern France," Lafayette said.

The sentry's eyes lingered on Lafayette for a few uncomfortable seconds. "Stay in your vehicle," he said before taking Lafayette's papers into a grey tent set up on the side of the road. A black swastika, on a white circular field trimmed in red, adorned the near side of the tent's roof.

"Should we be worried?" Corporal Martin said from the driver's seat.

"I wouldn't try and run if that's what you are thinking."

Martin tapped on the door in a nervous, twitching rhythm.

After five minutes, the sentry returned with papers in hand.

"The Hauptsturmführer permits you to pass," the sentry said, and handed Lafayette the documents. "We must check the papers of the second truck as well."

Lafayette nodded and waved his driver to proceed.

They drove past the checkpoint and pulled over to await passage of the second truck. The deep growling of several airplanes interrupted the evening lull. Overhead, a formation of five aircraft passed south of the roadblock. Four Focke-Wulf Fw-90 fighters escorted an Fw-200 Condor transport plane.

"Must be somebody important," Martin said. He continued tapping on the door, the same nervous beat.

53

0010 hours, Tuesday, August 18, 1942, Les Alliés, Doubs Department, Occupied France

Hiram's team would have to wait to search for Barbara. After this mission, and assuming they survived, he planned to go after her. Anger and suffering fueled her disregard for the rest of the team. And grieving Maxime had gone along with her, an otherwise unlikely pair.

The convoy rolled through the dark, quiet commune of Mamirolle. He ordered a stop to pick up Danette, Rosette, and little Leverette, who opened his eyes for a brief moment as they passed him into the back of the first truck in the line-up to be reunited with his little sister. When Hiram asked about Garon's status, Rosette shook her head and moved on to take her place in the cabin of one of the trucks. Danette picked up a set of NVGs, chose a truck, and climbed in. They drove in darkness toward the French-Swiss border.

Hiram followed a dirt road onto a forested hilltop that overlooked Les Alliés. He led the convoy deep into the woods and brought the Citroën to a halt. The trucks and railbikes pulled up behind him.

"Stay put," he said to Petain.

Petain peered out the windshield. "I know better than to go running in the forest at night." He rubbed the spot on his chest where he had been pegged with the Taser.

By the time Hiram, Trembley, and Deborah climbed out of the car, Danette had set to work positioning guards around the parked convoy.

Several refugees climbed down from the trucks and helped the others out. The long ride had worn down Hiram in the posh Citroën. He could not imagine what the ride had done to those in the back of the trucks. *It's almost over.*

"Charlotte, Simone, get your drones up," Hiram said, Deborah repeating his instructions. "I want to know where every guard within ten thousand meters is located, on both sides of the border." The two women went to work.

"What about Barbara?" Charlotte said. "I think she disabled the tracker on the railbike. I put up a drone when we stopped in Mamirolle, but I didn't find her signal."

"We'll deal with her later," Hiram said. "We have more immediate problems." *Where the hell is Team Bravo anyway?*

"Danette, you're in charge until we get back. Captain Trembley, Deborah, and I are going to do some scouting. Make sure nobody wanders off, especially the truck drivers. And for God's sake, keep everyone quiet and maintain light discipline. We are close now and can't afford any screw-ups." Deborah passed a shortened version of Hiram's message to Danette.

Danette nodded. Hiram, Deborah, and Trembley headed through the woods, Deborah supporting Hiram as he walked. Trembley was still carrying the HF radio, but he now sported an M22 assault rifle.

They positioned themselves to look down on the dark, quiet town of Les Alliés. About a half kilometer south of the town, a road leading to the Swiss border cut through a shallow ravine.

"One checkpoint at the bottom of the ravine, another one at the top," Deborah said, adjusting her night vision goggles.

Trembley fought with his goggles as he looked up to the top of the ridge. "Two patrols walking the bottom of the ridge. I can't see the border at the top of the ridge though. Damn contraptions."

"I make the ridge about a hundred meters high," Hiram said. "The road through the ravine has a six, maybe seven percent grade. With an incline like that, the trucks will be noisy and slow."

Trembley pointed toward the hill leading to the Swiss border. "And that slope is about a twenty-five percent grade. Easy for you and your soldiers, but not for the civilians we busted out of the camps. The younger ones might be strong enough, but we've got a few that can't even walk. Well, maybe not so easy for you," he added after glancing at Hiram's leg.

"We're sending as many of them up that hill as we can," Hiram said. "Captain, would you mind monitoring the patrols? See if there's a pattern we can exploit?"

"My thoughts exactly," Trembley said. He settled into a more comfortable position and took out the powerful night vision scope. "Going to have a good look at that village, too." Deborah and Hiram headed back into the woods.

"Hiram, the only thing stopping us from taking these people through the checkpoint is documentation." She stopped walking. "The healthy ones and the children, they'll make it. But not the older ones."

Hiram turned to her.

"You've got all this technology. Remote controlled flying machines, silent weapons, robots. Don't you have a means of producing a handful of documents for the ones we know won't make the climb?"

"And then Petain can talk us through the border."

"He's gotten us this far. No one expected him to be our savior after all the damage his men have done."

"It's worth a try," Hiram said.

54

0100 hours, Tuesday, August 18, 1942, Les Alliés, Doubs Department, Occupied France

Petain sat in the passenger seat of Lebeau's Citroën. Several soldiers surrounded the car, most of them female. Hiram Halphen, the mysterious soldier with his advanced technology, had taken off into the woods in the cover of night along with the other two individuals who had occupied the car.

With the windows open, Petain heard a woman near the car ordering the others around. "Keep everyone close," she said. "Put the little ones back in the trucks."

Petain scooted over into the driver's seat of the car. Halphen had taken the keys. He adjusted the side view mirror so he could see the scene behind him without looking interested. They had approached the refugees' destination – the Swiss border. Given what was happening in France at the moment, escaping with the Jews to Switzerland might be his best option. Even if he managed to stop the Jews from getting out of France, he wouldn't be seen as a hero. With Locard dead, he'd be the person the Gestapo would hold responsible for all the problems they had caused since their escape. However, once the road trip ended, Petain feared he would be killed. He needed to escape before that happened. With hundreds of refugees wandering around, distracted by their unearned bit of freedom, he figured he better slip out soon, before Hiram Halphen returned.

He watched the guards, searched for his way out of this mess. Then, he found something better – a distraction.

Three of the escaped prisoners decided they wanted to head toward the Swiss border immediately. "We can't wait for him to come back. All these easy targets. We don't want to be among them," one of the men said.

"We made it this far," one of the female soldiers said. "Trust us. We'll get you all out of here."

But the men did not want to hear it. Petain watched through the mirror. The men headed for the woods.

"Watch him." The female soldier standing beside his window walked off and another took her place.

Two soldiers ran after the men on the other side of the clearing. A scuffle broke out and several individuals raised their voices to protest. After a few seconds passed, all the guards charged with babysitting Petain drifted over toward the fight to assist.

Petain opened the car door nearest the woods. No one seemed to notice. He climbed out of the car, inched around the door, and backed toward the woods.

"Petain!" a woman said.

"It has been a delight, but I must be going," he said as he turned and ran.

"Stop the captain!" another woman said, her voice deeper than the first.

"Irene, stay with the trucks," one of the soldiers said.

"He went this way. Use the NVGs."

Petain knew better than to take off at a full run in the woods at night. Trees, rocks, thick brush, and uneven ground would defeat him if he moved too fast. So he turned to the left and tried to head back toward the main road, which he hoped would take him toward the border.

The armed women near the trucks refocused on Petain. "Don't let him out of your sight."

He kept moving, his stride minimal to avoid any misstep. Debris cracked beneath his feet calling out his location to those following him, but he refused to stop moving.

At last he stepped out onto the road leading to the town and thence to the Swiss border beyond. An occasional flicker of light from the closest tower caught his attention. Someone lighting a match perhaps. *What I wouldn't give for a cigarette.*

Behind him, a voice called out. "Captain Petain, stop!"

"I think I've had enough of this game," he said. "I'll take my chances with the border guards."

"Stop or I'll fire," the woman said.

"I don't think you will," he said. "If you fire your weapon, the men up in that tower will see the muzzle flash. Then your precious Jews back there will be prisoners once more."

Petain picked up his pace. The sooner he made it to the border, the better.

The woman didn't fire. For a moment, he thought he imagined her. Then, he heard her running toward him. Petain waited to turn and grab her when she got close.

Petain bear hugged her and swung her around his body. He swept her legs out from under her and let her fall to the ground. She tried to roll away, but he fell down on his knees on top of her back, straddling her at the waist. He pressed her face down into the ground. She squirmed and kicked.

"I told you I didn't want to play."

She grunted beneath him.

"I'm going to do you a favor, right here, right now Madam. I'm going to put you out of your misery. All of your friends back there, all of those people you believe you've saved, are all going to die. But you, you don't need to see it. You're a fighter. I like that. So, I'm going to do this for you."

"Bastard," she said. At least, that's what Petain heard.

He grabbed the woman by the hair on the back of her head and slammed her face into the ground. After the second time, she stopped moving. Petain got up and ran into the night.

55

0125 hours, Tuesday, August 18, 1942, Les Alliés, Doubs Department, Occupied France

Hiram circled the empty Citroën. "Where's Petain?"

"Disparu," Danette said, morosely.

Deborah said, "She says he escaped." She looked at him but said nothing. Without Petain, their chances to get everyone into Switzerland lessened.

Danette continued, her words flying out fast. Deborah translated, no doubt condensing the story. "She was distracted when three of the prisoners decided to make a break for the border on their own. They realized Petain was gone and Isabelle went after him. He roughed her up, knocked her out. Danette and Irene stopped to help her. They lost track of Petain. Denise found a doctor among the prisoners. He's with her now."

"Petain could raise an alarm. We need to get everyone out of here," Charlotte said.

"Not yet. No need to incite panic. Which way did the captain go?" Hiram asked.

"She thinks he's headed toward the town," Deborah said after consulting with Danette in French.

"Probably heading for the border," Hiram said. "He has as much reason to get out of France as we do now, but we don't need him alerting anyone that we're not far behind. We'll find him. I put a tracker on him when I first captured him. Get someone to watch his movement. Worst case, someone does notice him. He's not in uniform and I'm holding his papers. He's going to have a hell of time getting someone to believe him. Don't worry about Petain for now."

Hiram turned to his two drone operators. "Charlotte, Simone, what did you find?"

Charlotte nodded and positioned her C2ID2 display so Hiram and the team leaders could see. Deborah translated. "The ravine appears to be the straightest shot to the border. With two checkpoints at the ends of this ravine, both manned by French soldiers and the machine gun nests here, here, and here, I think we need to find a better route" She handed the display over to Simone.

"The border is about one hundred meters beyond the top of this slope. It's a double barbed wire fence, three meters tall and topped with concertina wire. French soldiers patrol the northwestern side on foot, Swiss soldiers on the southeastern. A patrol road runs along our side of the fence, though I didn't see any vehicles using it. A fixed tower is positioned every hundred meters. Every fifth tower has a machine gun. Soldiers with rifles in the rest." Simone pointed out the towers with the heavy firepower. "I saw a few small warming huts in between, but no one's using them this time of year."

Hiram ran through Simone's assessment in his head, trying to find the best option for his soldiers and the truckloads of refugees. He zoomed out and searched for anything Simone might have missed. "What about this structure here?" He pointed to a building about six kilometers northwest of where the ravine exited the woods.

"Swiss barracks," she said.

"So, no nearby reserves," Hiram said.

Simone shook her head.

Hiram turned to face Deborah and Danette. "I need an honest assessment of whether or not these people can make the hike to the base of the ridge, climb up to the top, and then walk another kilometer or so to safety on the other side." Deborah translated for Danette.

The two women looked at each other. They exchanged a few words, their voices strained, angry.

"No," Danette said, and she stepped in between Deborah and Hiram. She spoke fast and her hands flew up dramatizing her rant.

Deborah waited until she stopped speaking to translate. "She worries about them all. She doesn't think we can get five hundred people up that ridge. Many of them are exhausted and weak. Some of the older individuals need assistance walking on a paved road."

"What do you think?" Hiram said.

"If Petain's no longer an option, then we need a Plan B?" Deborah said.

Simone spoke and Deborah translated. "What if we take out their communications? Jam their radios?"

"Might slow down the response from towers farther away. I assume they have field telephones at the checkpoints, machine gun nests, and guard towers. We'd have to take everything out at the same time," Hiram said.

"There's not enough of us," Charlotte said.

After the desertion of Barbara and Maxime and the deaths of Nora and Catherine, seventeen soldiers remained, including himself and Trembley. Diane and Isabelle were in no state to fight. Rosette refused to leave her children.

"What about them?" Deborah pointed to their intended refugees, some now milling about around the trucks.

"You think you can find thirty willing and able?" Hiram said.

"At least thirty," Deborah said. She headed for the trucks.

A rustling in the woods near the Citroën drew the eyes of a few of Hiram's soldiers and they adjusted their weapons to fire.

"Hello ladies," Trembley said as he emerged from the darkness and raised his arms. No one pulled the trigger, but the tension in the clearing lingered well after the soldiers relaxed.

"I'm hoping you've got good news," Hiram said.

"The five-man patrol along the base of the hill is moving like clockwork. We should be able to avoid them fairly easy."

"What about the town?"

"No signs of life. Looks deserted. Of course, it's still early."

Irene's eyes lit up as she spoke. "Then, we won't have to worry about a lot of civilian casualties when we blow our way into Switzerland with one of your nuclear weapons." Deborah almost laughed as she translated.

"How welcome do you think we'll be in Switzerland if we set off a weapon of that magnitude?" Hiram asked.

When Deborah finished translating, Irene shrugged.

"Sarah's last transmission said the Americans have arranged for the Swiss to accept us on the condition we'll be let into the United States," Charlotte said.

"I'm not sure our neutral friends would honor such an arrangement if we kill a couple dozen of their border guards," Hiram said.

"Have you got a better idea?" Trembley asked.

"I don't know," Hiram said. "We could follow a couple of combat robots up the ravine. We'd probably make it."

"If a machine gun burst hits one of the trucks, the casualties are going to be high," Deborah said.

Hiram glanced at Charlotte's display. "Zoom in on the town." She adjusted the view and he moved closer to look. "What's this?" he said pointing.

"Church?" Charlotte said.

"A mostly intact church," Trembley said. "I looked over the steeple pretty carefully, searching for spotters or snipers. Didn't see anyone."

"You think I could get a clean shot on the checkpoint from there?" Hiram said.

"Good possibility," Trembley said.

"I could clean out the checkpoint at the bottom of the hill before our convoy comes into sight. That would give us a little more time. How many guards did you see?"

"I counted five heat signatures," Charlotte said.

"Can you shoot that distance?" Deborah placed her left hand on top of Hiram's right, which was trembling slightly.

"Yes, I can shoot," Hiram said defensively. Turning to the others, he said "Deborah and I can visit the church and check out the sightlines from the steeple. And maybe pick up Captain Petain along the way. Trembley - you and Team Charlie will head up this hillside and get in position to take out the upper checkpoint. If we can take out both checkpoints, we'll send a pair of combat robots up the ravine to eliminate the machine gun nests in these areas."

"That leaves the guards at the top of the ridge." Trembley smiled. "And I think your soldiers are quite capable of knocking out a few stragglers."

56

0225 hours, Tuesday, August 18, 1942, Les Alliés, Doubs Department, Occupied France

Hiram stared at his C2ID2 display as Deborah drove the railbike into Les Alliés. "Turn left here," he said. "Petain should be moving down the right side of the street."

Deborah swung the bike in a tight arc, and the tires offered a half-hearted squeal on the cobblestone street. Petain, a couple hundred meters ahead, turned at the sound. As Deborah accelerated towards him, Petain cut into an alley to his right and disappeared.

Deborah pulled up to the alley. She slowed to make the turn, then slammed on the breaks.

Hiram pitched forward into the cowling of the sidecar. He put his foot out to steady himself and the impact shot a fresh and intense surge of pain up through his leg. He hissed.

"Sorry," she said. "I didn't expect the stairs."

In the alley, several flights of stairs, broken by short flat stretches, led up to the next cross street. Petain had made it about two-thirds of the way up.

"We can go around and cut him off," Deborah said.

"Let's see if I can slow him down a bit first." Hiram brought his sniper rifle to his shoulder. "Might give us a blood trail to follow if he decides to take cover in one of these buildings." Hiram settled his weapon's sight picture on Petain's lower back, then lowered it to put a bullet into his right leg.

Hiram's left arm trembled as he tried to bite back the pain in his ankle. The sight picture wobbled a bit too low. He corrected and jerked the trigger.

Petain's head exploded in a red mist.

Hiram said nothing as he lowered his rifle and settled back into the side car.

Deborah put a hand on his shoulder. "Plan B it is."

* * *

Deborah parked the railbike a block from the church. The sign in front said Église de Sainte-Foy. Hiram leaned against a shed with his weapon ready while Deborah crept up the steps to the rear entrance. If she ran into trouble, his bad ankle would hinder his ability to help her. Deborah disappeared through the door and the helpless feeling grew.

Five minutes later, her voice came across his C2ID2. "All clear."

Hiram hobbled his way up the stairs and into the church. He had never been inside a Catholic church. He recognized the altar and crucifix mounted on the wall behind it, but the layout was unfamiliar. He said a brief prayer asking forgiveness for using a house of God to kill. They needed God's protection, now more than ever.

Deborah met him at the base of the curving staircase that led up to the steeple. "No need for you to make the climb," she said. "The checkpoint is beyond the curve of the hillside. Can't see anything."

"Kak," Hiram said. Without a clear shot at the lower checkpoint, they needed to scratch the effort to sever the communications lines. He stood at the bottom of the staircase, admiring the brave woman before him and wondering why he hadn't taken both Deborah and Danette away from this madness. He couldn't shake the feeling that he was setting them both out as targets – as sacrifices – to save the others.

"Hawk, this is Raven, over." He jumped at the sound of Sarah's voice coming from his C2ID2.

"Raven, this is Hawk. Good to hear your voice, over."

"Hawk, Falcon's request has been approved."

"Raven, say again."

"Hawk, ETA for the British SAS Commandos is fifteen minutes. Touching down in the field north of Les Alliés."

"Roger, Raven," Hiram said. "We'll be waiting for them. How many?"

"Two full troops. Thirty-two soldiers, plus Major Thompson and Sergeant-Major Wilkes."

Deborah's eyes widened along with her smile.

"Roger, Raven."

"Good luck Hiram. I'll see you all on the other side," Sarah said. "Raven out."

Deborah's hands flew up into the air and she let out a relieved laugh. "We're finally going to get some help," Deborah said.

"It shows how badly they want the nukes," he replied. "And I'll be surprised if that's all they want."

Deborah helped Hiram hobble over to a pew near the back of the church. He contacted his team leaders and Trembley via C2ID2 and passed along the good news.

"Trembley – I could kiss you," Hiram said.

"Not necessary, Hiram. I've got a team of lovely ladies over here that are a bit more appealing. I'm taking Irene with me to coordinate with Major Thompson and his men. Maybe she'll be the lucky one."

"Remember, she's got a big brother in one of those trucks," Hiram said. "Danette can get our refugees ready to move. Have Simone keep that drone focused on the French. The next surprise of the day might not be in our favor. We're headed to the northern edge of town. You can pick us up there."

"Roger Hawk. Falcon, out."

Hiram sat in the pew and opened up a private communication channel with Charlotte. *"Find Barbara and Maxime."*

"Looks like we're not going across the border," Deborah said.

"You are."

"The hell I am." She stood up and crossed her arms. "If you're going after Barbara, I'm coming along. It's not open to discussion. You can barely walk two meters on your own. You need me." Hiram sighed. He did need her. At least Danette would be safe.

Deborah guided Hiram out of the church and they took the railbike to the northern edge of town. He adjusted his NVGs and looked toward the open field. Human forms floated down from the sky. "The cavalry has arrived."

57

0335 hours, Tuesday, August 18, 1942, Les Alliés, Doubs Department, Occupied France

"You trust this, Captain?" Thompson asked Trembley, pointing to the C2ID2 display Irene held. Small infrared heat signatures dotted the outer edge of the map. Thompson looked out toward the ravine, eyes squinting as he searched for the thing capturing the images.

Simone stood a couple of meters away controlling the drone circling above the ravine.

"With my life, sir," Trembley said. "But the drones can't see everything." He pointed to a farmhouse and barn about two hundred meters north of the lower checkpoint. "We haven't seen any signs of life there, but we've no idea what might be inside."

"Jolly good, then. Seems straightforward. We kill a bunch of Frogs, drive the trucks up the hill into Switzerland, and we can all go home." Thompson turned to his two troop commanders and began issuing orders.

"We can help," Irene said in French.

Thompson seemed to understand. "Best to leave the soldiering to the menfolk." He responded to Irene, though his eyes stayed on Trembley. "Looks like these ladies have been through the wringer themselves. Why don't you hang back and keep everyone out of our way? I'll radio when we are ready to move. Cheerio." Thompson walked away without a look back.

Irene looked at Trembley. "What did he say?"

"Nothing worth repeating. Let's go find Hiram and brief the others."

241

* * *

0540 hours, Tuesday, August 18, 1942, Les Alliés, Doubs Department, Occupied France

"What? We're just supposed to trust that they will get the job done?" Danette said when Trembley finished briefing Hiram and the team leaders.

"They are quite good at their jobs," Trembley said. "We can watch them via drone and step in if they need support."

Danette glared at Trembley as Hiram addressed his soldiers. "In terms of the convoy, we're going to modify my original idea. Two combat robots out front, followed by two railbikes with light machine guns." Deborah translated for them.

"Team Charlie will take that mission," Irene said.

"Good," Hiram said. "Captain, I'd like you to drive the Citroën, with Simone, Charlotte and Danette inside operating the drones and robots."

Trembley nodded.

"Spread out through the convoy," he said to the others. "I want one of you on every fifth truck. Danette and I will take up the rear in the last railbike. Let's move."

* * *

Soon, the convoy was in motion, the robots dictating the pace. They stopped inside the village and waited for the order to move forward. The low ridge provided cover for the trucks.

Gunfire erupted along the ravine. Trembley watched flashes of light blossom on the display of Simone's C2ID2 as the British commandos eliminated each of the French positions in a well-coordinated attack.

The victory seemed complete, until a pair of French Laffly armored cars emerged from the barn north of the lower checkpoint, each spitting Hotchkiss machine gunfire at the British commandos. Two squads of infantry followed in their wake. The British dove for cover and returned fire.

Danette leaned her head out the window and yelled at the railbike sitting in front of them. "Go, they need your help."

Irene nodded, signaled the bike next to her. Team Charlie headed toward the firefight, two combat robots leading the way. A moment later, Danette saw Deborah and Hiram roar by in the third railbike.

58

0610 hours, Tuesday, August 18, 1942, Les Alliés, Doubs Department, Occupied France

"Stop here." Hiram reached into his backpack, through the portal, and unlatched the IDF missile launcher mounted near the opening of the pod.

Deborah brought the bike to a halt to the left of a break in the trees that provided a perfect view of the armored cars now spitting machine gun fire at the British commandos.

Hiram pulled the missile launcher through the milky surface of the portal. "You're going to have to fire it," he said. He grabbed another missile.

Deborah dismounted and walked around the bike to help him out of the sidecar. "Hiram?"

"My hands are shaking too damn bad. I'll be fine, but I need your help."

She nodded and took the weapon from him, setting it on the ground to help him swing his bad leg over the cowling of the sidecar. "You'll have to refresh me on how to use it."

"It's like riding a bike," Hiram said. "Take a kneeling stance, right knee down, left foot forward, weapon on your right shoulder,"

Deborah assumed the position as he had instructed.

Hiram knelt just behind her left shoulder. He reached for the button on the left side of the weapon's trigger housing. A video display jumped to life in front of Deborah's right eye, overlaid with a set of crosshairs. "Ready?"

She took a deep breath, the weapon rising and falling with her body. "Ready."

"Set your sight on the lead armored car," he said. "Keep it there. Once the missile fires, keep the crosshairs centered on the armored car as it moves. The missile will self-correct."

"Then let's kill these bastards," Deborah said.

"Fire," Hiram ordered.

Deborah squeezed the firing trigger. The missile leapt from the tube, streaking towards the French armored car. As the vehicle exploded in flames, Hiram slammed the second missile into the launcher.

"Ready," Hiram said.

Deborah hit the second vehicle and the machine gun fire stopped.

59

0640 hours, Tuesday, August 18, 1942, Les Alliés, Doubs Department, Occupied France

The Citroën crested the hill as the smoke cleared, leaving two mangled heaps of flaming metal. One of the gunners survived and he managed to remove the machine gun and distance himself from the burning vehicle. The driver of the other car ran toward Trembley screaming, his body engulfed in flame. He collapsed after a few meters while the flames feasted. The surviving French infantry fled east, toward the base of the lower ridge and positioned themselves to defend what was left of the checkpoint. The gunner raked the field in front of them with machine gun fire.

Team Charlie abandoned the railbikes and took cover in a drainage ditch along the east side of the road. Trembley maneuvered the Citroën off the road into a small stand of trees. He jumped out of the car, seeking the cover of a large oak tree, as the two combat robots rolled by, still under the control of Team Charlie.

One robot was equipped with a heavy machine gun, the other an automatic grenade launcher. With their seemingly impenetrable body casings, machine guns and rifles posed little threat. Hiram once voiced concern about the optics, but Trembley believed the monsters would be no less formidable flying blind.

The robots advanced toward the French. Once they got within range of their target, they let loose a storm of fire. A moment later, another of Deborah's missiles arced in and the French position evaporated.

Trembley, Charlotte, and Danette joined Team Charlie and together they moved across the field, Simone providing surveillance via the drone. The lone survivor of the attack surrendered as Irene approached his position.

Hiram and Deborah arrived a moment later. While they huddled with Charlotte and Danette, Trembley and Irene walked towards the remains of the nearest armored car.

Trembley rolled the body of a young French soldier over. *Too young to be dead.*

Major Thompson arrived as Trembley knelt beside the body, three SAS commandos trailing behind him. Thompson kicked the dead man's foot. "Well done," he conceded. "Thanks for your help."

* * *

The convoy reassembled, the vehicles settling into a similar order as before. Trembley, searching for unwelcome surprises along the way, headed up the ravine toward the Swiss border. Not a French soldier in sight as they approached the border crossing. Team Charlie, in the lead, pulled their railbikes off to the side of the road to let the Citroën pass as they neared the gate. Trembley stopped the car and he and Danette stepped out and walked toward the border guard. Major Thompson, who had found a place in the lead truck for the ride up the hill, joined them.

The Swiss corporal leading the guard detail at the gate watched the trio approach, hand over the pistol on his hip.

Trembley held a hand out to the man. "Captain Joseph Trembley, Major Archibald Thompson, and Mrs. Danette Halphen. I believe someone's expecting us."

The corporal took the man's hand and nodded. He said a few words to the other men nearby before summoning a lieutenant, who radioed a captain, who phoned a colonel, and then the gate opened.

"That's how it's done," Thompson said.

The lieutenant stepped through the gate. "These men will escort you to a nearby field where you can park the vehicles. A representative from the Swiss Foreign Office will be along soon with further instruction."

One of the men jumped into the driver's seat of the lead truck and set the vehicle in motion. Without hesitation and, Trembley was sure, grateful to be as far from the French border as possible, the rest of the trucks followed. Trembley stayed behind, chatting with the Swiss guards as truck after truck rolled past. Cheers emanated from each truck as they passed the checkpoint.

He'd catch a ride on the last truck, once he was sure everyone made it across the border.

"Here's the last of them," he said to the guards as the thirtieth truck approached. "I expect a sidecar motorcycle bringing up the rear." Hiram and Deborah had made the call to move through last. The final truck passed Trembley's position and behind it stood only empty road. Trembley slipped on his NVGs and tried to search along the ravine, the contraptions not offering as much help as he had hoped. Hiram and Deborah were nowhere to be found.

60

0730 hours, Tuesday, August 18, 1942, Vichy, Allier Department, Vichy France

Corporal Lafayette passed through six additional checkpoints on his way into Vichy, all manned by the LVF. At each stop, he offered information in hopes of getting something in return, a trick he learned from Captain Petain. And the LVF, proud of the current state of things in Vichy, wanted to talk. At the first stop, he learned that Rene Bousquet remained in office as the General Secretary. When they pulled into the second stop, he passed along the information about Bousquet, adding that "he's been cooperative with the SS these past two years."

"I guess cooperation doesn't mean much," the guard said. "Look what happened to Prime Minister Lavall."

"At least they haven't executed him yet," Lafayette said at the third stop. "Detained for an undetermined amount of time I hear, but quite alive."

At the fourth stop, he heard Marshall Petain sat comfortably in a prison cell alongside Prime Minister Lavall.

"The LVF control's Vichy now," a guard at the fifth stop said. "Except for the prefecture. The German's hold sway over the government center. A Waffen SS battalion's taken up residence there, or so we've heard."

"The German 15th Infantry Division made a move into Unoccupied France." The guard at the sixth stop called out the information from his small hut, radio earpiece pressed to the side of his head.

"Any word on the Pyrénées-Orientales?" Lafayette asked as the guard passed his papers back through the window. He had been out of touch with his family for a few days. He hoped trouble had by-passed his home.

"No news today," the guard said. "I supposed that is good news."

At the prefecture, German soldiers formed a cordon extending two blocks out from the edge of the compound. The officer in charge, a grizzled Waffen SS Sturmbannführer, decided to let Lafayette pass after a careful review of his papers.

"Just you," he said.

"Yes, sir." Lafayette turned to Corporal Martin. "Find a place to park the vehicles, then come back here and wait for me. Stay alert." Martin acknowledged his orders and led the vehicles away from the well-guarded entrance.

Lafayette entered the prefecture with papers in hand. His papers passed through three more sets of hands as he made his way through the complex of buildings that constituted the seat of the Vichy government.

Bousquet's personal secretary appeared disinterested when Lafayette arrived in the ornate office suite. "Can I help you?"

"I am here to meet Captain Louis Petain, Chief of Police for the Pyrénées-Orientales Department. I understand we have an appointment with the General Secretary."

The secretary stood and reached across her desk for his papers, leaning far enough to expose the topmost bulge of her large breasts that seemed to be squeezed upward by the same force that created her narrow waist. She had a pretty face framed by short, sculpted blonde hair. *Rank does have its privileges.*

She reviewed his papers. "I am not aware of this appointment." she said. Her accent confirmed Lafayette's suspicion that she hailed from Marseilles, a place known for producing such beautiful specimens of the female form.

"We captured an American spy that has provided advanced equipment to the partisans. Captain Petain sent me here with several of the weapons. The General Secretary will want to see the weapons for himself. Quite an impressive collection. I'm surprised Captain Petain has not arrived yet."

"I'm afraid the General Secretary-"

"General Secretary Bousquet is meeting with the Führer and Reichsführer Himmler," said a voice in passable French. His voice carried a strong German accent.

Lafayette turned to face the man who had entered the room behind him. Black fedora, long black leather jacket, despite the moderate temperature, a Nazi armband, jackboots, wire-rim glasses, and dead blue eyes. *Gestapo.*

"The Führer is here? In Vichy?" Lafayette asked, dumbfounded. "Why?"

"The Führer is not accountable to you," the Gestapo man said.

"Of course not," Lafayette stuttered. "I'm surprised that he has decided to honor the people of Vichy with a visit. Will there be a public celebration of the event?"

"The only public event will be the execution of the French cabinet," the man said.

"Execution?"

"If the Reichsführer's investigators believe the French orchestrated the *event* in Saarbrücken, the entire French cabinet will find themselves lined up in front of a firing squad," the Gestapo man said. "And the Führer might purge their families as well. Messy business." He nodded back toward the closed door.

"It was the Americans," Lafayette said.

"Perhaps they played a part. Is this what your American spy has told you?"

"No. He didn't say much of anything before he-" Lafayette stopped.

"Before he died?"

"No, sir. He managed to escape."

"Escaped. Hmm. You did say your captain's name was 'Petain', correct?"

"Yes, sir," Lafayette said. "The Marshall is his grandfather's brother. He barely knows the man."

"Except when he needs something, I'm sure."

"I-"

The Gestapo man held up a hand, then pulled a small notebook from an inner pocket of his jacket and made a note. Before he finished writing, he said, "You'll take me to see the advanced weapons you mentioned."

"I'm sorry, sir," Lafayette said. "The cache has been secured in a heavily armored trunk in my truck outside. Captain Petain has the key."

"And where is Captain Petain, then?" the Gestapo man said.

"I assume he arrived some time ago," Lafayette said. "As I told Bousquet's secretary, I was ordered to meet him here."

The secretary carried Lafayette's papers around the desk and handed them to the Gestapo man. He considered the contents for a moment, then turned and headed toward the closed door to Bousquet's office. Quietly he opened the door and walked in, closing the door behind him.

"Friendly guy, isn't he?" Lafayette said to no one in particular.

The secretary straightened her skirt. "*Kriminaldirektor* Hans Huber," she spat the name out as if it had gone sour in her mouth. "Friendly is the last word I'd use to describe that man, Corporal Lafayette."

Lafayette swallowed hard. *Kriminaldirektor* was the Gestapo equivalent of a major. He knew who had all the power here.

61

0830 hours, Tuesday, August 18, 1942, Les Bayards, Val-de-Travers, Switzerland

Charlotte leaned against the tire of the lead truck, grateful to be out of the stuffy confines of the crowded vehicle for a while. The drone she had sent out hours ago had located three motorcycles travelling west. She zoomed in on the image. "Found them!"

"Found who?" Danette leaned over her to see the display on the C2ID2.

"Barbara, Maxime, *and* Team Bravo," Charlotte said.

Simone squatted in front of her. "They are together? Where?"

"On the road to Vichy." Charlotte held the C2ID2 display so the others could see. "Barbara probably swung south to meet up with Team Bravo. They're headed west."

"Why would they be headed toward Vichy?" Danette said.

"I'd only expect one reason if Barbara's involved," Charlotte said. "Revenge."

Danette looked at Charlotte. "What do the six of them think they can accomplish?"

Simone stood and crossed her arms. "Depends on the tools they have with them."

"What?" Charlotte and Danette asked in unison.

"It's possible that Team Bravo's hyperbaric nuclear weapon is fully functional," Simone said.

"That's not possible," Danette said. "How would Team Bravo have gotten a hold of a fully functional nuclear weapon?"

Simone let out a deep breath. "Do you remember when Team Golf was disarming the weapons Hiram intended to present to Captain Trembley? He wanted to show him we had the weapons but didn't want them to be functional. After Saarbrücken, I can see why. I mean those weapons are quite unbelievably powerful."

Charlotte stood and faced Simone. "Spit it out!"

Simone scratched the back of her head. "Emma may have switched out one of the backpack portals for one of the weapon portals."

"What?" Danette said.

"Well, we thought it was a failsafe in case something happened to Hiram. I think Agnes ended up with the pack."

"Get Hiram on the radio, now!" Danette said.

"I thought Hiram and Deborah were going to catch up with us here. Didn't they follow us across the border?" Charlotte said.

Danette shook her head. "They went after Barbara and Maxime."

"On their own?" Simone asked. "Do you think Hiram can stop Barbara and the others?"

"Barbara's got a good head start." Charlotte calculated Hiram's distance from the rogue team. "Doesn't seem likely."

"Let Hiram know about the weapon," Danette joined Charlotte.

"He's been monitoring my drone feed. He knows where they are," Charlotte said.

"Yeah, but does he know they have a nuclear bomb?" Danette said.

62

1130 hours, Tuesday, August 18, 1942, Oyonnax, Ain Department, Occupied France

Hiram and Deborah moved south through the Jura Mountains. The railbike drew little attention despite traveling in broad daylight.

They turned west toward the more heavily populated lowlands, careful to avoid checkpoints with the help of the drone scouting ahead of them.

Danette's harried voice boomed through the speaker in his helmet. He translated a few words on his own before Deborah was able to respond.

"Hawk. Team Alpha. Bad. Barbara. Maxime. Team Bravo." He turned to Deborah, her expression concealed by the helmet.

When Danette stopped talking, Deborah translated, the calm in her voice forced. "Danette says Barbara and Maxime met up with Team Bravo."

"At least we'll only have to track one group down," Hiram said as he swerved around a large rock in the path.

"Hiram," Deborah said, her voice shaky.

Hiram guided the railbike off to the side of the road. "What is it?"

Deborah looked up from the overhead drone feed she monitored. "Agnes is in possession of a portal and electronics package from one of the nuclear weapons."

"What? How did they-"

Danette spoke again.

"Simone confessed that Team Golf switched out one of the portals for a backpack weapons portal and pocketed one of the electronics packages from the nukes."

Is it possible? Hiram tried to go back to the night Team Golf helped him prepare the dummy weapons for Trembley's arrival. He remembered counting the portals…*No, I counted the stacks – six stacks.* But they had been in a hurry and he had felt as though a Mark XII had been detonated inside of him. *It's fucking possible!*

Hiram powered down the railbike and climbed off.

"What are you doing?" Deborah asked as she maneuvered her way out of the side car.

He ignored her and tapped an icon on his C2ID2. The portal in his pack activated and Hiram dove into the portal head first. He rolled as his body connected with the mat on the floor.

He found the two bags used to store the parts from the six sample weapons. He tore the bags open and counted the contents with uncooperative, shaky hands. A single portal from one of the backpacks had been slipped into a stack of the weapons-grade discs. "Traveler" had been etched into the metal disc surrounding the portal. He found only five sets of the hyperbaric electronics packages as he fumbled through the electronics pile. *It doesn't matter. The weapon won't function without the PAL code.* He looked at his C2ID2. With a shaky hand, he withdrew the unit from its protective sheath. The titanium finish appeared brand new. The one he'd carried for the last three years had been scratched, dented and marred by continual use. At some point when he had been sleeping or fighting off Hagar's ungodly curse, someone – Barbara – had switched his unit and he'd never noticed. He swallowed hard despite the sudden dryness in his mouth. The PAL code he had copied over from Jacob's C2ID2 was stored on the device she had taken.

Why? Why in the hell would they have taken them? But the answer was clear. His soldiers needed a contingency plan.

Hiram hopped back up the ladder, doing his best to disregard the excruciating pain that had settled all the way up to his knee and now seemed so insignificant.

Deborah rushed to his side as he collapsed on the ground beside his pack.

"Agnes has a hyperbaric nuclear weapon portal and a firing mechanism. I can only guess that she's reinstalled the disc in Team Bravo's weapon. And Barbara has the code to set it off."

His stomach turned and saliva pooled in his mouth as the world around him twisted. "It was one of the big discs." He took in a deep breath. "Six hundred kilotons. Fuck. Fifty times the size of the one used in Saarbrücken.

255

Hundreds of thousands of innocent people could die if that weapon goes off."

"Then get up!" Deborah put an arm around him and helped lift him to his feet. "We've got to stop them."

* * *

0730 hours, Wednesday, August 19, 1942, Bost, Allier Department, Vichy France

The railbike sped west through the lowlands, past long stretches of idle farmland and a handful of small quiet towns. In the dark, Hiram and Deborah travelled unnoticed. As the sun came up, their odd vehicle caught the eyes of several farmers tending their fields and a petite old lady who sat at a small table in front of the burned-out husk of her home sipping from a delicate teacup.

They followed a well-travelled trail through the mountains west of Vichy. The city came into view an hour after Barbara and her rogue soldiers.

63

0730 hours, Wednesday, August 19, 1942, Bost, Allier Department, Vichy France

The hyperbaric nuclear weapon sat at the center of the warehouse floor. Barbara, Maxime, Agnes, Ida, Nathalie, and Isadore surrounded the metallic canister. They stared in silence as Barbara pulled up the weapon's interface on the C2ID2.

"I'll give you all a head start to get out of here," Barbara said. "I don't know what the radius of the blast will look like, so you need to get as far away from here as fast as you can."

"You should come with us," Ida said.

Barbara shook her head. "I need to stay here to make sure no one interferes."

Maxime touched Barbara's shoulder. "I'm staying too."

"No Maxime. You can't. You've got a family out there somewhere."

"No," she said. "I don't. Not anymore." Maxime looked down at the floor. "The rest of you need to get out of here now. Drive the bikes straight out of town. Put as much distance away from this place as possible."

"When you see Hiram, tell him I'm sorry," Barbara said to Agnes. "We need these people to suffer for what they've done."

Agnes nodded. "We can all walk away. Pretend this never happened."

"Like all the others?" Barbara took Maxime's hand. "Our fellow Frenchmen watched this horror play out. Our political leaders joined hands with the Germans. They tried to convince us that if we just played along, it would all work out in the end."

"I understand," Agnes said. "We pray for your success." Agnes and the others walked out of the warehouse, leaving Barbara and Maxime.

"What now?" Maxime asked as she circled the device at the center of the room.

Barbara climbed on to a stack of dusty wooden crates and sat with her legs dangling a few inches above the concrete floor. "We'll give them some time to clear out and then we'll activate the device."

"And maybe I'll get to hold my little girl again," Maxime said under her breath.

Barbara wanted to sit back and enjoy the show, to feel the warmth of the explosion blanket her before taking out every living thing from here to who-knows-where. She would see the faces of those who had wronged her people when she crossed over into Olam Ha-Ba. Maybe then, just maybe, they would see how many lives had been extinguished by the hatred that had infected her homeland. And in that place, she prayed, war would cease to exist and the truly righteous would stand with honor a step – or two – above those who had turned their backs when France needed strength.

"How much longer?" Maxime said as she peered out one of the windows.

"Do you think ten minutes is enough?"

64

0734 hours, Wednesday, August 19, 1942, Bost, Allier Department, Vichy France

Charlotte's directions led Deborah and Hiram to a warehouse on the east bank of the Allier River. Peering across the wide river through his high-powered binoculars, Hiram searched for signs of Barbara and the others. He had trained them too well and saw no sign of the railbikes or the women. "They could detonate the weapon at any moment."

"Are you sure Barbara and Maxime have the weapon?" Deborah asked. "Charlotte said Team Bravo left the warehouse headed south. What if they took the device?"

"They're moving too fast to be carrying anything that heavy," he said.

"Hiram." He waited for more, but she said nothing.

He turned to Deborah, her face white as she stared at the display. Her mouth moved as if trying to force words out. "What is it? What's wrong?"

"I – I think Barbara activated the weapon."

"What?" He took the C2ID2 display from Deborah. "It's counting down! Six minutes, forty-nine seconds." Without the PAL code now in Barbara's hands, he couldn't stop the countdown.

Hiram activated the portal in his backpack. He slid down the ladder, the impact on the floor of the pod bringing him to tears. He grabbed a small guided missile launcher and passed it up through the portal and went back for a parachute. He slung the RediChute over his shoulder and hopped up the ladder.

"Three minutes, thirty seconds," Deborah said as he emerged.

He tossed the parachute on the ground and grabbed her by the shoulders. "Take the bike and head back east. Don't stop for any reason, don't turn around. Shoot anyone who tries to stop you. Go now!"

"I'm not going without you," Deborah said. "From what you've told me about this weapon, I'll never make it far enough in time. So, tell me what you are going to do so I can help."

"I'm going to reset my pack to open an aerial portal directly above us. I can lock the missile on the C2ID2 signal. If I know Barbara, she's not going too far from that weapon. We'll knock out her C2ID2 and destroy the bomb too.

"You're down to two minutes," Deborah said.

"Go!" Hiram said.

"You can't possibly orient and control the chute, program the missile, aim, and launch before the people on the ground start firing at you. I can help," Deborah pleaded.

"You have to get out of here!" Hiram shouted.

"No! You need my help."

He stared at her for a few seconds, waiting for another idea to pop into his head that might save her. He had no more time.

"Fine." Hiram reset the portal, then got to his feet and pulled the parachute onto his back. "Take this." He thrust the missile launcher into Deborah's hands and spun her around. He pulled off her backpack and replaced it with his own. With Deborah strapped to his chest and the parachute on his back, he couldn't carry the pack that carried the portal himself.

"This probably won't hold, and the chute is too small anyway." He hooked his parachute harness to the D-rings on her new backpack with a pair of snap links. "We'll both fall to our deaths."

"Nonsense," she replied as he ran a rope between her legs to finish off the harness. "The Germans or French will shoot us out of the air before that happens."

Hiram tapped the C2ID2. "Jump on three. One, two, three." Hiram and Deborah disappeared through the milky white portal in his pack.

65

1530 hours, Wednesday, August 19, 1942, London, England, United Kingdom

"Tea, Ms. Mendelson?" Lord Mountbatten said. The British delegation at Camp Griffiss took a break for afternoon tea daily, and today Lord Mountbatten invited Sarah to join him. They sat at a thick wooden table in a quiet corner of the camp cafeteria.

"Yes," Sarah said. "Thank you, my Lord,"

He filled her cup, then his own, and placed the teapot on the silver tray. "Please, call me Monty."

"As you wish, Lord Monty."

Mountbatten smiled, though she wasn't sure he appreciated the quip. Sarah had always addressed individuals in office by their appropriate title and the idea of calling this man anything less than Lord discomforted her.

He offered her milk, which she refused. Sarah added two cubes of sugar to her tea and stirred it well. Sweets had been few and far between before she arrived in London.

It had been a hectic day. Aerial surveillance had detected a detonation – a very, very large detonation – in Vichy around 7:40 a.m. Reports came in from French partisans describing the devastation, including the destruction of an SS brigade. Sarah was shocked that Hiram used another nuclear weapon on French soil, let alone in a place that offered so little in the way of tactical advantage. She had spent the last hours alternately trying to contact Hiram, with no luck, talking via C2ID2 to her friends that had made it to Switzerland, talking by radio with Captain Trembley, and discussing the implications with the Allied High Command, trying to make sense of it all.

Four scones sat on a plate between them. Mountbatten picked one up and reached for the margarine as his aide burst though the cafeteria door and hurried to their isolated corner.

"My Lord, Miss Mendelson, you're needed in operations immediately," the man said.

"Surely it can wait until we've had our tea, William," Mountbatten said as he smeared margarine on his scone.

The major's eyes darted from Sarah to Lord Mountbatten, breathing hard. "My apologies, sir, but it is most urgent."

Mountbatten hesitated as if he considered dismissing the man in favor of Sarah's company. "Very well, William. Miss Mendelson, if you please?" They followed the aide out the cafeteria door and across the cobblestone street to the Operations Center, European Theatre of Operations, United States Army. General Eisenhower greeted them.

"I have good news," Eisenhower said grinning from ear to ear. "And better news."

"Tell us for heaven's sake," Sarah said.

"We've learned, with high reliability, that Hitler and Reichsführer Himmler were visiting Vichy when the bomb went off."

"Oh my God," Sarah said.

"Jolly good news," Lord Mountbatten said.

"And," Eisenhower continued, "a group of Wehrmacht generals and important industrialists seized power in Berlin. They have proposed an armistice. I think the war in Europe is over."

66

Midnight, Thursday, December 31, 1942, Chicago, Illinois, United States of America

Music and laughter drifted out of the Jewish Community Center across the street from where Sarah Mendelson stood alone hugging herself in the cold. The New Year's party was well underway inside.

For the first time in weeks, she had made it out of the lab early enough to attend any kind of social event and still she managed to arrive late. After her relocation to the United States, Sarah had been recruited by the Italian physicist Enrico Fermi to assist in the work taking place in a metallurgical lab, Chicago Pile-1, hidden beneath Stagg Field at the University of Chicago. Her knowledge of the events that took place in Saarbrücken and Vichy earlier in the year awarded her a strong recommendation by General Groves, the general in charge of the Manhattan Project, as well as General Eisenhower. She had been on-site, standing beside Fermi, when the world's first nuclear reactor attained criticality just a few weeks ago. The research and documentation effort that followed had kept her contained on campus ever since. And, she loved it.

"Happy New Year!" Sarah shouted when she found the familiar faces she had been longing to see.

"Happy New Year!" Emma echoed in English with a thick French accent.

"Glad they let you take a few days off from Rock Island," Sarah said.

"She's still learning English," Trembley said, switching to French. "I think Happy New Year's the only thing she's really learned."

"Happy New Year!" Emma shouted again in English as she mingled with the others nearby.

"She's been heading the team to reverse engineer a few of Hiram's weapons with the American munitions experts. I heard she's too good at her job and the weapons teams can't keep up," Trembley said as he sipped his drink.

"Sounds like Emma," Sarah said in French.

Trembley smiled. "I believe Congratulations are in order for your work with Fermi."

"Fermi's the genius. I'm thankful for the opportunity to work with him," she said.

"He's the one who should be thankful," he said.

Danette pushed her way through the group. "Hey, my turn." She spoke loudly, the glass of champagne in her left hand obviously not her first drink of the evening. Silas trailed along behind her. She put an arm around Sarah and kissed her on the cheek, careful not to spill her drink.

Emma stepped in with an extra glass of champagne that she handed to Sarah. "Almost time."

Rosette had followed her. "Good to see you, Sarah."

"I'm so glad to see you all," Sarah said.

Behind them, the host of the celebration stood up on the small stage and began to count down to the New Year. Sarah and the others counted down with him. "…Three, two, one. Happy New Year!"

Beside her, Major Joseph Trembley kissed Emma and Rosette. He said, "Happy New Year!" and pulled Sarah in for a kiss too.

Irene was locked in an embrace with her husband, Ephraim. He had been one of the survivors rescued from the train.

"A toast," Trembley said as he held up his glass. "To those we saved."

"And to those we lost along the way," Sarah added.

"Here, here," said the assembled survivors of Rivesaltes, most of whom had settled in Illinois.

Everyone drank deeply. An odd yet appreciated quiet followed.

"I wonder what happened to Deborah and Hiram," Rosette said. Her children, Leverette and Sophia, slept on a sofa in the next room. Sarah guessed they had been too sleepy to stay awake for the midnight celebration.

"Depends on where they were when the bomb went off," Sarah said.

EPILOGUE

45°25'41"North Latitude; 4°35'12"East Longitude; 4,104 Meters Altitude

Hiram tightened the grip on Deborah's makeshift harness, praying she wouldn't slip out. He held his breath as he pulled the ripcord. The chute deployed with a hard jerk. Deborah's body tried to jump free, but the D-clips kept her anchored to him.

"That's not Vichy," she shouted after a moment.

He expected to see the haphazard gridwork of buildings and roads that made up the capital city of Vichy growing as they approached the ground. Beneath them, a forest grew from the shattered ruins of a city, and they were speeding toward the treetops. Towering hardwoods blanketed the floor of the valley below, springing up between the broken foundations of absent buildings. It was an *old* forest.

"We're falling too fast," Hiram said. "Drop the missile launcher and your rifle. We can find them later." Hiram dropped his own rifle, then turned his attention to finding a safe spot to land.

"Look, a road." Deborah pointed to a north-south track off to the west.

"Too narrow. Let's try for that area a little farther west, looks like a meadow. I think we can make it." Hiram tugged on the left riser, steering the chute toward the small glen. They continued falling at an uncomfortable rate.

They passed over the road. Rows of men marched south.

"Hiram, where are we?"

"I don't know," he shouted. *But we probably shouldn't have dropped the weapons.* He looked a little closer as they passed over the marching columns.

A thousand identical faces turned toward them. They weren't the faces of men. Alien, yet familiar. Optics glinted in the sun.

"What the hell are they?" Deborah yelled, horror in her voice.

Hiram couldn't take his eyes off of the mechanical things. The faces reminded him of combat robots. He closed his eyes, squeezed them tight for a few second before opening them. The optics caught the light of the morning sun and threw it back at him. "Robots," Hiram said. The ground was coming up too fast to speculate more on the subject.

"They look like mutilated relatives of the combat robots," she said.

"We'll find out what they are soon enough." Hiram wrapped both arms around Deborah. He closed his eyes and took in a deep breath, preparing for another rough landing on his bad ankle. "Remember to bend your knees and roll when we hit."

At least I'm not alone this time.

ABOUT THE AUTHORS

Steven Landry is a husband, father, soldier, engineer, and consultant. He is a retired U.S. Army officer, a former FEMA training and exercise planner, and a risk management consultant specializing in weapons of mass destruction. He holds degrees in Chemical Engineering and Business Administration from Worcester Polytechnic Institute and a Ph.D. in Chemical Engineering from Stanford University. Steven lives with his family in Maryland. His first novel, *The Legend of Indian Stream*, a science-fiction based alternative history novel of the Civil War, is available on Kindle and in print at:
https://www.amazon.com/dp/1545487561
Steven is also the editor and co-writer (with Kate Lashley, Dan Cassenti, and Larry Garnett among others) of the comic science fiction anthology *Old Farts in Space* which is available on Kindle and in print at:
https://www.amazon.com/dp/0692187790
Steven is on Facebook and The Legend of Indian Stream has its own Facebook page.

Katie Rae Sank lives with her husband and daughter in Maryland and works as an IT project manager in the Finance industry. She focuses her creative energy on reading and writing science fiction and wrestling with the characters living in her head that all think they deserve the lead role in her next literary project.